BAY AVENUE III:
"Pratt-ically Speaking"

I hope you enjoy the journey!

Jill Hicks

Jill Hicks

This book is a work of fiction. Names, characters, businesses, organizations, places, events, and incidents either are the product of the author's imagination or are used fictitiously. Any resemblance to actual persons, living or dead, or events is entirely coincidental.

Cover photograph and design by Bill Hicks

1st Edition 5/2/15
2nd Edition 10/18/16

Originally published in 2014 as "Will Power III: Pratt-ically Speaking"

This book is dedicated to my very patient, understanding, and encouraging best friend, husband, and the love of my life, Bill Hicks.

PROLOGUE

I dreamt that he was tall and strong. He had dark hair and soft somber eyes. His voice was deep, rich, and gently soothing, conveying his empathy for my complicated world. He knew how to console me and how to make me laugh. He always put me first, and was willing to lay down his life for mine. He had everything, except the white horse.

I never saw a white horse in my dreams. I had no need for one: I saw him.

CHAPTER ONE

COURTNEY

It took months of planning. I wanted a small affair, but to no one's surprise, my father wanted a big bash. He argued that the wedding ceremony belonged to the bride and groom; however, the reception belonged to the parents of the bride, and he was determined to go all out. His description of "all out" meant free-flowing wine and champagne, several fully stocked bars with two or more bartenders assigned to each, a wide array of hors d'oeuvres served by no less than 40 waiters, a sit-down dinner with a waiter assigned to every table so that every table was served every course at the same time, a decadent wedding cake, and a coffee bar serviced by two baristas. He wanted a live band and an experienced MC to keep things moving. He brought in a photographer from New York City, someone he knew personally.

My father's guest list was an extensive "Who's Who" of Delaware, Maryland, Virginia, and Pennsylvania.

"Daddy, I know you're very excited about this, but don't you think you're going a little overboard?" I asked cautiously.

"What do you mean? This is how it's done."

"It is? I have never attended a wedding of this magnitude. Have you?"

"Many."

"OK. That's because of the company you keep."

"What are you talking about? You know all of the people on the guest list," my father challenged confidently.

I scanned the list in more detail, looking for names of proposed guests that I would not recognize.

"OK. I do know most of these people, but Dylan doesn't. The size of Dylan's guest list is miniscule compared to this," I said, slapping the list against the opened palm of my hand. "Won't you please consider cutting this back, for Dylan's sake? It's a little overwhelming, don't you think?" I suggested, waving the rolled up list in the air.

He took the list from my hand, unrolled it, stared at it momentarily, and then abruptly shoved it back into my hand.

"No. I will not cut it back. I'm paying for it, so that's that."

In the wake of my mother's death, my father had become increasingly impatient and less able to consider a compromise in most areas of disagreement. We had all been tiptoeing around his wounded heart, picking our battles carefully.

One February night, in our "new to us" home, Dylan and I discussed the not too distant celebratory firestorm. I was snuggled up against his warm body. His arm was wrapped around my shoulder, pulling my head in to rest on his solid chest that rose and fell like a gentle bellow. I found comfort in his breathing the way one finds it relaxing to fall asleep to the rhythm of the ocean's waves. I felt a sense of security in the sure, strong steady beat of his heart.

It was a good thing that we enjoyed cuddling up together. Winter had claimed its stake, and we were learning just how cold and drafty the new old house was going to be. Dylan had warned me.

"This place will need a lot of work, but the potential is endless!"

Dylan had repeated the exact same sentiment he had expressed when we signed the Agreement of Sale back in December. Those were his exact words. Those were "Carter" words. I had vaguely remembered Dan—Dylan's brother now deceased—saying the same things about the original Carter beach house, several months after he had inherited it in his father's Will.

"So, Dylan, my dad has a huge guest list," I blurted out of nowhere, kind of like the burp that escapes before you even begin to feel it bubbling up to the top.

"I'm not surprised. He does know a lot of people. How many are we talking about?"

"I don't know exactly. Three, maybe four hundred. Every time we talk, the list gets longer."

"Wow, that is a lot of people," Dylan whispered, failing to hide his surprise. "Where are we going to find a place big enough to accommodate that many people?"

"Trust me, my dad will find a place, or build it himself."

"No doubt."

Dylan shifted so he was on his side and facing me. He rested his chin on the top of my head and stretched an arm around my waist. His breathing slowed. He began nodding off.

I lay awake, trying to envision my father's plans and exactly how they were going to match up with our dreams for a more intimate and long awaited wedding day. After visualizing my walk down the aisle, our first dance, cutting the cake, and waving goodbye to everyone, I began daydreaming about our future. I was going to be a Carter.

A Carter? So what will become of the firm? Will it become Sable & Carter? No, my father and I have worked too hard to build our reputation as an accomplished father-daughter team. We had become a prominent and highly sought-after law firm in Sussex County.

GINNY

As expected, her father spared no expense. Once the date was set, Mr. Sable pleaded with Courtney to hire a wedding planner. As Courtney tells it, her father wanted BIG, but was nervous about taking it on without his beloved Elizabeth by his side. Dylan vouched for Courtney, saying she had tried to keep her father in check, but she was no match for his "I'm without my Elizabeth" pout that he would don at Courtney's great expense, and his, too, literally. The wedding planner did exactly as Mr. Sable had expected; she set everything into motion.

Following the planner's recommendation, Mr. Sable rented the Nassau Valley Winery for the entire day, and most of the night. I don't know the exact number of invitations mailed out; however, approximately 400 guests were expected. Dylan would be lost in a sea of pomp and politics. That was a given.

For a guest list that large, the wedding party was comparatively small. Ava and Bridget would serve as Courtney's bridesmaids. Dex and Pratt would serve as Dylan's groomsmen.

The weather was perfect for an early June wedding. A light nor'easterly breeze moderated the effects of the full summer sun in a cloudless sky. Birds were dancing from limb to limb as they sang their brilliant songs in the trees surrounding the venue, and the vineyards encompassing the winery were in flower. The excitement of an approaching new season of life was in the air. The "Pegasus Trio," from Wilmington, provided a popular mixture of classical through contemporary music as Dex and Pratt seated hundreds of guests. The ensemble consisted of an acoustic guitar, violin, and flute. I think what I loved most was the violinist's voice as she sang "From This Moment" during Courtney's procession. Never had I heard anything as beautiful. Gracing the arm of her father, Courtney appeared under the floral arbor and began her procession toward Dylan. He was completely undone by the sight of his beautiful bride. His handsome grin became a beaming smile as a happy tear escaped from the corner of his eye.

Courtney originally requested a Judge or Justice of the Peace to perform the ceremony. Dylan preferred that they be married in the "eyes of God." He asked Courtney to please consider a pastor.

"How about a Justice of the Peace who knows how to say a short prayer and something nice about God here and there?" Courtney bargained.

Dylan agreed to the compromise. They had not been attending church on a regular basis—more like not at all—so it was probably as close as Dylan was going to get to the "eyes of God" with Courtney as his bride. Mr. Sable, being socially and politically well connected, requested the honor of Robert Felts, the Mayor of Lewes, to officiate the ceremony. Mayor Felts readily accepted.

"What about our vows?" Dylan had asked.

"Do we really need to do all of that?" Courtney whined. "Seriously, I just want a short ceremony to make it all legal, nothing drawn out."

Now, Dylan was the one pouting. Courtney stared in disbelief at her fiancé before continuing her reign over the ceremony.

"Seriously, Dylan? You really want the whole religious shebang?"

"Yes."

I was glad that they had agreed to declare their vows. What is the point of having a wedding ceremony if you are not willing to recite your commitment before all of your invited witnesses? Four hundred witnesses, to be exact.

Their vows were beautiful, and I had forgotten to pack tissues. Luckily, Susan had some tucked away in Zoe's diaper bag.

Dylan began:

"Courtney, I never knew what it meant to chase after life and love until the day I met you. I want to run this race with you from this day forward, forever. You are my oxygen when I am drowning. You are my oasis in the midst of a drought. You are my way home when I am lost. You are the light in my darkest storm. You are beyond my wildest dream. Court, please accept my heart, my mind, my body, and my soul. I give it all to you. I promise to stand by you and with

*you. I promise to share my dreams with you and to do
everything within my power to make yours come true. I
promise to protect you, laugh and cry with you, and love you
forever. You have me completely. I give myself to you for all
of eternity."*

I began crying in the middle of his recitation. The
tone of his voice was identical to Dan's. Hearing him speak
gently to her with such commitment took me back. I could
feel Dan's fingers wrapped around my hands, nervously
fidgeting as he had given himself to me.

Courtney spoke beautifully, too:
*"Dylan, I have waited a lifetime for you, and now that
you are here, my life is complete. You have saved me in so
many ways; you even saved me from myself. I promise to love
you forever, and to stand with you and by you, forever. I
promise to be faithful, truthful, and always hopeful, for
together, we will conquer our worst fears and celebrate our
greatest victories. Dylan, I give myself to you completely:
heart, mind, body, and soul, for all of eternity."*

They exchanged rings and sealed the day with a kiss.
They became, now and forever, Mr. and Mrs. Dylan Carter.

I remembered that glorious feeling when Dan and I
ran over the dune after being introduced as Mr. and Mrs.
Daniel Carter. I remembered all of us sitting in the dunes
late that night around a campfire that Dex had built, and we
filled the night sky with lanterns that Courtney had given
us.
I allowed my mind to drift back to the Hotel Blue
where Dan and I had spent our one and only night as a
married couple.

I remembered the accident. My body shuddered as
tears began to well up in my eyes.

I looked up at Dex, hoping the sight of him would grant me courage. He was standing stoically between Dylan and Pratt. When he saw me, he flashed a warm smile that was meant only for me, albeit in front of 398 other guests. He was so handsome in his tuxedo, just as he was on our first big date, more than two years before. So much had happened since that night. Indeed, it was only by the grace of God and the courage of Dylan and Dex that we were gathered at Nassau Valley Winery to witness the marriage of Courtney Sable to Dylan Carter. She would now and forever be a permanent fixture in the Carter family.

As the wedding party prepared to recess and form the receiving line, Dex's eyes caught mine once more. A pout formed on his usually chiseled lips. He knew. He always did. But there was nothing he could do. As a member of the wedding party, he was obligated to perform certain duties, namely escort Courtney's oldest sister, Ava.

It was no secret that Ava was a man-eater. She loved men. She ate them up and spit them out. Like her two sisters, Ava was a self-made woman, but she was perhaps the most ruthless of the three. I was not worried about Dex, he could handle himself around her. I just did not appreciate her attempts. It seemed to be a thing with the Sable women. They were magnetically attracted to Dex. For me, it was tiring to watch.

Susan noticed my stares, and it did not take her long to figure it out.

"Ginny, as soon as we're able, let's go get a glass of wine," she suggested.

"I would like that very much."

Susan, who was carrying 13-month old Zoe on her hip, and I, carrying the memory of a wedding past and the annoyances of the present, made it to the receiving line. I told Courtney how beautiful she looked, and she was just that: drop-dead gorgeous. She was an absolute vision in her Cerelia Amaro gown. I could not begin to imagine how much it cost. Add in the price tags for the two bridesmaids' gowns, and I was sure that Mr. Sable had forked out well into 5-digits for all three ensembles. Assuredly, the Sable women wore them like runway models.

I congratulated Dylan, who was absolutely over the moon and ready to party. I greeted Mr. Sable and gave him a hug and a kiss on the cheek. He was like a father to all of us.

When I reached Dex near the end of the receiving line, he pulled me in for an embrace.

"Are you going to be OK?" he breathed into my ear.

I stepped back so he could look into my eyes and have confidence in my answer. I nodded. I overheard him ask Susan to please keep an eye on me until all of the ceremonial stuff was over and he could join us.

Reaching the end of the receiving line, Susan walked with me to the bar. Zoe happily babbled away, smiling at every guest we passed along the way.

DEX

Weddings. By the time Dylan's rolled around, I had already participated in more ceremonies than I cared to remember. The first one was my mother's second marriage. Like her first, that marriage had ended badly. Sadly, I am not aware of my mother's current marital status.

When I was young, I equated marriage to fairy-tales where the brides and grooms were the villains and villainesses, always successful in their prowl to destroy all that was good. Because divorce seemed to be the best thing for my mother, my world-view version of nursery rhymes and children's books did not conclude with the customary "happily-ever-after." If only she could have stayed away from men altogether.

Now, after living with Ginny for almost two years, I was beginning to see things differently. First and foremost, even though Ginny and Dan's marriage lasted less than twenty-four hours—due to their horrific car accident—I knew in my heart that theirs would have been one that lasted forever. Watching Ginny cross the dune that day in front of the original Carter beach house, I began to believe in the possibility. Even before we began dating, she had a positive impact on my perception of many things, marriage being just one of them. Up to that point in time, my mother's marriages had only shown me cruel treatment and the traumatic impact. I grew up in a dark world until Ginny entered my life. Once she arrived, I was beginning to see things beyond the struggle of day-to-day survival.

I had high hopes that Dylan and Courtney's marriage would stand the test of time. If they failed, it would send Courtney over the edge with all of her self-esteem issues, which were absolutely ludicrous. Courtney was a brilliant, hard working attorney, and to top it off, she was undeniably beautiful. Sadly, she was never convinced of either. For Dylan, if their marriage failed, he would receive scars he never deserved. He would bury himself in a sea of self-doubt, always managing to paralyze his best intentions with a game of second-guessing.

Which brings me back to my current relationship with Ginny. We had an unspoken and mutual understanding about wedding nuptials. Both of us were in "wedding recovery," so the topic was off-limits. It had been a little over three years since Ginny lost Dan, and it had been a little over a decade since I had escaped the wreckage of my mother's dismal attempts to survive.

I should probably stop blaming my mother for everything. If I really examined the root of her actions, I would most likely discover that she was only trying to provide for me. Her husbands always put a solid roof over our heads and fine food on the table, which were her first priorities. What she failed to find was love, the kind of love that makes a house a home, or a family thrive in its truest sense.

I have heard it said that life is about choices. However, I will always add that our choices are largely governed by our priorities.

When I was eighteen, my mother saw fit to turn me out. She probably thought I had injected enough turmoil into her relationships. Perhaps she felt that I had ingested enough poison from my stepfathers, as well. I was old enough to leave, yet still young enough to heal and recover from everything I had experienced and witnessed. She said it was time for me to go.

Ginny and I never talked about marriage. In fact, we had made an art form out of avoiding the subject. Attending Courtney and Dylan's wedding posed no threat to our status quo. We had become an impenetrable fortress when it came to preventing that discussion from entering into our guarded, yet treasured, relationship.

SUSAN

Unlike my wedding, which was a full Catholic mass at the behest of my mother, Courtney's was held outdoors in the middle of a vineyard, and the ceremony was very short and sweet. We were seated, Mayor Felts prayed a short prayer, Courtney and Dylan exchanged vows and rings, Dylan kissed his beautiful bride, and it was over.

I walked with Ginny through the receiving line. When we approached Pratt, I extended my hand. I had planned on saying something polite like, *"You look very handsome in your tux, "* or, *"It was a lovely ceremony, wasn't it?"* But he never gave me the opportunity to let the words form in my mouth. Instead, he pulled Zoe and me into his arms and whispered in my ear.

"After all of the pomp and ceremony is through, please save your dances for me, okay?"

"Why Pratt, that's a little possessive, don't you think?"

" *'Completely'* seems to be the word of the day," he smiled back.

Bridget Sable cleared her throat. She disapproved of her escort flirting with someone else.

"Thank you, Pratt. However, as you can see, I have my hands full," I responded, giving Zoe a boost up on my hip. "I make no promises."

"Not ever?"

"Never. I've sworn off of them."

"Well, we'll see about that."

Pratt bowed slightly, as if to tip a hat, and winked.

At the bar, Ginny and I ordered two glasses of Pinot Grigio. Ginny would have preferred something stronger, but we were at a winery, so it seemed the proper thing to do. Courtney and Dylan were kind enough to have us seated at Mr. Sable's table. Everyone else we knew was in the wedding party and seated at the head table. Someone had even thought far enough ahead to have an infant seat in place for Zoe.

Probably Dylan's doing.

After the first dance was in the books and everyone was seated, it was time for the toasts. Having composed one together, Ava and Bridget went first, sharing in its delivery. Mr. Sable fought back tears as the girls retold their favorite stories of growing up together as a threesome. They emotionally expressed how they were indebted to Dylan, Dex, and Pratt for bravely saving their little sister. Everyone there knew Courtney's story and gave the three humble heroes a standing ovation. Courtney's sisters concluded with how happy and proud their mother would have been. Tears flowed down Courtney's cheeks. Everyone at our table was sobbing. Elizabeth Sable had touched so many lives.

Next, Dex stood, looking extremely handsome in his tux. He gave a toast that centered on Dylan being his "little brother all grown up." He welcomed Courtney into the family, even though she was his little "sister," which made the whole thing sound totally wrong. Those who knew laughed, but I could see other faces that were clearly confused.

Mr. Sable leaned over to me. "That will give them something to talk about," he chuckled and shook his head.

Dex finished by telling Courtney that she had found a wonderful man with whom to spend the rest of her life. He told Dylan to make sure that he always did what Courtney asked, never try to win an argument, and everything would be just fine! His closing remark drew laughter and approval.

Then it was Pratt's turn, which seemed out of order, because Dex was the best man. I could not imagine what Pratt was going to say. Apparently, neither could he. He rose from his seat and strolled over to the piano, where a mic was at the ready and mounted on a stand. Clearly puzzled, Courtney looked over at Dylan. Pratt sat down on the piano bench, adjusted the mic to his height, and tapped on the head to make sure it was on. He shook out his hands, and placed them on the keys. The room went completely silent as he began playing a familiar introduction. Speaking softly into the mic as his fingers continued playing, he addressed Courtney.

"This song is for the lovely Mrs. Dylan Sable-Carter, as requested by the very lucky Mr. Dylan Carter."

Pratt, looking at the newlyweds, launched into "The Way You Look Tonight." He put his heart and soul into the song, sounding very much like Harry Connick Jr. I was taken by the soothing sound of his voice and his command of the piano. My mouth dropped. I had no clue.

"Some day, when I'm awfully low,
When the world is cold,
I will feel a glow just thinking of you
And the way you look tonight.

Yes, you're lovely, with your smile so warm
And your cheeks so soft,
There is nothing for me but to love you,
And the way you look tonight."

How did Dylan even know Pratt could sing and play like that? Even Dex seemed to be in on the newly revealed secret. Ginny and I were absolutely spellbound by the very romantic gesture. Every woman's heart melted like ice on hot black macadam. We were left as puddles evaporating in the hot summer sun.

". . . and the way you look tonight."

I was breathless and would have laid across a brass bed at that very moment to feel that kind of love directed toward me. His voice had taken me prisoner. I would have been his to do with as he pleased.

Pratt received a standing ovation as Courtney rushed over to plant a kiss on his cheek, and Dylan shook his hand. Pratt returned to his seat beside Bridget who leaned over, took his arm, and looked into his eyes as she offered words of praise before kissing him on his sublime cheek. I have to admit, a pang of jealousy stabbed my heart. I quickly looked away and turned my attention to Zoe.
My heart was breaking.

At the completion of dinner, one more obligatory dance was announced that demanded the wedding party's participation. Dylan led Courtney onto the dance floor, and after the first several phrases of their song, they motioned for Ava and Dex, and Bridget and Pratt to join them. Ava moved in close to Dex and was all about making eye contact while smoothing her fingers up and down the narrow lapel of his tux. Dex, being the gentleman that he was, returned the smiles but managed to fend off what looked like Ava's attempts to dance cheek-to-cheek and lock lips. I could sense Ginny's discomfort with Ava's mating dance.

Bridget, on the other hand, was not as overt in her attempts. Moving politely in Pratt's arms, it appeared that they were sharing a humorous conversation. Still, a pang of jealously stabbed me, slicing through my chest, again. They seemed so at ease and familiar with one another. After the dance, Pratt politely thanked Bridget before they separated.

Dex tried to quietly leave the dance floor, and Ava.

The evening became a whirlwind of drinks as the celebration escalated quickly.

PRATT

She was absolutely captivating in the way she moved. She studied the width and depth of the open area surrounded by the vineyard, taking in the enormity of it all and the sea of unfamiliar faces. When she spotted Dex and me standing by the arbor and waiting to seat the guests as they arrived, I detected a sense of relief cascade across her lovely face. I shoved Dex aside.

"May I have the honor of escorting you and your beautiful daughter to your seats?" I asked, extending my arm to her.

Holding Zoe on her hip, Susan accepted my invitation. As we made our way down the aisle, she moved in lockstep with me.

"How far are we going?" she asked hesitantly.

"You're family, so you get a front row seat on Dylan's side," I responded.

Susan protested at first, suggesting that Zoe might fuss and disrupt the proceedings.

"I think Dylan would be hurt if he didn't see you and Ginny there."

I have attended many weddings, and I have been a part of them, too, but few were as extravagant as this one. It was just on the precipice of "over the top," yet tastefully so.

While Courtney was beautiful, I could not take my eyes off of Susan. She was stunning. She had unknowingly committed one of the first offenses of proper wedding etiquette: "Thou shalt not outshine the bride."

DYLAN

Our day had finally arrived, and it was no easy task getting there. Courtney had physically survived the kidnapping and degradation carried out by one very sick bastard. However, the mental assault was equally horrific and brutal, if not worse, than the physical abuse and molestation. Courtney and I sought professional counseling as individuals and as a couple. In the months immediately following her kidnap and assault, we went to counseling three times a week. Ten months later and just before the wedding, we were able to pare back our appointments to once a week. Time was becoming such a precious commodity, yet we had so much to overcome.

I had taken another man's life in a very violent way, albeit to save Dex from being shot again. Looking back, it scared me to think that I could actually pick up a knife, or in this case a sword, and thrust it into the back of another person. At point blank range, Max was aiming at Dex's head. If Max had pulled the trigger, Dex's skull would have been blown to pieces. Pratt repeatedly said my instincts were right. Still, it was not that easy for me to gloss over so automatically, because after I drove the sword into Max, I did nothing to help him. Instead, I watched him die. Again, Pratt repeatedly assured me that even if I had tried, there was nothing I could have done to save him. Nonetheless, I was scared, frightened of what I was capable of doing.

Would I, could I, do it again? Is there a part of me that is as callous and as ruthless as my brother Derek?

I needed to be reassured that some deep, dark, lurking evil was not a part of my DNA.

It took a long time before we were able to joke about Dex being a marked target. He admitted many times that he felt like a ghost: that somehow he was not meant to be walking on the earth. Clearly, the opposite was true. Dex had literally "dodged a bullet," twice. If anyone had nine lives, or a guardian angel, it was Dex.

Courtney rose from the ashes in dramatic fashion. Fueled by all that had happened, she soared through her recovery. She became an advocate for abused women, and took cases pro bono to protect those who did not have the means or resources to protect themselves or their families. She was fierce and spared no time, expense, or mercy to punish those who preyed on the helpless, especially when children were involved. Her father and I worried that her work and close association to the very evil that sought to destroy her would cause her to backslide and drown in the recall of her attack.

What if she wakes up one day and everything comes crashing in on her?

To the contrary, Court found strength in the fight. She took what had been her worst moment in life and turned it for good. Her cause had become her healing medication. She found herself telling others that they could survive and find a better life waiting for them and their children beyond the suffering and the struggle that was currently trying to paralyze them. Because she believed in what she was saying, her advice and encouragement of others became her own source of restoration. Court was, as always, amazing to watch when she was in her zone.

In a very strange twist of fate, Max Black, in a handwritten Will, had named Courtney as sole heir of all his holdings. Courtney was repulsed by the notion, to say the least. To her, it was his way of compensating her for his dirty deed. In fact, "repulsed" does not come close to describing how it made her feel. Was it possible that he never intended to kill her? I knew he was crazy about her. I had underestimated just how crazy he was. Was he delusional enough to believe that he could force Courtney into some sick relationship? It became another issue she would have to deal with in her counseling sessions.

Max had no immediate family. However, his mother had a sister, Cheryl, who had taken Max in after his mother's disappearance and subsequent death. Attorneys for Cheryl Trimmel filed an injunction to contest the handwritten Will, stating that Max was not of sound mind when he wrote it just three days prior to kidnapping Court. Long story made short, Courtney hired her own attorney who was able to bring about an out-of-court settlement. Everything was to be sold, except for the large property where Max's field office trailer sat. The settlement stipulated that the proceeds would be split down the middle: half would go to Aunt Cheryl, and the other half would fund a foundation Court had created for the purposes of building and supporting a safe haven for abused women and their families. The facility would be built where the field office trailer once stood, the very property where Max had assaulted Courtney.

The future residents would not only be provided with food and shelter; they would also receive legal and personal counseling services. Courtney's sisters also pledged to provide pediatric and dental care, pro bono. Later, Cheryl Trimmel also donated half of her inheritance to the cause, demonstrating her commitment to make things right.

Construction of the facility would begin after we had returned from our honeymoon. If you have not already guessed it, the construction firm that employed Dex was hired to build the center, and I had promised my carpentry skills wherever needed.

Immediately following Courtney's rescue, I had closed up my home in Unionville and moved into the

Sable's garage apartment. In our spare time, of which there was none, Court and I went to work on finding a place for us to relocate. With Dex's and Pratt's help, we quickly found a place where we could live and I could also reestablish my shop. It was actually Pratt who knew the owners of the small farmette that had become available for rent.

Pratt brought both parties together in a conference room at the offices of Sable & Sable. The farmette needed a lot of work, and knowing that I was an excellent carpenter, the owners practically begged us to move in. Our rent was something short of a song.

Courtney never reentered her townhouse at Five Points. Her sisters, Ava and Bridget, graciously took care of listing and selling it. Together, Court and I moved into the farmette, and the owners subsequently sold it to us. It cost us more than a song, but once Court's townhouse sold, we were in a position to pay their asking price. I, on the other hand, was not ready to part with my home in Unionville. Unfortunately, my unwillingness to let it go had become a point of contention for Court, one that we had to address in our couple's counseling sessions, too. Court had convinced herself that I was not willing to sell it because, to her way of thinking, deep down inside I was not committed to our impending marriage. Nothing could have been further from the truth.

If she really believes that, why would she want to marry me?

Regardless, we had somehow made it to the altar.

I will never forget how beautiful Courtney was on our wedding day. A gentle breeze played with her long brunette hair that she wore down just for me. She knew that was how I liked it. Circling her head and holding her veil in place was a crown made of baby's breath. Her gown was soft and flowing, accentuating every voluminous contour of her slender enticing body. When she made her entrance under the arbor, she took a deep breath, looked up at me, and smiled. Rather than wait for her to reach me, I wanted to run down the aisle and intercept her.

Dex leaned over and whispered, "Are you ready for this?"

"Yes. Completely," I smiled through tears.

During the reception, Court's father introduced us to everyone who was anyone in Sussex County and the Delmarva Peninsula. Not to anyone's surprise, Pratt was on a first name basis with almost everyone who was there in attendance, as well.

"That guy should run for office," I thought as Pratt easily mingled, shaking hands with gentlemen and kissing the cheeks of their sophisticated ladies.

Mr. Sable explained that the Pratt family members were well known benefactors, and when Pratt's father could not attend social, political, and other fund raising events, Pratt would attend in his father's stead as the family's ambassador.

I also noticed that whenever Pratt was not with Bridget to fulfill the day's ceremonial obligations, he had Susan on his arm, making introductions. Something was definitely developing between those two.

GINNY

I did not know Ava all that well, but she apparently knew Dex well enough to maul and paw at him whenever she had the opportunity, all under the guise of the "wedding party show," of course.

Seriously?

I took small comfort in Dex's obvious discomfort with Ava's hands-on approach.

The Sable women were nature's artistry personified. They were tall and slender with soft curves in all the right places. Their long brunette hair had body and shine to die for. Their sky blue eyes could capture kingdoms, and they always seemed to move in slow motion like a fragrance or shampoo commercial. They were so easy to hate, in an envious way. And as of that day, thanks to Courtney and Dylan, they had become a part of the Carter family. We would be seeing a lot more of them.

Ava would obviously like to see a lot more of Dex.

Finally, the ceremonial first dances and toasts were completed. Throughout dinner, Ava never stopped talking to Dex. Seated one table away, I tried not to stare at them. She had the gift of gab and kept Dex occupied and engaged. He was too polite to shut her down. I probably would have tolerated it much better if she had not constantly had a hand on his arm, or anywhere else she thought she could without notice. Plus, whenever she thought she was losing his interest, she would lean into his shoulder, nudge him, or burst out in fake flirtatious laughter.

After dinner, the band turned up the volume and ramped up their set. Guests started making their way out to the dance floor. Dex excused himself, stood up from his chair at the head table, and removed his jacket, slinging it over his arm. He smiled in my direction and walked straight over to me. After carefully hanging his jacket over the back of my chair, he offered me his hand. I believe he left Ava mid-sentence, her mouth still hanging open.

Dex escorted me on to the dance floor. Courtney and Dylan danced their way over to us. Soon, Susan and Pratt joined us. Adorably, Pratt had Zoe on his hip as he danced with Susan. My tension eased. With Dex and my closest "family" members surrounding me, I was back in my comfort zone.

SUSAN

The sister duo of Ava and Bridget Sable was a force to be reckoned with. They were outgoing, uninhibited, gorgeous, mingling experts, and great dancers. Plus, each was independently wealthy. They were the whole package.

Why are those two alpha felines still single?

We were out on the dance floor loosening up and having our own little party when Ava and Bridget danced their way over to us and stole the spotlight. Our circle soon expanded as other guests, drawn out by all of the commotion, joined in. Ava and Bridget took "center stage" and danced away, causing a near frenzy. They were fluid and mesmerizing as they left it all on the dance floor. The other wedding guests began propelling the two Sable bridesmaids on with raucous clapping and cheering that reached a crescendo and acted as their catapult. Ava and Bridget reached out and grabbed Dex and Pratt, pulling them into the center ring of their circus. Dex and Pratt, being the hams that they were, went along with it, and the four of them killed it. Zoe loved watching Dex dance by like a crazy person. She clapped and squealed each time he went flying past us. I truly believed he was putting on a show just for Zoe. Ginny did not see it that way. It was all too much for her, and she sulked away to the ladies' room.

When the dance was over, Pratt and Dex walked breathlessly to where I was standing with Zoe, bouncing her in my arms.

"Where did Ginny go?" Dex asked with some apprehension.

"Ladies' room. I think she feels abandoned."

I probably should have left my commentary out of it.

"Oh. I'll go wait for her."

Dex hastily walked away, especially because Ava was making her way over, and Bridget was right behind her.

"Susan, it looks like Zoe would like to dance off some energy. Would you like me to take her?" Pratt kindly offered.

I was sure Pratt's offer had something to do with Bridget, who was closing in.

"Sure!"

I happily handed Zoe over to Pratt who twirled her around and carried her back out onto the dance floor while I was left to stand completely alone and thoroughly entertained by the charming man dancing with my delighted daughter. Courtney and Dylan, unknowingly, came to my rescue.

"Having a good time?" they asked in unison just as Ava and Bridget reached us.

"Oh, yes! This is a great party! Just look at Zoe on the dance floor with Pratt," I pointed out.

Everyone appropriately gushed.

"She really is sweet," Bridget complimented. "And Tom is so good with her! I think he is really into you, Susan."

That was not what I had expected to hear from Bridget.

"What? Really?"

I was totally caught off guard and almost lost my balance.

"You and Zoe were all he talked about during dinner, and I caught him gazing at you more than once," Bridget elaborated and winked.

My curiosity was piqued. I pulled her aside while Courtney, Dylan, and Ava continued their discussion of whatever.

"How well do you know Pratt?" I asked.

"Actually, I know his ex-wife better than I know Tom . . . uh, Pratt," Bridget whispered as if she preferred that no one else would hear her secret admission.

Shock sucked the oxygen out of my lungs. I was sure Bridget heard my gasp.

Pratt was married? How did I miss that? Why didn't he tell me?

"His ex-wife is a piece of work, let me tell you," Bridget added with humor.

I was ready to dig for more information when Pratt and Zoe came off the dance floor and were headed in our direction. I politely cleared my throat, signaling to Bridget that we should change the subject quickly.

"Well, ladies, this little one has completely worn me out! Would either of you care for a drink?"

"That is very kind of you, Tom. However, I have a friend I need to catch up with on the other side of the room. I'll see you two later!"

Bridget excused herself and was gone.

"Wow, I think I completely misjudged her," I corrected myself, thinking aloud.

"No surprise. Of the three Sable sisters, she is the sanest, and unfortunately, I think she is often wrongly accused because of the other two. In truth, Bridget is most like her mother. The other two are very different. If the three of them didn't look so much alike, I would've sworn that they were not related."

"Courtney?" I questioned, shocked that Pratt would defame the bride on her wedding day.

"Don't get me wrong, Courtney is a professional at work and fun to be around, but you have to admit that she can get a little crazy at times."

"Well . . ."

I was stalling, trying to get my head around what Pratt was saying and how to appropriately respond without throwing the bride under the bus.

"However, there are not many who could take what she has been dealt, rise above it, and convert what could have been negative energy into a positive force. She will emancipate many, and heal the masses. Very admirable, wouldn't you say?" Pratt completed his eloquent soliloquy by concluding with a rhetorical question.

"I guess so, when you put it that way," I nodded in agreement with Pratt's assessment.

Very well stated, Pratt. You should run for office.

He continued.

"Now, Bridget has always been a very sweet person. Rock steady. She is the one I took to the Arrest Pediatric Cancer fundraiser two years ago."

Oh, that explains so much. . . .

DEX

I waited a good ten minutes for Ginny to come out of the ladies' room.

"There you are. Are you going to be OK?" I searched for an answer, fearing that Ginny thought I had crossed some imaginary line.

She took a deep breath and looked up at me.

"Dex, I know you have ceremonial things that you have to do. And I know that you have to pretend that you are having a good time, even if you're not. I get it. But watching you with someone as attractive and as successful as Ava is very difficult for me. I don't know if I can stay and watch much longer. This is torture for me."

I combed my fingers very gently through her exotic amber hair. She pressed her head into my hand and lifted her eyes to mine. We were in a secluded area with no one else around, lending us a moment of treasured privacy.

"You're the one that I'm madly in love with, and I don't see Ava the way you just described her."

"Then how do you see her?"

"What I'd rather do is describe how I see you. You are the most extravagant woman I have ever known. You are strong in spirit, smart as a whip, funnier than hell, a culinary artist, and a maestro at the piano."

"Oh?"

"Wait, there's more. I'm just getting warmed up."

I grinned and moved closer, wrapping my arms around her waist and sliding my hands down to massage her buttocks. Aroused, I found myself pressing into her.

"You, my dear, have an effect on me that is hard to control, literally."

Taking her hand, I pressed it into the fly of my rented tuxedo pants.

These pants should be so lucky!

My whispers became heated and labored as my hands went back to gather her into my body.

"You are stunning and elegant, and you bring out the bad boy in me," I growled into her neck as she tilted her head back.

"Hmmm . . . this bad boy is certainly making himself known," she encouraged.

"You are so fascinating, and when we get home, this bad boy is going to explore every exotic inch of you: mind, body, and soul . . . completely. Did I say 'body?' "

"Yes, you clearly said 'body,' " Ginny chuckled at my mocking of the vows recently spoken by the newly married couple.

My hands moved to her face and brought her lips to mine. Feeling deprived, she was hungry and ravaged my mouth. Her body shuddered and I nearly went over the edge. When our lips separated, I laid my forehead against hers and looked into her eyes.

"Baby, you have ruined me. I could never look at another and see them the way that I see you. You are my one and only. You are my only distraction."

"I'm sorry, Dex. I don't doubt or blame you. It's just difficult for me to witness someone else clawing at you for your attention. And yet, who can blame her?"

"I'm sorry, too. I'll do my best to hold Ava at bay, but know that I am yours, completely yours."

Yes, "completely" certainly seems to be the word of the day.

COURTNEY

"Bridget, it's my wedding day. Do you think she could stop with the flirtations, just once?"

"I have my doubts. She has been after him for the last several months."

"Really? How do you know that?"

"Because every time I run into her, she asks about him. Today, she wanted to know if he was ready to start dating."

"You have got to be kidding. How rude is that? You're his daughter. We lost our mother. And she is inconsiderate enough to ask you that question on my wedding day? I don't care if she is a city councilwoman, I will call her out on this!"

"I'd let it go, Courtney. It's not worth getting riled up about. Daddy's a big boy. He can handle it."

"Oh, it just frosts me that we even had to invite her."

"It's what you do when everyone on your client list travels in the upper social and political stratosphere," Bridget defended our father's well-intended all-inclusive guest list.

"It's all crap, when you come right down to it. But I get it."

Shit.

I threw down the rest of my champagne and went looking for my husband.

"My husband"... I like the way that sounds!

SUSAN

I thought I was getting to know him. Apparently, I knew very little about the tall and very handsome Officer Tom Pratt. He handed Zoe back to me and smiled.

"Have dinner with me tomorrow night," Pratt blurted out of nowhere. "I know of a little place on Franklin Avenue where the seafood is incredible and the chef has the day off, so he can certainly create a plate of delectable, fresh fare just for you."

I had attended several functions with Pratt in the past, and he had always behaved like a perfect gentleman, but I have always been leery about letting my guard down when we were alone. Fortunately, most of the time when Pratt was around, we had been in the company of Dex and Ginny, or surrounded by hundreds of other people at some public function. This time, Pratt's invitation sounded a little more intimate.

"When were you going to tell me that you were married once before?" I asked while looking down at the wine I was nervously swirling around in the bottom of my glass. "And when were you going to tell me that you've dated Bridget Sable?"

I paused to let my questions breathe like fine wine, and then I looked up at him.

Pratt had blurted out his invitation, so I felt like I had the right to hasten my request for information that he had withheld from me in the past. I tried not to sound upset, but in truth, I was.

"Whoa!" Pratt raised his hands and took a step back. "I just assumed you knew about my previous marriage.

When it fell apart, it seemed like everyone in town was involved. I just assumed it was common knowledge and there was no need for me to wear a sign that says, 'I'm Divorced.' "

Pratt mocked me by pretending that he was holding a sign in front of his broad chest.

"Really. Did you forget that I live in Valley Forge? How would I have known?"

"You *lived* in Valley Forge, and I just thought that Ginny or Dex would have told you, especially because Ginny acted as my character witness before our first date."

"I am willing to bet that Ginny doesn't know, either. She doesn't get caught up in everyone else's business like some people do."

"And yet, here we are, discussing something that I have worked hard to put behind me."

Pratt placed his hands on his hips and shifted, looking slightly annoyed.

"And you used to date Bridget? Is that why you spoke so highly of her?"

I should have let it go. Did I even hear his earlier protest? Obviously, I had chosen to ignore it.

"Do I detect a note of jealousy?" Pratt jabbed back, crossing his arms in front of his chest.

"Jealousy? Why would I be jealous? I am just surprised that you never shared these little details with me before."

"I didn't see the need. So, Susan, dinner tomorrow evening, yes or no?"

He dropped his arms to his narrow hips again, signaling the end of our debate. Pratt always had a way of ending a conversation by simplifying the complicated with something black and white.

I was hesitant to answer quickly, so Pratt took the opportunity to further elaborate on his offer.

"Listen, Susan, I'd really like to get to know you better and answer all of your questions. Why not ask Ginny and Dex to watch Zoe, and come have dinner with me, just the two of us."

COURTNEY

The day was everything I had hoped for and more, way more. My father, as he had threatened to do, spared no expense. From the moment Dylan and I said, "I do," until we packed up and left at midnight, we had danced and partied like never before. My dad, Dylan, and I were the last to leave. Even the band—which had already played an extra hour—had packed up and was long gone. I know, very unusual for the newlyweds to be the last to leave, but Dylan and I were enjoying the party. Besides, the flight to our honeymoon destination did not leave until 2:00 PM the following day.

"Dad, thanks for a wonderful celebration," I said as I gave him a parting hug.

"Not too big?" he asked, hoping his big bash for his little girl was not too overwhelming, yet grand enough to impress his list of celebrity clients and friends.

"No. It was just right."

Dylan shook my dad's hand.

"Thank you, Mr. Sable."

"Dad. Please, call me Dad."

"I'll try, sir."

Was it possible that my father intimidated Dylan? It was something my new husband would have to work on.

Our drive to the Boardwalk Plaza Hotel in Rehoboth was a bone-weary, quiet one.

"How are you doing, Baby?" Dylan asked.

Dylan kept his left hand on the wheel of my Porsche and gently rubbed my arm with his right as I started to doze off on our way to the hotel. Dylan had booked a fabulous oceanfront suite for our first night as Mr. and Mrs. Dylan Carter.

"Hmmm . . . I'm exhausted. Did you have a good time?"

"I did. And you?"

"Yes."

I swiveled in my seat to study his handsome profile as he kept his eyes on the road.

"I can't believe we've landed here, you and me."

"You can't? I can't," Dylan replied. "Never in a million years would I have believed that someone like you would ever want to spend the rest of her life with a guy like me."

"What's that supposed to mean?" I snapped back.

There was something authentic lingering in the core of his sarcasm.

"You know."

"I don't think I do."

In truth, I had had my suspicions. I just wanted him to say it so we could put it to rest.

"Well, you're a high powered attorney, and a damn good one at that, and I'm just a lowly carpenter."

Before I could verbalize my response, I just started laughing.

"Jeez, Dylan. Jesus was a lowly carpenter, and if you're anything like him, then I should be so lucky to just kiss your feet, like Mary."

Dylan took his eyes off the road for a split second and looked at me with a quizzical cocked eye.

"Since when do you know so much about the Bible, Court?"

"Cover-to-cover, my friend."

"What? Why would you do that? I didn't think you had a religious bone in your body."

" 'Religious' is an often misused and misinterpreted adjective. I'm religious about a lot of things like brushing my teeth every morning when I wake up and every night before I go to bed, or starting every morning with a cup of coffee . . ."

"I know, strong and straight up," Dylan finished my sentence.

"Right. Just the way I like you."

I rubbed the metaphorical rise in his pants.

"Hmmm . . . so that makes me like Jesus and a strong cup of black coffee?"

"Let's not get carried away before you get a big head."

We both laughed at the accidental innuendo.

"Baby, I think you just did!"

Dylan grabbed my hand and added force to its placement.

"You need to drive faster!" I suggested.

We laughed again. Dylan shifted in his seat to get more comfortable with his latest development.

"Seriously, Court, you've read the Bible cover-to-cover?"

"Yes. Your dad gave one to me. He said I should read it, and he added that it was chock full of scandal, sex, violence, and romance."

"Whaaaat? My dad? When did this happen?"

"Shortly after I brought Dex and him into my office for their 'Come to Jesus' meeting."

"Really? Is that what you called it?" Dylan asked, obviously in a "full Court press" below the steering wheel.

"Probably. One of us did. Anyway, it was a chronological Bible, so it read like a story, and he was right: it was full of scandal, sex, violence, and romance. Who knew?"

"Yeah, who knew?" Dylan echoed incredulously.

I stopped my assault below the belt so he could focus on the road and what I was about to say.

"Maybe I don't subscribe to everything the evangelicals preach, but I did discover that Jesus was probably the best attorney who ever walked the earth," I professed.

"Really? And yet, you don't believe in Christianity."

"Nope. The whole thing is a little difficult to swallow."

I felt Dylan clutch. I continued.

"However, having said that, the Bible is a book worth reading, and there are a great many lessons worth reflecting upon, proverbs worth memorizing, and parables to ponder."

"You are a mystery, Mrs. Carter."

"Good. I intend to keep it that way."

We received applause from the desk clerks as Dylan carried me, and my overnight bag, past the check-in desk and directly to the elevator. Dylan was in his tux, and I was still in my wedding gown with white crepe silk de chine flowing in our wake.

Inside our suite, he put me down on my feet and gently kissed me.

"Welcome to our honeymoon suite, Mrs. Carter."

"Thank you, Mr. Carter."

I took my bag from his shoulder.

"Now, if you don't mind, I would like to get out of this wedding gown."

"Yes, I would like that, too! Do you need any help?"

"Nothing more than the zipper. I can handle the rest."

"Given the opportunity, so could I!" Dylan beamed.

DYLAN

That night, I left the balcony door ajar so we could hear the ocean throughout the night and wake up to it in the morning. What happened next was thoroughly embarrassing.

COURTNEY

It was not how I had envisioned my wedding night.

Ava, Bridget, and I had gone shopping several weeks earlier so they could help me pick out some wedding accessories, clothes for my honeymoon vacation, and lingerie for my wedding night.

Inside the hotel suite, I excused myself to slip out of my wedding gown and into something much more seductive.

DYLAN

"What time is it?" I asked drowsily.

"About 7:00."

"Really?"

Gazing out over the ocean, I shot up in bed and rubbed the stubble on my face as the penetrating sun showed no regard for my eyes.

"What happened?"

"Nothing. Absolutely nothing," Court smirked as she sat up and gathered her long hair, pushing it back over her bare shoulders.

"Oh, Baby, I am so sorry," I apologized, realizing what had *not* happened.

"It's OK. You were tired."

I looked across at the sheer negligee barely covering her body.

"No, looking at you, I am *reeeeeeally* sorry."

Courtney laughed again.

"It's all right, Dylan. Watching you sleep was one of the most romantic things I have ever done. The moon was full, casting its soft light across the bed, the ocean waves provided calming background music, and you were here with me. What more could I want?"

"You could have wakened me."

"Yes, I could have, but last night and all day yesterday was not about great sex."

"It wasn't? What's not so great about it?" I asked as if I was mortally wounded and had made a huge miscalculation about all things vital for a good marriage.

Courtney jabbed me.

"DYLAN!" she scolded. "The sex *is* great, as far as I can tell with my very limited experience. However, I am here because, even without the sex, I would want to spend the rest of my life with you."

"So, if I had been involved in an accident and could no longer, you know . . . you would have married me anyway?" I had intentionally asked, knowing that she would have to say "yes."

"There are other creative ways to make love, you know," was the answer I got from my self-proclaimed naive wife.

"Oh, and that's coming from your very 'limited experience,' is it?"

"Are you mocking me, Dylan Carter?" Courtney accused with a straight, agitated face.

I could not tell if she was annoyed or joking. I chose to believe the latter.

"Maybe. But rather than argue the point, I think I'd rather spend the next hour or two getting creative with my very snarky wife."

"You would?"

Her voice became instantly soft and seductive as her hand slid under the sheet and across my naked torso. Wrapped in sheer erotic fabric, her body drifted across mine as she lowered herself on top of me. The sensation of silk, warmth, and weight was arousing, to say the least. Her hips were moving in time with the ocean waves as they lapped against the coastline. Her lips met mine, and a low moan escaped her. She was going to send me over the edge.

I carefully rolled Courtney over to her side, wrapping her outside leg up and over my hip. With the next exertion, she was totally mine. I brushed the hair from her face and kissed her, again. She responded by pressing deeper. Instinctively, our bodies moved in and out with the timing of the rolling ocean just outside our balcony doors. Sometimes they crashed onshore like thunder, and other times, they rippled along the shoreline with small vibrations. Some gathered steam before the strong undertow curled beneath them. Others sneaked in like a cleansing breath before gathering more momentum.

In the morning light and the reflection of the glistening water below, Courtney and I consummated our vows with the various ebbs and flows of the ocean's pulse.

CHAPTER TWO

PRATT

She said, "Yes."

She would arrive within the half-hour, and I was ready.

There it was—the much-anticipated knock on the front door. (My house was so small, I had no need for a doorbell.)

"Come on in! Did you have any trouble finding the place?"

"No, not at all. Right next door to the Presbyterian Church parking lot, just like you said. In fact, I parked in their lot. Is that OK?"

"Perfect. How's Zoe?"

"She's good. She loves Dex and Ginny, so leaving her with them has never been an issue."

"Good. I hope you don't mind my asking for an evening alone."

"Mind? Not really. Just a little puzzled by it."

"Don't overthink it, Susan. That's how relationships become complicated. Are you looking for complicated?"

"No. As a matter of fact, I'm not looking at all."

"Good. That will definitely keep things simple. Would you care for something to drink? I have a nice unoaked chardonnay you might enjoy."

"That sounds nice," she answered politely.

As I uncorked the bottle of wine, I watched her out of the corner of my eye. She was studying my house: my very small and humble abode.

I lived in a very confined two-story cottage that was adjacent to the Presbyterian Church property in town. The location was perfect because I could walk to the police station when on duty and to church on Sundays. When you entered my house through the front door, you were standing in the living room. Immediately behind the living room was the eat-in kitchen. There was no formal dining room. Upstairs were two small bedrooms that shared the only full bath. I had turned the second bedroom into a well-organized, pseudo office/storage area. It was all I needed.

Over dinner, our conversation drifted toward some of the more life altering events in our separate pasts. So much for uncomplicated.

"So, Pratt, what brought you to Lewes?"

Susan was the more inquisitive one.

"My parents own property on the Lewes-Rehoboth Canal. We would spend several months a summer there. When I graduated from the University of Pennsylvania, I applied to several police academies near the water on the East and West Coasts, Sussex County being one of them, and this is where I landed."

"I see, and when did you meet your wife?"

"That would be my EX-wife."

"OK, your *ex*-wife."

"We actually met here, in Lewes."

"How old were you?"

"We were just out of school."

"How long were you married?"

"Just a little over two years."

"What happened?"

"You are full of questions tonight, aren't you? And here I was beginning to think that you couldn't care less about me."

"Just answer the question, Pratt. That's if you're up to the same interrogation you gave me the first time we met."

"Oh, so that's what this is all about. Are we trying to even the score?"

"Who's keeping score? I have no need for a competition to prove anything. I'm fine with who I am."

Susan was getting a little feisty. I liked it.

"Yes, well, to prove that I am not intimidated by your over abundance of self-confidence, I will answer all your questions. Continue."

"So, I repeat, why did your ex-wife leave you?"

I laughed. Susan had tried to maneuver me into admitting that my ex-wife had left me, insinuating that I was the reason for my failed marriage.

"What makes you so sure that she left me, and why is that so important?"

"Just a good guess. A guy like you probably has many temptations."

"And many faults."

"There's that, too."

"The truth, Susan, is that she walked out on me. I came home one morning after my night shift, and she was gone."

"Just like that? There were no warning signs?"

"There were plenty of warning signs. I just chose to ignore them."

"Did you love her?"

"Of course, I loved her. I loved her more than I had ever loved anyone, or anything. I thought I would die that day and many months thereafter."

"Oh, Tom, I am so sorry. I didn't know."

"Thank you, but it really doesn't matter anymore. Immediately after, she would never take or return any of my phone calls, or voicemails. The divorce papers arrived several weeks later, and her attorney made it clear that she had no intention of reconciling, so I eventually signed the documents. It was the worst year of my life."

SUSAN

It was probably the worst date of my life. I left Pratt's house that evening convinced that he would never call me again. For some strange reason, that bothered me.

Pratt had gone through a tremendous amount of trouble to prepare one of the best dinners, ever. With Frank Sinatra, Nat King Cole, and Ella Fitzgerald crooning in the background, I watched Pratt prepare a thick, creamy New England clam chowder. He followed it with a cranberry spinach salad. Then he served la pièce de résistance: Dungeness crab, with sides of macaroni and cheese and stewed tomatoes. Most people boast about Maryland blue claw crab for good reason; however, if you want to taste a sweet meaty crab, order Dungeness. We polished off a bottle of unoaked chardonnay during dinner, and then retired to the living room where we finally relaxed with homemade strawberry banana gelato and a cup of coffee.

Unfortunately, I had ungraciously hit him with a barrage of impertinent questions during dinner. Pratt endured my inquisition and answered them all, always remaining the perfect gentleman, despite my bad manners.

"Is there anything else you would like to know about me, Miss McCabe?"

"No, I am really sorry. I didn't know."

"And now that you do know about my blighted past, do you think any less of me?"

"No, not at all. I didn't mean to make you sound like the bad guy."

Conversely, I wanted to tell him that his honest recounting of his personal history made me appreciate him all the more. Perhaps we had a common bond, after all. But I feared that I had already said too much.

The tapers were burning down and the music was drawing to a close. I could feel Pratt shift.

"Susan, there is a reason I asked you here, tonight."

Where's he going with this?

"Oh? What might that be?"

"At Courtney and Dylan's reception, do you remember Mayor Felts pulling me aside?"

"Yes, I do. I figured he had police business to discuss with you. Anything serious?"

"Yes and no. It depends. What I am about to tell you stays in this room. You and I have been friends for a while now. We even had a date or two, which I have enjoyed immensely . . ."

I knew it. I overstepped with my interrogation of his private life.

" . . . and I have grown to respect your sensibility and opinion."

Great. Here comes the "but" let down.

"So, I'd like to ask your opinion about a very important matter."

"Oh? OK."

I waited on pins and needles.

"Mayor Felts will not be running for re-election this May. He thinks I should consider running. What do you think?

"Holy shit, Pratt. Of course, you should! You know every person in town. No, make that the entire county. You're on the boards of a gazillion organizations, including the Sable-Carter Women's Shelter. Yes. You should do it. Mayor Felts wouldn't pull you aside if he didn't think you were the person for the job. From what I know of Mayor Felts, he would be a great endorsement for you."

"See, that is why I asked you. There are other implications. I will have to resign from my current job. Otherwise, it would be a serious conflict of interest."

"Oh. Is that something you want to do?"

"Not really. I enjoy what I do. At least, I did before Dex moved back and started wreaking havoc again," Pratt remarked straight-faced.

Really? Is Dex that much trouble? Well, he did start that one ruckus at the yacht club shortly after I had met Pratt.

"If Dex had kept his doors locked, I may have never met you." Pratt stared into my eyes.

I felt my blood rushing to my face, causing me to blush.

"Oh. So you were kidding about the 'wreaking havoc' part?" I felt stupid.

"Not entirely. Meeting you hasn't been altogether free of its own unrest."

"I don't know if that's good or bad."

"Neither do I," remarked Pratt. "At least not for now. I guess we'll have to wait and see how this all plays out."

"True. The last thing you need is a liability like Zoe and me."

"What does that mean?" Pratt looked annoyed at my suggestion.

"I don't know what any of this means, Pratt."

Around 10:00, I thanked Pratt for a wonderful evening. I wanted to tell him how much I enjoyed his company, but the words were not forthcoming. He walked me to the door, thanked me for joining him for dinner, then placed an obligatory kiss on my cheek. He watched from his stoop as I made my way to my car and waved one last time before I drove off.

Dammit.

When I arrived back at Ginny's, Zoe was already asleep for the night. Both Dex and Ginny were in the great room on the third floor, having a beer, sharing popcorn, and watching a movie.

"Hey, how was your dinner?" Dex called out as I went to the fridge to pour a glass of wine.

"Very nice. Dinner was absolutely wonderful and Pratt was, as ever, a perfect gentleman, almost too perfect. In fact, I doubt that he will ever call me again."

On cue, my cell phone rang.

"Hello?"

"Hi, Susan."

"Oh. Hi, Pratt."

I tried to conceal my surprise.

"I was just calling to make sure you got home OK."

"I'm here, and I'm fine. Thank you for your concern."

"No problem. Good night, Susan."

"Good night, Pratt."

"That sounded dandy!" Ginny stated sarcastically. "What went on with you two?"

"Everything got off to a great start: wine, soup, salad, and casual conversation. But after he served the main course, I launched into an interrogation about his marriage."

"HE'S MARRIED?" Dex and Ginny gasped in unison, nearly spewing beer and popcorn.

"No. He *was* married. Now, he's not. Didn't you know?"

"I had no idea," Dex said reflectively stunned.

"Yes, he was married for about two years to someone he was obviously very crazy about."

"Wow. I had no idea," Ginny echoed in disbelief.

"So, I have my doubts that he will ever ask me out again, which is a shame because I was beginning to believe that he was human, with real unfortunate circumstances, like the rest of us. I was beginning to believe that I could actually like the guy. Oh, c'est la vie."

"I'm sorry," Ginny pouted.

"It's OK. This dating thing is not for me, anyway. I have Zoe to look after, and that is enough, for now.

I had difficulty sleeping that night.

PRATT

The next night, when I walked into the station to begin the night shift, two federal agents were waiting for me.

"Daly, Wilson, what brings you here?" I asked, surprised by their late night visit.

We had history.

"Let's step into the conference room," Daly suggested, though it was more like a direct order.

The dispatcher watched as I escorted the agents into the conference room and shut the door.

"Pratt, we've done a little investigation of our own into the matters of Sussex County inmate Derek Carter and Mr. Marco Corelli of Malvern, Pennsylvania, as you had suggested we should."

"What did you find?"

"More than we expected. First, Mr. Corelli did order the DNA test as you had suspected. We have no proof that Corelli broke into the Carter beach house to steal the dirty diaper that provided the infant's DNA, but we highly suspect that he either ordered the break in, or carried it out. Also, there is sufficient evidence to believe that he is siphoning money from Valley Forge Graphic Design, just as you had suspected, and has taken kickbacks from several of its vendors.

"The bigger issue is what we discovered he may be doing with the money. From what we can gather, last year he probably siphoned half a million and raked in another 2.5 million."

"His dealings are bigger than even I suspected," I admitted.

"It's not drugs," Daly clarified.

"What's he selling?"

"Children. Some orphans, some not."

"What? I'll kill the bastard. How long has this been going on?"

"Our guess? He could be into his third or fourth year. Again, we're building the case now. It's going to take time. He's been pretty good at covering his tracks."

CHAPTER THREE

DYLAN

Courtney had refused to help with our honeymoon plans. She justified her lack of cooperation by reminding me that she had to handle all of the wedding details and arrangements with her father, so the honeymoon was on me. Because she wanted to be surprised, I was not permitted to discuss any of it with her. I was on my own, somewhere way out of my comfort zone.

She had left me no choice but to call the two most world traveled people that I knew of at the time: Mr. Sable and Tom Pratt. We met at Agave. Dex came along, too. It had something to do with a margarita that Mr. Sable had owed him.

"What does she like to do?" Pratt asked.

If Courtney's dad had not been sitting across the table from me, I could have answered that in any one of a million ways. Courtney may have been the last one out of the gate, but she sure had an imagination that made up for anything she lacked in experience.

As you can imagine, the trauma she suffered at the hands of Max Black had slowed her down considerably. The medication to treat her anxiety and depression had initially put a damper on her ability to enjoy our intimacy. Her days became void of all the lows, as well as her highs. However, without medication, she may not have been able to handle much at all, let alone our lovemaking. Our therapists told us to be patient. They said that as long as we were talking to each other and were careful not to isolate ourselves, we would survive. We continued to make progress every day.

"Let's see, what does Courtney like to do?" I mused. "She's not much of a beach person."

Mr. Sable agreed.

Good, I was on the right track.

"She loved our long ski weekends in Vermont," I recalled out loud.

"That's it!" Pratt blurted out. "I know the perfect ski resort in Argentina. It's winter there in June. I'm assuming you both know how to ski?"

"Yes, we do. In fact, Stowe was not much of a challenge, especially for Court."

"Good. I'm sending you to San Carlos de Bariloche, in the province of Rio Negro, for ten glorious days," Pratt chirped as if it was that simple and a done deal.

"You're sending us?"

"Yes, your flight will leave Wilmington on Sunday afternoon. After two stops to refuel, you'll land in Bariloche on Monday morning. A driver will meet you on the tarmac and take you to the lodge. We'll make sure you are booked for my parents' penthouse suite. Everything will be fully stocked and room service will be comped."

Pratt went on throwing out times and places like he was our personal travel agent.

"Whoa! Whoa! Who's we?" I tried to slow him down.

"Sorry. My parents own a ski lodge in Bariloche. The skiing is fantastic there, and there's plenty to do in the village. You'll love it."

"That's insane, Pratt. Your parents own a lodge in Argentina?"

"Yes, and they would love it if you stayed there. In fact, they'd be honored."

"How do you know that?"

"Because they are always bugging me to go, or asking why I don't send my friends."

"I don't know. Round trip airfare has got to be $3,000, or more, per person. That's very kind of you to offer, but I'll have to give it some thought."

"No, no. The airfare is free. I'm sorry I didn't make that clear. My parents own a Learjet. You'll be doing them a favor. They'll probably take advantage of your flight and send some parcels down for the lodge staff. They always do."

"Pratt, this is really too much."

"Dylan, I know his parents. Believe me, they would want you to receive this. It's what they do," Mr. Sable added convincingly.

"It's what they do, huh?" I repeated at a near whisper. "I really need to give this some thought. What is the name of their lodge?"

"I'll write it down and give you the website address so you can do the research and give it proper consideration. You won't be able to see their penthouse and its accommodations, that's private information. But believe me, you won't regret it."

"Thank you, Pratt. I am really grateful for the offer. It's just a lot to take in."

Courtney and I landed in San Carlos de Bariloche on Monday morning, as promised. She was thrilled. Pratt made Mr. Sable, Dex, and me vow not to divulge the givers of the gift.

Of course, I was going to tell Courtney, if she asked. She was my wife. No secrets.

COURTNEY

It was wonderful to get away from the summer heat and humidity blanketing the East Coast. Landing in an area surrounded by snow-covered mountains was surreal. Landing in a private Learjet with Dylan, my husband and the only other passenger onboard, was beyond my wildest dreams.

The crew catered to our every need and beyond. Once we reached cruising altitude, we were served champagne and chocolate covered strawberries. Dinner included salmon with creamy dill sauce, perched on top of a Parmesan risotto with a side of steamed baby asparagus. It was so good! Dylan said everything tasted better at 30,000 feet, including something he wanted after we excused ourselves and moved to the private bedroom suite at the back of the jet. We joined the Mile High Club that night and exercised our membership privileges several times before landing.

After we had touched down the next morning and just as Dylan had promised, a limo was waiting for us on the tarmac. The driver, who introduced himself as Javier, greeted us by name, escorted us to the limo, and gathered our luggage. After he gave a few brief instructions to the pilot, co-pilot, and the flight crew, he got into the driver's seat of the limo and we were on our way. Javier explained that he would be at our service throughout the duration of our stay. He said that our ski equipment had been delivered the day before, and he would attend to it whenever we needed. He recommended several shops, restaurants, and sites. When we neared the lodge, Javier drove the limo up a private drive and through a gate that he operated remotely. The limo stopped at a secluded entrance to the lodge, and Javier quickly jumped out to open my door for me. Once Dylan and I were out of the limo, Javier reached into his pocket and took out a wireless device.

"Mrs. Carter, please look this way," Javier instructed. "Now you, Mr. Carter."

"Mrs. Carter" . . . I like the way that sounds, and I love the way it rolls off Javier's tongue in his native Argentine accent!

Javier tapped his device several times, the same device that had opened the gate.

"There, you're all set. To enter your exclusive penthouse lobby, stand on this carpet, look directly ahead, and the doors will unlock. You'll do the same at the elevator, which will take you directly up to the penthouse."

Javier handed a card to Dylan and one to me. He continued.

"Here are the numbers to call for the car. Arrival time will be no more than ten minutes after you make your request. If you wish to use the jet, we request three hours lead time so we can have pilots and crew onboard and a flight plan filed. If the jet is unavailable, we can provide a helicopter; however, the downside is that it will increase your travel time. Any questions?"

I was still trying to process that the limo and Learjet, or helicopter, were at our disposal.

"Good. I'll deliver your luggage. Congratulations and enjoy your stay," Javier smiled as he immediately got to work unloading our luggage.

The elevator door closed behind us and we were jetted up several stories. Within seconds, the doors reopened.

The "penthouse" was not like anything you would find in a major city. The decor and view was from the cover of a travel magazine. It sat atop a rustic lodge. Three sides were glass, opening up to a view of a large lake with the Andes Mountains in the background. It was breathtaking. The kitchen, dining, and living areas formed one large, open space. The master suite was up two steps and was also constructed with three walls of glass that showcased another breathtaking view.

"Dylan, there are no curtains. . . ."

DYLAN

Most people would not list curtains as one of their required accommodations. I had never thought to ask! I thought we were well beyond Court's shyness. In truth, *we* were. It was other people she worried about.

"Court, no one can see us up here. Look out these windows. No one has a view of us! Overlooking the lake and the mountains, we can make love in the middle of the day, and not one single soul will see us. We'll have the Andes Mountains and Lake Nahuel Huapi at our feet. This place is spectacular!"

"OK. I'll try. Let it never be said that I passed up a great adventure."

"Babe, everything with you is a great adventure."

"Yeah, but it would be nice to have just one slice of normalcy every now and then. You know, every once in a while, all I want is cheese pizza, no exotic toppings. Just plain, carb and dairy overload, comforting pizza."

"Come here." I took Court's hand and drew her close. "I never expected normalcy when I proposed to you. Don't go and get all stale and stagnant on me. Not now. Not here!"

Court took a swipe at my arm.

"You make it sound like I'm eighty years old!" she sniped.

I grabbed her arms and drew her in for a long hard kiss while my hands moved down to her firm butt and pressed her into something that was rising quicker than thick pizza dough. Courtney moaned and melted. There was a quiet knock at the door that startled my softening wife.

"I'll get that," she whispered. "It's probably Javier with our luggage. You stay right here and keep your motor running until I get back."

Court was anything but stale and stagnant. She embraced adventure, and that day, in full view of the lake, she undressed for me and left all of her cares and hang-ups at the foot of the mountains. The climb was incredible: slow and deliberate. We worked in tandem, each taking the lead when the other tired. When Court was in control, she loved to entertain me and take me to the edge of my limits. Looking down a crevice that would surely plummet me to my death a thousand times over, she would catch me just before I reached the point of no return. After regaining stamina, we would move forward, again, picking up momentum as we ascended together. It was a long, slow climb to the final climax. Breathless. Exhilarated. Spent.

An hour later, we ordered a pizza. Double cheese pizza with thick crust.

PRATT

I hated things about my job for the very reasons I had gotten into it in the first place: I could not stand by and let defenseless people get hurt. This particular case involving Corelli cut deep because its victims were young families and their children. I also knew that he was taking advantage of Susan's kindness and trust, something he should have treasured.

To make matters worse, I was getting too involved. My worst fears had been substantiated, and my suspicions were becoming my worst nightmare. Because it involved Susan, it was going to become personal, rapidly, no matter how hard I tried to prevent it from happening.

I had strict orders not to disclose or discuss any of the findings with anyone, especially Susan McCabe, her friends, associates, and her family. Because of her part-ownership of Valley Forge Graphic Design and her association with Marco Corelli, Susan was also a person of interest. She was being investigated, caught in the web, despite the lack of her knowledge or physical presence. Fortunately—as if anything could be fortunate about this investigation—the case was receiving top priority because children were involved.

My skin bristled at the thought of Marco Corelli, a favored associate and toady for Derek Carter, benefiting from such a heinous crime against the innocent. It took every ounce of self-control not to run out, find Corelli, and beat him senseless. Instead, I would have to remain quietly impatient and let justice take its course.

In the meantime, I had to harness my heart. This was clearly not the time to get wrapped up in a deeper relationship with Susan. Besides, I had a campaign to put together and the investigation could become a liability.

How is this even possible? She is the kindest, most straight-up person I know, which is why I asked her about my interest in potentially running in the first place.

Was I really going to be the candidate and elected official that allowed the media to dictate my life?

CHAPTER FOUR

GINNY

"Courtney and Dylan got married!" Even when I said it out loud, it still seemed unreal. Dylan, the one who second-guessed every decision he had ever made in his life, the one who Dan always said had a real string of bad luck with women, one of the most handsome bachelors left on the face of the earth, had tied the knot. And not with just any woman: He married a woman who was a real contradiction of terms. Dex believed Courtney was crazy half of the time. At work and before Dylan entered her life, Courtney was a ferocious tiger, taking no prisoners. However, once Courtney had found love, she became insecure, self-deprecating, and pulled some pretty stupid stunts.

Having said all that, Courtney did manage to survive a horrifying kidnap and assault, followed by the subsequent death of her mother from cancer. Her mother was a woman we had all grown to love and respect. The two tragic events, one on top of the other, would have thrown any of us into a tailspin.

"Call her crazy," I said to Dex, one night, "but I would never have been able to endure what she has gone through and come out whole."

Before the wedding, Courtney had founded an organization to provide support and shelter for abused women and their families. When she and Dylan returned from their honeymoon, construction of the facility began. Incredibly, it was built on the large property where Max Black had held Courtney hostage in a trailer.

Still to this day, it makes my skin crawl to think about it and how that man had actually visited my house to see Dex's work first hand.

Courtney had sold her townhouse because she said she would never be able to live there in peace. However, she wanted the property where Max Black's field office was located to be the site for the women's shelter, because it would always remind her of what it felt like to be held prisoner and to have her life threatened by her captor, someone she thought she knew well. She said that being in touch with that sense of fear, and the reality that others were experiencing it in their own lives, would spur her on, no matter how difficult the project became to build and maintain. Courtney had found a way to rise above her personal tragedy and compartmentalize her life in each extreme. Even I had to admit how admirable she was.

Dylan and Courtney had located a farmette available for rent on Route 24. They eventually ended up buying the place, and Dylan moved his business into the barn. It was bigger than the one he owned in Unionville, therefore requiring more work to renovate. He had a long list of repairs and upgrades that were needed before winter set in and only two to three months, tops, to get it done. You can imagine where Dex spent most of his weekends. Tom Pratt went out to help when he could.

Funny thing about Pratt, we all thought he had a thing for Susan. Then, very suddenly, the chase stopped. Pratt would ask Dex and Dylan how Susan and Zoe were doing, even though he had stopped pursuing her.

At least, we thought he had been in pursuit at one time.

Maybe it was just Pratt being Pratt. He never seemed to take an interest in women that ran after him. As far as we knew, Susan had not made one single assertive move toward him.

"Have you heard from Pratt?" I asked Susan one day when the guys were out working on Dylan's place, and we were on the beach with Zoe.

"No, but I had a feeling he would never call again."

"What happened, Susan? He seemed so interested."

"I guess I pried too much into his past."

"Well, he certainly didn't have to answer, did he?"

"No. I don't think I made him feel like he had to. He freely offered up his tale of woe."

"Well, when you say it like that, I can see why he might not be interested in being around your insensitivity. Which, in hindsight, is really not like you. What's gotten into you?"

"Paybacks."

"Paybacks? Paybacks for what?"

Susan proceeded to tell me about the night she thought someone had broken into the beach house while Dex and I were out on the Right Tackle. When Susan described how Gilda had barked and gone berserk, upon hearing her name, Gilda came over and laid her head in Susan's lap. Susan proceeded to tell us how Gilda had escaped and chased something or someone down the beach.

"Why didn't you tell us about all of this? What if that person had been Max?"

"Pratt assured me that our location and activity did not fit the serial killer's M.O.," Susan answered, trying to justify her rationale for not divulging the information sooner. "That was after Pratt had already asked *me* far too many questions about *my* private life."

"Susan, you should have told us. You and Zoe could have been in danger. Didn't you think that we would want to know?"

"Sure, but then you two would never go out again, and I would become the 'Great Imposition.' I didn't want that to happen. I like it here."

"We love having you here, too, but you have to promise: No. More. Secrets!"

"No more secrets," Susan repeated in a whispered surrender.

"So, let me get this straight: You knew Pratt before we knew you knew Pratt?"

"Something like that, yes."

"So, when he visited us the next day and told us to keep the doors locked, you two had already met?"

"Yes."

"Dex was right! Pratt really is into you!"

"Yeah, well, not anymore."

It explained Susan's somber mood, but I was finding it hard to believe that a man would give up on a woman like Susan just because of a few insensitive questions. Fortunately, with little Zoe growing like a weed and on the move, Susan was forced to bounce back quickly.

Later that day, I heard Susan calling me from the great room.

"Ginny, come quick! Zoe just took her first step!"

SUSAN

One week after the grand Sable-Carter wedding, Zoe and I were coming back from the Food Lion at Five Points when a Lewes patrol car caught my eye. Actually, it was the officer standing beside the patrol car that distracted me. Pratt was so tall, fit, and handsome that he should not have been standing anywhere near an intersection. Before I knew it, I drove right through the red light at Front Street and straight onto the drawbridge.

Shit!

On the downside of the bridge, I saw the flashing lights and heard the siren crest the top of the bridge and fly up behind me. I pulled over into the bike lane, and as I had suspected, Pratt pulled in directly behind me. With the lights still flashing blue and red, he got out of his cruiser and quickly approached the driver's side of my car.

God, that man is so damn good-looking.

"Susan, I need you to pull up and into the next drive so we're out of traffic and not blocking the bike lane."
He was very official and not very friendly, at all.

So, this is what it has come to.

My heart flopped like a half-baked pancake on a hot griddle.
The second time Pratt approached my car, he was moving at a much slower pace. He exhaled deeply, and I noticed the half twisted frown on his face. As he got closer, it was the belt around his waist that rocked on his hips and the fly of his pants that filled the field of vision in my side view mirror, now distracting me further.

Dear God . . .

My heart was racing and my palms were moist before he even spoke his first words to me in almost a week.
"Susan, do you make a regular habit of running red lights through congested intersections?"
"No. And whatever happened to 'Hello, Susan. How are you today?' "
"Yes, there's that, too. First, let's address your traffic violation, and then we'll get to the more important issue."

Important issue? What does he mean by that? He hasn't called me since our disastrous dinner date. There was nothing left undone, other than my heart. What important issue can he be talking about?

"Can I see your driver's license and registration, please?"

"Really, Pratt? You know who I am."

"They provide me with a legitimate way to look into whatever havoc you've been wreaking around town."

"Me? Sheesh, alright."

While I was fumbling with my wallet and digging through my glove box, Pratt leaned down and looked into the back seat. Zoe was sound asleep.

"How's little Zoe?" he asked in a much different tone. It was the sweet voice I remembered from the other side of the table that night in his home. I instantly relaxed.

"She's great. She just had her one-year check-up."

"How'd she do?"

"Perfect. She's just perfect!"

"In every way, just like her mother," Pratt added.

My heart softened with his compliment. I really regretted that I had botched things so badly.

How I would love to hear such kind words from a caring man every day . . .

Pratt took my information and walked back to his cruiser, leaving me to sit alone with my regrets. He turned off his cruiser's flashing lights, thank God. He could slap me with a heavy fine, but I did not care. Speculation of what I had screwed up was weighing heavier than any legal fine he could levy on me at the time. I had run a red light; that was all. However, at his house that night, I must have crossed a line into a sensitive area that was really none of my business. Plus, he would announce his candidacy soon, and Zoe and I could add nothing, other than a possible campaign liability. As a matter of fact, maybe he was trying to gently tell me that we would become obstacles to his election. He was letting me down easy.

Pratt strolled back with my cards and politely handed them back to me.

"Susan, it appears that you have been on your best behavior for most—not all—but most of your life."

What the hell does that mean?

"So, I'm going to let you go with a warning. However, I will need you and Zoe to have a private lunch with me tomorrow. I'll pick you up at noon."

"What? What if I'm busy?"

"You're not busy tomorrow."

"How do you know that?"

"Trust me, I know."

"I think you're a scoundrel, Pratt. I don't know if I should further expose my daughter to the likes of you."

"The two of you could do a lot worse, believe me."

Pratt flashed a magnificent grin.

"See you at noon," he further ordered.

Pratt patted the door of my car in confirmation, which, for the record, I never offered. Then he turned and walked back to his car. Watching him in my rear view mirror, I saw him shake his head, open the door of his cruiser, slide into the driver's seat, and drive off. I was left without a breath of air in my lungs.

What just happened?

I needed to get back to the beach house and find Ginny.

"Slow down, girl. Where's the fire?" Ginny asked me as I came running up the steps, carrying Zoe to the third floor.

"Oh, my gosh!" I huffed out of breath. "She's getting too big to carry up all these stairs."

As soon as Zoe saw Ginny, her little hands reached out. Ginny swept Zoe out of my breaking arms and swung her around, causing her to squeal loudly. Ginny then set Zoe down on the floor. Zoe happily padded over to Gilda and started patting her on the head and pulling her ears.

Gilda was such a good dog, she never seemed to mind when someone, anyone, paid attention to her.

"So, what's up?" Ginny asked, again.

I had caught my breath and was able to speak.

"I just ran into Pratt. Actually, he pulled me over."

"Not again!" Ginny responded.

"Yes. And this time, I deserved it. I ran the red light at Front Street and Savannah Road."

"Susan, that's a busy intersection. You could have run someone over," Ginny reprimanded.

"True, but it was Pratt's fault. Anyway, he's taking Zoe and me to lunch tomorrow!"

"That's excellent. Where are you going?"

"I have no idea. Someplace private."

PRATT

She was vivacious, intelligent, and beautiful. And worst of all, she knew it. She knew how to play games like a master, and she knew how to get her way. What she could not win with words, she used her most powerful weapon: sex. She was a goddess in bed. Her foreplay was beyond any possible escape and her teasing hurt to the far side of pleasure and back. She was an artist when it came to manipulation, in any sense of the word.

When she left me, I was sick. I became physically ill. She refused to take my calls or return my messages. I took off work for a week and hunted her down. When I eventually found her, she refused to see me. Her attorney threatened me with a restraining order, stating that I had physically abused her. Never. She was the one that liked it rough. Our lovemaking never left any marks, and I only did the things that involved props and restraints because she had requested them. No, she begged for them. Even her begging was a turn on. I was not in my right mind when I had allowed myself to do those things.

Did I enjoy it? Yes and no. In the moment, it was all hotter than hell. Afterward, I felt deviant, dirty, and detestable. What man treats the love of his life that way? I rationalized that I had done it to please her, keeping a wedding vow that I had made.

". . . and I will to do my best to bring you joy for the rest of your life."

The last time I remembered making love to her during our married life, it involved handcuffs and a leather belt. Afterward, I regretted it. At the time, I truly believed that was how she wanted to "make love." Looking back, it was raw sex.

When did we stop "making love?"

Our behavior haunted me.

* * *

When Gwen showed up at my door, three years ago and long after our divorce, I was in shock. I had not seen her since our split. Unfortunately, she showed up minutes before I needed to leave to pick up my first date as a second-chance bachelor. Needless to say, I did a very awkward and unkind thing: I decided to stay home with Gwen, and I called my date and cancelled.

I remember it well.

"You had me threatened with a restraining order. I would be crazy to let you in, again," I reminded Gwen with the door half open.

"Yes, I had considered my attorney's suggestion, but I never had it executed."

"What is it that you want, Gwen?"

"Who says I want anything from you? Are you going to let me in, or not?"

As soon as I opened the door, I knew it was a mistake. I was headed down a dead-end road, once again.

Gwen was wearing a very sheer white blouse with a pink camisole beneath. Believe me, she had no need for padded or push-up bras. Her body was naturally sized and arranged in a way that other women spent fortunes trying to recreate for themselves. That day, like many times before, her nipples were deliberately commanded to stand at attention by the silky fabric that brushed up against them. She had left little to the imagination. For me, it required no imagination at all. I was quite familiar with her body. Her shorts were about six inches too short, and her long legs met with only an inch of fabric to cover what was between them. Gwen meant business.

Some things never change.

"So, Gwen, to what do I owe the pleasure of your uninvited company?"

" 'Pleasure.' Now that's a word that could mean many things, on several different levels, in many locations," Gwen suggested.

She took a step closer and ran her hands down my chest, then wrapped them around my waist, pulling her torso into mine. In her heels, the apex of her legs was positioned directly above mine. She knew my anatomy so well. My arousal was nothing more than a human reflex, a very detectable one, I was sure of it.

Gwen never gave up easily. In fact, Gwen never knew when to quit. The woman had determination and a competitive streak like no one I had ever known.

After that first post-divorce encounter, Gwen made a habit of tracking me down if she thought I was getting too close to another woman. She always showed up like an unannounced firestorm. For example, the first time I had taken someone else to an Arrest Pediatric Cancer fundraiser, she showed up at my house the very next day and succeeded in seducing me, again. The morning after, she asked about my date, who happened to be Bridget Sable. I spoke honestly and admitted that I had no long-term interest in Bridget. I explained that Bridget and I were just friends supporting a good cause. As soon as Gwen's curiosity was satisfied—very satisfied in all the locations she had desired—she disappeared, again. I was hurt. Looking back, I think that deep down inside I was hoping that our little tryst would lead to a second chance.

When I took Susan as my date, Gwen showed up again, the very next day. Hoping against all hope that Gwen had intended to stay, I ignored the lessons of my past. I made love to her that afternoon. She gave me mind-blowing sex. When I returned from my shift that night, she was gone. I was crushed. She was slowly killing me, and I could not let go.

Feeling lower than low, I also avoided Susan after that. Deep inside, my conscience suggested that I would be dishonest if I continued seeing Susan with any romantic intention, especially because Zoe and our friends would eventually get involved in my tangled mess. My contact with Susan continued only as friends when the group managed to get together, or we crossed paths.

Then there was the Sable-Carter wedding. Susan was as beautiful as ever, and my interest in her was becoming undeniable, once more. No surprise, Gwen reappeared two days later—the day after Susan and I had dinner together. Gwen came close to bedding me that day had it not been for a phone call. Gwen was actually undressing, just inside my front door, when my cell phone rang. I recognized the ringtone.

Lori Caruso, one of our dispatchers at the station, was old enough to be my mother, and she treated me like a son. In the days following Gwen's and my separation, Lori had witnessed first hand what it had done to me. She kept a close eye on me for months after the divorce was made final. Lori could always tell when Gwen had made her reappearances and subsequent vanishing acts. Lori knew my roller coaster. Her husband had treated her poorly with one affair after another, always returning with the promise of repentance and becoming faithful. Lori, bless her broken heart, knew my pain.

That day on her way to the station, Lori recognized the car parked on the street in front of my house. She immediately called me.

"What is that bitch doing there?"

"Lori, you don't want to know," I answered shakily as Gwen was unbuttoning her blouse. Soon, it was evident that Gwen had chosen to leave her place without wearing a bra.

"Do you want her out of there?" Lori asked sternly.

It was the million-dollar question. I gaped at Gwen's beautiful body. I had not been with a woman since her last visit. I tried to rationalize my immediate desire as being acceptable, because we had been married at one time, and I had been with no one else. Gwen stepped out of her panties and posed for me wearing only her red stilettos.

"Yes, I'll be there right away," I answered loudly for Gwen's benefit. Then, I disconnected the call. "I have to go into the station, which means you have to leave. I'm sorry."

"Tom, I think you should park yourself right here, right now."

Gwen lifted her right foot up onto the arm of my sofa and touched an intimate area that I knew all too well. She knew how crazy that would drive me.

Lord knows how many others have parked there since our divorce.

I foolishly pondered my options before trying to convince myself that I should leave right away.

"I'm really sorry, but you'll have to get dressed, I have to leave."

I picked up her blouse and gently handed it back to her.

"Wouldn't you much rather stay here and enjoy my company. I could give you an up close and personal view of what you've been missing."

Gwen swayed her hips. My head was spinning. What she had just said was so hurtful. We were supposed to have been inseparable for life. Now, she was presenting an invitation to what she had promised years ago like it was some sort of carrot, or grand prize. I was at war with myself. I was so lost in her power over me. My body was acknowledging her gifts and trappings as my blood heated and throbbed in my lower extremities, though I tried hard to conceal it.

What are you waiting for? She is so ready for you. A couple of minutes, maybe an hour or two, could never hurt.

"Come on, Tom. We have some catching up to do, for old times' sake."

Gwen threw her blouse over her shoulder, spun on her toes and started walking her beautiful bare ass toward the stairs leading up to my bedroom—a room that was once *ours*.

I quickly grabbed her arm and pulled her back around. Gwen quickened the reverse momentum and laid her naked body up against mine, pressing her lips and tongue into my mouth. Her moan almost sealed the deal.

I am not sure why, but in that moment, I thought of Susan and Zoe. I felt a need to stay true to them, even though Susan and I had never kissed or had any such physical intimate connection.

I immediately overpowered Gwen and pushed her away.

"Please, pick up your clothes and get dressed," I said sternly. "You have to leave, or I will have to push you out the door, naked."

"You can't do that."

True. I could never do that, but I needed to get her out before I did something I would surely regret later.

"You need to go."

Gwen put on her blouse, and continued taunting me as she pulled on her panties.

"I know you're not serious about that woman. She can't hold a candle to me. And what do you want with someone who's already got a kid, anyway? Oh, I see. You just want to make sure the next one can make a baby. Is that it?"

"Gwen, that's not fair. Is that what this is all about? We could have adopted. I would have been happy to adopt a child. You're the one that left! I waited for you. I tried to call you a dozen times a day. I came after you. You still refused to see me and then had me threatened with a restraining order. And now, here you are, naked, and in my house."

"Our house. This was our house, Tom."

"Get help, Gwen. Please, I'm begging you to get help."

I was beginning to see straight.

"Okay, I get it. I'm outta here."

Partially put back together, Gwen left quietly. The last thing I heard was her car's engine fading into the other noises around town.

Once again, she had forced her way back into my life like a windswept brush fire, kindling memories and past hopes. When she left, my world fell silent, sad, and empty, once more.

After I began breathing normally, I called Lori. "Thanks, Lori. I owe you."

* * *

Thank God, I had not seen Gwen in several days and hoped that I would be able to keep her from learning about my plans to spend an afternoon with Susan and Zoe.

SUSAN

Pratt called in the morning and said that in honor of the beautiful weather, he was taking us on a picnic, so Zoe and I should dress accordingly. I packed a diaper bag for Zoe and changed into a pair of Bermuda shorts and a T.

Pratt picked us up at noon. Not having a toddler car seat of his own, we decided to take the Explorer. Pratt drove. It was the first time a man had driven the Explorer since Derek's imprisonment.

I looked over at Pratt as he backed the Explorer out onto Bay Avenue. It felt good to be in the passenger seat again. It felt even better to have a gentleman to drive us.

"Where are we going?"

"To one of my favorite spots in the whole world."

"Oh? Are you letting me in on another one of your secrets?"

"You are incorrigible, Ms. McCabe. And, yes, it is another one of my secrets. I used to enjoy this spot as a child and thought Zoe might like it, too."

"She's walking now, you know."

"I didn't know. Well then, she'll love it there all the more!"

We only drove a short distance before reaching our destination. Pratt made a left turn directly after the drawbridge and followed Gills Neck Road away from town. The road ran alongside the Canal and past several magnificent homes and boathouses. Winding down and around, we came to a large estate that sat far back from the road and fronted on the Canal. Pratt made a left into the long drive.

"Who lives here?" I whispered, obviously overwhelmed by the size of the estate and the magnificence of the grounds.

"A very nice couple occupies the third floor."

"Do you have permission to be here?"

"Yes."

Pratt parked in front of the large estate home. An older gentleman came out through the front door to greet us.

"Tommy! How good to see you!"

Tommy?

Pratt jumped out of the Explorer and came around to open my door as his older friend approached us. They shook hands.

"Thanks, Kirk. How have you been?"

"I've been well, thank you."

Pratt took my hand and helped me out.

"Kirk, I'd like you to meet Susan McCabe and that's her daughter, Zoe, in the car seat."

Kirk bowed slightly and gently shook my hand while Pratt moved to open the backdoor.

"It's a pleasure to meet you, Ms. McCabe."

"Please, call me Susan."

"Yes, ma'am."

Ma'am? What's with all the formality?

"Have you heard from Javier and the others?" Pratt asked Kirk, as I reached into the backseat to remove Zoe from her car seat.

"No, sir. Knowing Javier, that's probably good news!" Kirk chuckled. "Would you like me to call him for an update?"

"No, no. I'm sure everything is fine. They'll be back tomorrow, and then we'll know how it all worked out."

"Very good, sir. Janice has your picnic ready for you. Shall I have her deliver it?"

"Heavens, no. We'll go in and retrieve it. Thank you, Kirk."

Someone prepared a picnic for us?

Kirk escorted us up the steps of the grand portico, leading to the opulent double front doors. He stepped back and held a door open as we walked into the entrance hall.

"This place is so beautiful. Is it some kind of museum?" I asked, confused by the huge investment in furnishings, carpets, paintings, and window dressings.

Pratt did not answer me, at least not right away.

The interior was furnished with authentic Victorian period pieces. The wallpaper and window dressings were right out of "Victoria Magazine." All of the brass was polished and the crystal was clean and dust free. The floor of the entrance hall was polished marble, likewise the steps of the grand staircase. The ornate ceiling of the hall had to be at least twenty feet high. The slightest whisper seemed to be amplified and echoed around the elegant cornices and crown moldings.

"Follow me. I want you to meet Janice. She probably put a fabulous picnic together for us," Pratt directed as he took my arm to keep us moving. He was extremely happy and at ease.

We walked through the long entrance hall, past several large rooms, past a long dining room, and back through a smaller hallway that opened into a huge kitchen. Everything about the kitchen was on a grand scale and double capacity. It could have easily serviced a fine restaurant.

"Wow!" escaped from my jaw-dropped mouth.

"Janice! How are you?" Pratt gushed as he rushed to hug an older woman about half his size, yet sure to carry a lot of authority.

"Tommy! It's so good to see you!"

Tommy? What's with everyone calling him Tommy? It makes him sound like a little boy. A little boy . . .

Their embrace was sweet and endearing as he lifted the woman off the floor and swung her around. She laughed and reprimanded Pratt at the same time.

"Put me down, you ruffian!" she scolded.

As the woman straightened out her apron and adjusted her large bosom, Pratt introduced us.

"Janice, I want you to meet two dear friends of mine, Susan and Zoe McCabe."

Dear friends?

"Nice to meet you, Susan."

Janice, fully recovered from her twirl, shook my outstretched hand, and then she gave Zoe's cheeks a little pinch.

"She is everything I had imagined! You did a great job describing her, Tommy," Janice exclaimed as her eyes gazed at Zoe who was acting shy by turning her face away.

Then Janice addressed me.

"Susan, I hope you enjoy your lunch today at the 'Pratt Canal House.' "

Canal House? This place looks more like a flippin' plantation! Did she say—Pratt—Canal House?

Janice continued.

"For Zoe, I made little finger sandwiches using thin whole grain bread, thin sliced roasted turkey and avocado. I packed a juice box, a water bottle, a fruit cup, and applesauce. For the two of you, I packed turkey club sandwiches, a cheese and grape platter, and a fine bottle of white wine. You said to make it special, Tommy! I hope you like it."

"Janice, you're the best! I can always count on you to impress our guests."

"Our guests?" What kind of place is this? How many "guests" has he entertained here?

Pratt carried the large wicker picnic basket and a blanket while I held Zoe's hand. Zoe could only toddle so fast, but Pratt was willing to take his time getting out to our picnic site. We stopped a short distance back from the bank of the Canal and alongside a tall sweeping weeping willow tree. The grass was long and lush. The reflection of the sun on the water looked like a cluster of a million floating diamonds. A gentle breeze added a random soft whispered mystique to a place that already seemed magical.

"I can see why you love it here. By the way, where are we?"

"Well, that's the Lewes-Rehoboth Canal, and we're less than a mile from town."

"I know that, but what is this Pratt Canal House?" I asked, sweeping my arm in a large circle.

"Oh, this? It's just a name my family gave this place."

"This place? Does your family own this place?"

"Yes, it belongs to my parents."

"Are they here?"

"Oh, no. They're in and out during the summer months. They're at the Cape, now."

"Cape May?"

Pratt chuckled at my assumption before answering.

"Cape Cod."

"Do they have a place there, too?"

"Yes. Are we back to the great inquisition, again? I'd much rather know more about you."

Pratt's deep brown eyes met mine, and I knew he was sincere.

PRATT

When I was with her, I was relaxed and time seemed to stand still. The world and all of its troubles seemed to dissipate at the sound of her voice. She spoke like the song of a quiet brook and moved like a gazelle. I was mesmerized by her beauty and drawn by her kind heart and inquisitive mind. While I teased her about her constant barrage of questions, I really found it quite endearing. It reminded me of just how natural and innocent she was.

Little Zoe flopped down in the soft grass while I spread out the large square blanket. After positioning the basket on one corner, I stood and watched Susan and Zoe play a game of chase. Zoe was trying to run on her short wobbly legs while Susan pretended she could not catch her. Susan was bent over and running in double-time behind her little one. Zoe was running circles and figure eights, laughing so hard, her little body toppled several times. Together, they defined all things good.

My mind drifted to all the children that had been taken from their families with the promise of a better life in the United States, sneaked in under the cloak of a lie. I knew Daly and Wilson were working the case, but I had not heard from them in several days, and I was growing more impatient. Children could be at risk of being stolen and sold every minute that it took to identify those who were involved and put together the indisputable evidence against them. We had no jurisdiction to rule against what had been done in children's native countries. What we had to prove was their illegal transport and the subsequent receipt of payment for their illegal adoptions. The break came when a child died of a genetic defect and the adoptive parents wanted to know why they were not notified of the child's medical condition before everything was finalized and they had taken custody of the child. They were heartbroken and angry. It was their private detective who discovered that the adoption agency appeared to be a scam and that the parents had been taken for an expensive ride, all to end in enormous heartbreak. Daly and Wilson had learned through further investigation that the biological parents were told that their daughter was being adopted into an American family who could provide for the medical treatment that she needed and that her life would be spared. Daly, Wilson, and I were on a mission to make sure that the child had not died in vain. She was a toddler, like Zoe. My heart was filled with remorse and needed an outlet to express its heaviness; however, it was part of my job to keep silent so that nothing would be compromised.

Susan caught me watching them. She scooped up Zoe in the middle of her run. Zoe's little legs continued kicking in the air as if they were still on solid ground. Zoe giggled and squealed as Susan swung her around in the air. Susan, still carrying the wiggling Zoe, walked toward me, out of breath, and smiling.

"She has far too much energy!" Susan exclaimed.

"Let's take her under the weeping willow. It's nice and cool under there, and it makes for a natural playhouse."

I led the way, pushing aside the willow's long tendrils that reached the ground and swayed gently in the breeze that was coming off the Canal.

"Wow, this *is* the perfect escape!" Susan remarked upon entering the green canopy. Zoe stopped kicking and looked around her new surroundings.

"Exactly. I used to hide under here all the time."

"What were you hiding from?"

Susan was always full of questions.

"Ahhhh . . . it's my turn to ask the questions," I stated in an attempt to turn the tables.

Susan put Zoe down, so Zoe could explore beneath the branches of green and around the roots that jutted in and out of the ground like knotty fingers. Then Susan turned to me.

"What is it that you want to know?" she asked.

I could tell she was fearful of what I might ask. Her body stiffened, a sure sign that she was bracing herself.

There are a million things I want to ask you, Susan, like:

How did a sweet girl like you ever end up marrying a philanderer and pyromaniac like Derek Carter?

Why would you ever trust a person like Marco Corelli?

When was the last time you had the company books audited by an outside company?

Do you know what I know?

Do you know how much I already know about you?

Would you find it upsetting?

Are you in any way involved with the illegal adoptions?

Everything I knew about Susan screamed innocence. However, I had been thoroughly and painfully wrong about Gwen. I was still smarting from that one.

Like me, I wonder what deep hurts Susan has learned to cover up?

"OK, for starters, how did you end up in Lewes?"

Susan gave thought to how she would answer, while Zoe circled around Susan's legs.

CHAPTER FIVE

DYLAN

Sadly, it was time to gather my beautiful bride and head for home. Our stay in Bariloche was far too short. Courtney and I had had the time of our lives on the ski slopes and in town. We had befriended several other couples and found ourselves out on the town every night. Every morning, we slept in and had brunch served in our penthouse suite as we lazily lounged and played. It was every man's dream to sit across the table from a beautiful half-naked woman like Court with the snow-covered Andes in the background.

After drinking too much the night before and eating too much late in the morning, we would head for the slopes and ski for several hours. To change things up, we even tried snowboarding. Court picked it up quickly and became poetry in motion as she carved her way down the trails. I watched from behind, way behind. Snowboarding was definitely not my thing. I ditched the board when we finally reached the lodge and put my skis back on.

In the late afternoon, Court and I would immerse ourselves in the steamy Jacuzzi and then usually head to bed for an afternoon romp. Court, cured of her shyness around bright light and full-view windows, morphed into a vixen in our private playhouse. She was insatiable, and I was the luckiest man alive.

Our last day there, we spent the afternoon in the shops, rather than bed, purchasing gifts for friends and family.

"How shall we ever repay Pratt and his parents?" Court asked.

Court had learned the truth. By our second day, she had grown concerned about the amount of money the trip must have been costing me. After making her promise not to share it with anyone else, I had to tell her the truth.

"I don't think we can thank them, especially because you're not supposed to know."

"Did they really think I wouldn't figure out that something wasn't adding up?"

"Maybe?"

The next day, our flight was scheduled to leave at noon and land in Wilmington the following morning. It was the only time we had to set our alarm. After shutting it off, I rolled over and gathered Court into my body.

"Hmmm . . . you're so soft and warm."

Court turned over in my arms and sobbed softly.

"I love you so much, Dylan. I don't know where I'd be right now or what I'd be doing had you not walked into my office that day and acted like such a goof!"

She was laughing and crying at the same time. She looked into my eyes.

"I probably wouldn't be alive if it weren't for you and Dex."

"You're safe, Court. I'm always going to be there for you. We're a team, now. You're part of a big family and a close circle of friends."

"And you're part of my family, too," she sniffled.

I kissed her, and touched her, and made love to her one more time before we had to head for home.

We had lost track of time and were packing in a flurry of flying clothes, lingerie, shoes, and cosmetics, when my cell phone rang.

"Good morning, Mr. Carter. I hope I did not wake you and your beautiful bride."

"No, Javier, we were just packing. We'll be ready in a couple of minutes."

"That's why I am calling. Mrs. Pratt has asked that we make a stop in Bolivia on the way home. It seems that she has some precious cargo that she wants us to deliver to the States."

"Oh?"

"I hope you don't mind. Mrs. Pratt has asked that we pick up two ill children and bring them back with us to receive treatment at Children's Hospital in Wilmington. The children are being sponsored by the Healing Wings Foundation."

"Mind? No, not at all."

"They will require the Learjet's master suite for their comfort and care. Their nurse has asked that we allow the children to rest and to be mindful of their right to privacy. While we cannot disclose their illnesses, we assure you that you will not be at risk."

"That is most understandable, Javier."

"Thank you, Mr. Carter. Our arrival time in Wilmington will be delayed by an hour. We apologize for any inconvenience to you and your lovely bride. We will pick you up shortly, at 10:00, as planned. Will that be OK?"

"That will be fine, Javier. Let us know if there is anything we can do."

As promised, Javier had the limo downstairs at exactly 10:00. Court and I were packed and on time, but sad to go.

"We'll get you through customs and then out to the tarmac to board the jet," Javier directed as he retrieved our luggage and loaded it into the trunk of the limo.

"Thank you for a wonderful vacation, Javier."

I shook his hand and Court gave him a hug.

We had grown fond of Javier. During our stay, he drove us where we needed to go and directed us to sights and restaurants we may have otherwise missed. We were going to miss him when we returned to the States.

It was a long, quiet flight home. Court and I remained in the main cabin, dozing off and on in our seats. We made the stop in Bolivia to pick up the children, as requested. We made a second stop in Atlanta to go through

U.S. Customs and refuel. The customs agent was kind enough to meet the jet and come on board. It took less than an hour to get turned around and takeoff for Wilmington.

It was a brutal, boring, uneventful flight home. After our final landing, we thanked our pilot, co-pilot, and the crew. We caught a quick glimpse of the children as they were being ramped down the back airstairs and loaded into a transport vehicle. They looked so tiny, covered and strapped down on their large gurneys. I said a secret, quiet prayer for them. They were *so* small . . .

After departing the New Castle County Airport, in Wilmington, and staying awake for the one and a half hour drive south, we finally reached our farmette home at 2:00 in the morning. Court was completely wiped out and went straight to bed. As for me, I was profoundly energized, tossing and turning. I could not get my mind off of those children.

SUSAN

Pratt wanted to know how I ended up in Lewes. It was a difficult question for me to answer honestly. I was beginning to hope that Pratt and I might actually develop into something worthwhile, so I did not want to begin with a lie, or by trying to deliberately mislead him.

I was not sure how much Pratt already knew. I did remember Dex saying that he and Pratt were acquaintances when they were teenagers. As adults, they had become better friends after Pratt had organized several fishing trips on the Right Tackle for his fellow officers. If Dex and Pratt knew each other in their younger days, then there was a very good chance that Pratt had met my ex-husband, Derek. Anyway, I was certain that once I told Pratt that my ex-husband *was* Derek Carter, he would recognize the name. When it all went down, Derek's arson and attempted murder charges were pretty big news around the quiet seashore town of Lewes. If Pratt was a good cop, then he would have to recognize the name.

I was fairly certain that he only knew me as Susan McCabe. I had been careful, up to that point, not to identify myself as a Carter.

Dare I tell him, now?

"As you know, I, too, was married once before," I began.

"Yes, we established that the first night we met."

"Well, Ginny and I were good friends, and after Zoe was born, Ginny invited us to come and stay with her and Dex, so I would not have to be on my own with a newborn."

"That was really gracious of her. How did you and Ginny meet? I believe she grew up in Darien, Connecticut. Is that correct?"

"Yes, she did."

How did he know that?

"Did you live in Darien, as well?"

"No. Der . . . er, my husband and I lived in Valley Forge, Pennsylvania."

A near miss . . . whew!

Zoe was starting to whine and cling tight to my legs. Pratt had noticed my discomfort, so he suggested that we move to the blanket and have lunch. He added that we had better finish everything or Janice's feelings would be hurt.

Zoe was pleased to have a juice box and little sandwiches shaped like hearts and stars.

"Wow, Janice is really something! This is so thoughtful," I remarked.

"Yes, she and Kirk have been a part of the family for as long as my parents have owned the house."

"How does that work? Do they live here?"

"Yes, Kirk and Janice occupy the third floor in exchange for managing the property and serving when my parents are entertaining in town or having overnight guests."

"So Janice and Kirk are a couple?"

"Yes, they met while working for my parents and were married right here on this very spot."

"Really?" I startled, as if I were sitting on hallowed ground.

"Yes!"

"Why don't *you* live here?"

I was curious as to why he would own a separate smaller home in Lewes when this one was so spacious and seemed perfectly available to him.

"Ah, here we go, again—more questions from a very inquisitive lady."

Pratt opened the wine and handed an appropriately half-filled glass to me.

"My parents would have been thrilled to have me live here. They were really disappointed when I refused to move in after I was married. And, so was my ex-wife, by the way. She had dreams of living here and being waited on hand and foot."

"Ah . . . Did she marry you for your family's money, or for your good looks, or both?"

I can't believe I just asked that. What was I thinking?

Pratt grinned and shook his head at the thought.

"Who knows what Gwen was thinking?"

"That's her name? Gwen?"

"Yes," he responded softly and then looked over at the tree, his favorite place to escape from the world.

"She hurt you, didn't she?"

"Yes, Susan. She hurt me, and sometimes she continues to do so."

"How? Why?"

"By returning."

He turned back and looked into my eyes as if he had hoped that I could help him. Then he quickly looked away before continuing with his explanation.

"I will bet money that because you and I are here, together, today, she will be at my door by tomorrow."

"Really? Why?"

"That, my dear, is another million-dollar question."

His eyes returned to mine.

"What about you, Susan? Do you ever see your ex-husband anymore?"

PRATT

As soon as that question left my mouth, I wished I could retract it. I had entered dangerous territory for several reasons:

1. Up to that point in our very platonic relationship, Susan had not mentioned her ex-husband's name.

Should I act surprised when she finally gets around to telling me?

2. I did not believe that Susan knew of my visits to the Sussex County Prison to see Derek.

3. Because of the ongoing investigation, I should not have been having lunch with her.

Susan swirled the wine in her glass and helped Zoe with her sandwich before looking up to answer my question.

"Pratt, I have something I need to tell you. Please understand that this is something that I find really hard to live with."

"I am not here to judge you, Susan."

"Good. You see; my ex-husband is Derek Carter. Does that name mean anything to you?"

"Yes. It does."

"Did you know that I was married to Derek?"

"Yes, I did."

"You did? Why didn't you say so?"

"It's my job to know. It's not my job to go jawing about it everywhere I go. In fact, I don't think of you as Derek's ex-wife. I think of you as an incredible woman who is brave enough to raise a beautiful little girl on her own."

Susan got very quiet. She was shaking.

"Pratt, I have to go. Lunch was absolutely lovely, but would you be kind enough to forgive me if I take Zoe home, now?"

"Of course. Are you all right? Did I say something wrong?"

"No. You said nothing wrong. I just need to go home, please."

I quietly packed up the basket while she gathered up Zoe. No more questions.

"Janice is going to be so crushed when she sees that we did not touch her dessert or finish the wine," I stated in a contemplative whisper.

"Will you thank her for me, Pratt?"

"Of course, if you promise to come back with Zoe sometime in the near future."

"I think . . . actually . . ."

"Don't answer now, Susan. I'll call you in a couple of days."

It was not long after Susan and Zoe had left that I remembered my car was still parked at the Carter beach house. I ran to the barn to grab a bike off the rack.

"What happened to your lady friend? She didn't stay very long," Kirk remarked as I was strapping on my helmet.

"No, she didn't stay as long as I had hoped, and I left my car at their house."

"Would you like me to give you a lift?"

"No, I think I need to work off some of this frustration," I confessed.

"Understood, Tommy. Women will drive you crazy and make you wonder whether you're coming or going."

Kirk was a man of few words. However, the words he spoke were usually on point.

I was riding toward town along the Canal when Susan's Explorer passed me in the opposite direction, turned around, and came back. She pulled up alongside me.

"PULL OVER!" she yelled across the front seat and through the lowered passenger window.

Susan parked her Explorer in front of my bike. She got out of her SUV and walked back while I was removing my helmet.

Well, this is a strange juxtaposition!

"Your car is still at the beach house. Do you need a ride so you can drive it back home?" she asked rather directly.

"Whatever happened to 'Hello, Pratt. Are you having a nice day?' To which I would reply 'Yes, I was having a marvelous day until two beautiful young ladies walked out on me and left me without transportation.' "

"OK. I'm sorry. But I did come back for you, and I'm offering you a lift."

"Well, thank you for the offer, but I've decided to ride over and pick it up myself. The exercise will do me good. I have a few things I need to work out."

"OK. Don't say I didn't offer or that I left you stranded. And, . . . thanks again for the picnic. It was very nice."

I almost believed Susan was sincere, but then she quickly turned on her heels to leave. I grabbed her arm, which she immediately and violently shook loose.

"Susan, are you OK? Did I say something that upset you?"

"No. I'm fine."

"You're not fine. You left abruptly. Something upset you. What is it?"

"It's complicated. You don't like complicated, and you know what? I don't either. Let's leave it for another day."

Stalling for time to think of something profound or reassuring to say, I shook my head and looked at the ground. I had nothing. I had nothing that was simple enough.

"OK. Let's leave it for another day," I relinquished.

Susan promptly returned to her car, got back in, and drove off. I watched her Explorer reach the intersection of Gills Neck and Savannah Roads. She made a right turn and disappeared over the drawbridge.

Hoping to turn my frustration into raw energy, I pedaled hard and fast. I had not been that confused about a woman since Gwen first entered my life and then repeatedly left it, a pattern she continued long after we were divorced.

Sure enough, Gwen showed up at my door the next day around dusk. She appeared in the midst of a summer thunderstorm that had blown in from the west. Gwen was drenched and her car was nowhere in sight.

"How did you get here?"

"I walked. My car's parked in town."

"Why are you here?"

"I needed to see you. You're the only one who understands me."

"No. That's not quite accurate. I *thought* I understood you. Come in and get those wet clothes off."

I directed Gwen to change out of her clothes, put them in the dryer—the one she had picked out for us years ago—and put on my robe.

Fortunately, there were no shenanigans. She did not emerge from my bedroom—our former bedroom—naked and try to seduce me. She did not call me upstairs to help her undress. She did not try to coax me into bed by any of her old fail-proof methods. I was slightly disappointed, but mostly relieved. Her old games had become exhausting.

"Have you had dinner, yet?"

"No. Have you?"

"No. How about I order out."

"Sounds perfect, Tom. Thank you."

I could tell she was sincerely grateful.

It was unsettling the way the sound of her voice took me back to happier days.

* * *

It was true; the first year of our marriage was full of adventure and excitement. Everything was so new. We traveled whenever we had the chance, and Gwen had a thing about making love in every location possible.

"Every state in the nation, every continent and ocean on the earth," was her motto.

We had hit twenty-six states, four continents, and three oceans before she left me.

Whenever we were stuck at home, Gwen loved to play the time away. At the time, so did I.

Gwen and I never used birth control, and I just assumed that one day she would give me the good news. On many occasions, we had shared how much we wanted to start a large family. Then, on our first anniversary, I mentioned how I believed that our second year would be the year. I asked her if she would prefer a boy or a girl, first, and what names she liked best. I was ready.

Gwen became very quiet.

"I'm not sure I want children, Tom," she whispered antagonistically.

"Really? It's all we talked about before the wedding."

"A girl can change her mind, you know."

"Of course."

I decided to drop the subject for the evening. However, every time I brought it up afterward, Gwen gave me the same answer, complaining that a woman's body never recovers, and she was too young to worry about weight gain, a flabby belly, stretch marks, and sagging breasts.

What? Where did that all come from?

I loved Gwen. With all my heart, I loved her. If they really were big enough deterrents for her, I would have gladly adopted children.

"Gwen, as the mother of my children, I would cherish you whether those things happened or not!"

One evening, I even suggested we try other options.

"No adoptions. That's not on the table. It's out of the question," Gwen killed that idea with strong sentiments.

Gwen stomped off and we were in the midst of our first big fight. I chased her into the living room where she was getting ready to storm out the front door. I seized her by the arm. (She later claimed that I hurt her. I wished I had never grabbed her that hard.)

"Why, then, did you go on and on about children before we got engaged and before we married? It was something we both wanted. What's happened? What's changed?"

I failed to put two and two together at the time, but our arguing had begun about the time that our lovemaking turned rough, and she began making demands. The more we acted out in bed, the less we communicated outside the bedroom. When I thought I was losing her, I went to her mother for help.

Gwen's mother and I always had an open channel of communication, even if we knew we would not like what the other had to say.

Gwen was the product of her mother's first marriage and her father's second. Gwen had two older half-brothers from her father's first marriage, who were twelve and fourteen years her senior. As Gwen told it, there was no love lost between her and her half-brothers. The boys were estranged from their father and baby half-sister. They detested Gwen's mother.

Gwen believed she was the product of her parents' affair. She never wanted to talk much about growing up. Eventually, Gwen's parents divorced, as well, when Gwen was twelve. She had to adjust to her new living arrangements and a new middle school at the same time. I think that as part of her healing process, Gwen had erased much of her teen years from her memory.

When I spoke with Gwen's mother and described Gwen's change of heart regarding the possibility of having children of our own, her mother placed a hand on my arm and spoke softly.

"Gwen will never have children, Tom. She's known this since she was nineteen."

Gwen's mother continued on with tears in her eyes, describing how Gwen was diagnosed with ovarian cancer at a very young age and had to undergo a hysterectomy.

I drove home completely dazed.

Why didn't Gwen tell me? She was, is, and always will be the one that I want to share my life with. Had she told me, I still would have proposed and married her.

I was lost and overwhelmed in my state of mass confusion. I was upset for Gwen. I felt sorry and hurt for her. I wondered how she had covered it so well when we had spoken of children so fondly. She had suffered a severe loss at such a young age, and I never knew. Then I became angry because she had successfully kept the truth from me and deliberately lied about her medical history.

Did she think I would run?

I was crushed, and I have to admit that I did not handle it well.

As we climbed into bed that very night, I put the question forward that had been plaguing me all that day.

"Why didn't you tell me?"

"Tell you what?"

"That you've had a hysterectomy and cannot have children. Why did you hide it from me?"

"We are not having this discussion, not now, not ever!"

Gwen got out of bed and grabbed her robe. I caught the edge of it and pulled her back.

"Gwen, don't walk out on me. I don't care whether we have children, or not. What I care about is you. Why didn't you tell me?"

"If you care about me, you won't ask. You won't drag me into something from my past that I don't want to discuss."

"Don't you think I should have known in case you developed other related medical issues?"

"No. It's my body."

"Yes, it is your body, and you promised it to me the day we got married. I am responsible to care for you. Gwen, why would you lead me on about your ability or inability to have children? There are other ways. We could adopt.

"NO! Now leave it alone."

She yanked her robe out of my hand, stormed out the front door, and drove off in her car, wearing only what little she had on. I grabbed my keys and tried to follow her. She was driving like a crazy person. Fearful she would cause an accident, I backed off.

Gwen finally returned home at 3:00 AM. She reeked of alcohol, and with one look at her, I knew there was no way that she should have been behind the wheel.

"Where have you been?"

"At a friend's house."

"Who? Who allowed you to drive home like this?"

"No one you know. Let it go."

I wanted to shake her. I wanted answers. I wanted the truth. When I stepped closer to her, the scent left by the truth hit me hard in the face. She had been with another man.

"Get in the shower, Gwen. I'm sleeping on the couch."

It was the beginning of the end. Little did I know that the truth was about to set me free.

* * *

I ordered a thin crust veggie pizza for Gwen and a pepperoni and mushroom pizza for me. Not wanting to encourage her bad behavior, I told Gwen that I was out of beer and wine. She grumbled about it, but she drank my water and ate my pizza. We talked about normal things: the weather, the last trip we had taken as a married couple, the upcoming election, my decision to resign in order to focus on my candidacy, and cars. Gwen and I shared an affinity for cars. I liked fast, high-performance cars; she preferred sporty, luxury cars. After changing out of my robe and back into her dry clothes, I drove her back to her car. It was, perhaps, the most normal time I had spent with her, ever. Maybe things between us could become amicable.

I had not heard from Daly or Wilson, and I did not like being kept in the dark. I had to know that they were getting close to making arrests and pressing charges. I called both of their cell phones, but received no response. They were deliberately avoiding me.

My parents were going to be in town the following week. They were sponsoring an event to raise money for the Sable-Carter Women's Shelter. I desperately wanted to take Susan as my date; however, I did not know the status of the investigation. I called Dex and asked if he knew whether or not Ginny and Susan planned on attending.

"Yes! They wouldn't miss it for the world. Susan found a babysitter, so the girls are really looking forward to a night out. Will we see you there?"

"Yes."

Knowing that Susan would be there gave me something to look forward to. I no longer had to be concerned with Daly and Wilson's directive to stay away from her because of the pending investigation.

Susan and I will just happen to be at the same place, at the same time. What a serendipitous coincidence!

My world was looking up.

CHAPTER SIX

COURTNEY

Pratt's parents were so gracious to host such an amazing black tie affair to help raise money for the Sable-Carter Women's Shelter. Held at the Dover Downs Convention Center, we were expecting over 1,500 guests. Proceeds from the cash bar, casino, and auction would go directly to the shelter's building fund. At 6:30, the guests would be seated in the dining room and Mr. Pratt Sr., Tom's father, would open the evening with a short video and then introduce me. I was expected to say a few words of thanks and state the shelter's mission. Dinner would be served, and then another speaker would be introduced during dessert. She was a brave single mother who volunteered to share her story of spousal abuse and survival. After dessert, the dance floor and casino would reopen and a live band had been hired to play until 11:00 PM.

Dylan, my humble hero, was not raised in the public spotlight, nor did he crave it. Nonetheless, he acclimated quickly and helped me greet the guests. Surprisingly, he mingled comfortably throughout the evening.

When Dex, Ginny, and Susan arrived, they were like a breath of fresh air. Familiarity brings with it its own sense of peace and comfort, like a bowl of tomato soup and a grilled cheese sandwich at the end of a miserable, cold and rainy day.

"Hi guys! I'm so glad you're here!"

"Courtney, this is an amazing party! How did you ever pull it off?" Ginny asked as she looked around the hall.

"I didn't. Pratt's parents and their staff put all of this together. They're such a very generous family."

Dylan found us and hustled over to greet everyone.

"Hey, you guys are a sight for sore eyes. Court, I'm going to show them to the bar, would you like anything to drink?"

"A glass of white wine would be fabulous."

Dylan gave me a light kiss and escorted my new family over to the bar.

Tom Pratt was next to make his entrance into the crowded hall. He gallantly walked over and gave me a kiss on the cheek.

"You look lovely, Courtney."

"Thanks, Pratt. You're quite the knock-out, too."

"Have you seen my parents?"

"No, I don't think they've arrived yet."

'That's odd. I called them before I got into the shower and they said they were getting ready to head out the door."

"If I see them, I'll let them know that you're looking for them. In the meantime, everyone else is over at the bar."

"Splendid. Do you need anything to drink?"

"No, thank you. Dylan's got it covered."

Why does everyone think I need a drink?

Pratt must have spotted the family immediately, because he walked straight toward them. I watched as he shook hands with Dylan and Dex. They were a striking threesome: tall, fit, and sporting their rugged, bad-boy grins, all dressed up in black ties and tuxes. There is no way those three handsome men should ever be allowed to stand in one place together. It's just too much for a young lady's eyes. I secretly wondered what they were talking about. I saw Pratt slap Dylan on the back and raise his glass in a toast. It became obvious to me that they were talking about our wedding and honeymoon. Dylan looked very happy and alive, so they could not have been harassing him too much about it.

Ava and Bridget arrived together. It was the first time I had seen my sisters since the wedding.

"Ava! Bridget! Over here! How are you guys? I've missed you!"

"How are you? How's married life? How was the honeymoon?" they chimed in together.

"Slow down! One question at a time!"

"OK," Ava asserted herself ahead of Bridget, "where is that handsome husband of yours and his hot friends?"

I pointed in their direction.

"Oh my! Talk about eye candy! That is an orgasmic sugar high if ever there was one!"

"AVA!" I scolded. "Is that all you ever think about?"

"Yeah, and tell me you don't."

"No. I don't. I have a lot going on to keep me otherwise occupied."

"Did Pratt bring a date?" Ava demanded to know.

"Not to my knowledge."

"Well, listen. You two (meaning Bridget and me) can stand here and debate your dull lives. I am going to go over there and say 'hello' to that display of all-day suckers. Later!"

"Eeewwww, did she just say what I think she said?" Bridget gagged out.

"Who knows what she is thinking half the time."

Ava was off to salivate over Pratt, Dylan, and Dex. Bridget stayed to chat. Not far into our conversation about Bariloche, Bridget's mouth dropped and nearly hit the floor.

"Oh. Shit. Don't look now, but Pratt's ex-wife is here, and she is not alone," Bridget gasped in horror. "What is she doing here?"

I looked over my shoulder, and though I had never met her, there was no doubt in my mind who had just unnerved Bridget. The woman entering the hall was stunning. Her blonde hair was pulled up, revealing her bare shoulders that rocked seductively with each step. The fitted bodice of her strapless gown, which rose just high enough to cover her nipples, swayed back and forth with her shoulders. Her smooth stride provided just enough bounce to hold one's stare, ensnared by the possibility that her firm and plentiful mammilla were going to peek out at their audience. Her floor length gown was skintight, suddenly flaring out from her knees to her delicate toes. When she turned, the back was open, baring a long swath of her flawless skin. Even her spine and shoulder blades looked as though Donatello had sculpted them from heaven above. The opening in the back of her gown fell to a carefully placed point just above her perfectly heart shaped ass. The fabric clung to her and moved with her like a soft layer of supple, sexy leather. On closer examination, everything above the flare *was* leather, hugging her exquisitely curvaceous body enough to occasionally outline, in detail, her pelvic structure and then some. The flare had been constructed of soft glossy black satin. Her gown must have been a custom design and fit, costing a small fortune. She paraded in her gold stilettos like she was born to walk the red carpet. Pratt's ex-wife was a knockout. She was Roger Rabbit's Jessica, drawing the attention of every man in the hall, including my very own husband.

Just what is she doing here looking like that?

I looked over at Pratt. He was standing next to Susan and seemed to be enjoying their pleasant conversation. I watched Ava approach him, take his arm, and manhandle him as she spoke animatedly, much to Susan's dismay. It did not take long for Pratt's eyes to fall on his ex-wife and her escort. It was all over. I could tell that this night was not going to end well.

PRATT

"Gwen, may I have a word with you, in private?" I asked politely.

Gwen nodded to her despicable date and sashayed two steps in front of me. Half way across the room, I stopped and turned her toward me.

"Where are my manners? Would you care for a drink?"

"I would love one, Baby."

She spoke her response as she had so many times when we were married and she would allow me to fawn over her.

I ordered her a glass of chardonnay from the bar and then escorted her to a remote corner of the room.

"Gwen, you look absolutely stunning and somewhat underdressed tonight," I complimented with a heavy dose of honest sarcasm.

"Why, thank you, Tom," she chuckled, happy with her successful wardrobe selection.

"Do you remember buying this for me?" she asked, running her hands from her bodice down and around her hips. Then she spun around so I could behold the dip in the back of her dress.

"Yes, regrettably."

"Oh, Tom, do be a good sport. I must say; you've always looked irresistible in a tux. I especially like the black silk you've chosen for this occasion!"

Gwen took her hands and smoothed down my lapels while leaning into my chest and standing on one foot, striking a very enticing pose.

I had to pull it together. I had stolen her away from the crowd for a reason.

"Gwen, you know I still care about you, and I will always have your best interests at heart, right?"

"I love you, too, Tom," she whispered in my ear as she pressed into my neck. "There is no one as sexy and as charming as you."

She nipped my earlobe, sending a thrill down my chest and settling somewhere well below my waist. Gwen always had that effect on me, and she was well aware of it, too.

"Gwen, stop. Not here."

"Where, then?"

"Gwen, I need to know what you're doing here with that guy."

"Wouldn't you like to know?"

She twisted her body and stood back.

"Not to worry, Tom. We haven't done anything like what you used to do to me."

She reached out and fiddled with my tie, like she used to when we would dress to go out.

I grabbed her hands and brought them down to her side.

"Gwen, I'm serious. What do you know about that guy?"

"I know that he is hot, wealthy, and he doesn't care if He. Ever. Has. Children!"

She poked an index finger into my chest with each of her final four words.

Her words cut deep. They were deliberate, and they stung like a rusty razor's edge. My first reaction was to walk away from her and allow her to reap what she was sure to sow. However, my need to forgive her and to protect her was stronger.

"Gwen, he's a dangerous man, and I would prefer that you stay away from him."

"Dangerous? Says who?" Gwen laughed.

In light of the investigation, I had already said too much.

Marco Corelli walked over and put his arm around the bare shoulder of my ex-wife.

"Is there a problem here with Captain Terrific?" Corelli crowed like a hotshot.

The guy did not know me well enough to be that sarcastic.

"Tom tells me you're a dangerous man, Marco."

Gwen leaned into Marco, sporting a feigned pout.

"Come on, Gwen. Let me show you just how dangerous I can be!" Marco sneered with a salacious grin.

Marco dragged Gwen's shoulder around and they strutted off. A short distance away, he took a look back and made his threat clear while Gwen's ass swung with her hypnotic gait.

GINNY

"Who is that?" I asked anyone who was listening and noticed the spectacle playing out in front of us.

"That's Pratt's ex-wife," Ava answered disdainfully.

"That's Gwen?" Susan whispered.

Susan was shocked and mortified. First, she had to put up with Ava pouncing on Pratt in the middle of their conversation. Then two minutes later, Pratt excused himself to intercept his sizzling hot ex-wife.

Susan was so happy when we had first arrived. Now, her smiles were all turned upside down and her hopes for the evening had taken a steep nosedive. Susan tried to look away from the corner where Gwen was standing and stroking Pratt in any way she could. However, Susan's curiosity held her spellbound and her pain became increasingly evident.

More surprising was Dex's reaction.

"Susan, are you OK?"

Returning from the bar with our drinks in his hands, Dex had noticed her plummeting mood.

Susan nodded in Pratt and Gwen's direction and explained.

"That's Pratt's ex-wife."

When Gwen spun around, Dex's eyes popped with glaring disbelief.

"Holy shit! He married Gwen? You have got to be kidding me!"

"You know her?" I blurted out.

"Unfortunately, we all know her," Dex responded with annoyance in his voice.

"Whoa! Who's 'we all?' I had nothing to do with her, ever!" Dylan immediately and emphatically denounced his association.

Courtney approached our stunned gathering.

"Who are we talking about?" she was curious to know.

This time, I nodded in Pratt and Gwen's direction. Except now, another gentleman had approached them and was hanging all over Gwen, leaving Pratt obviously unhappy about it.

"What the hell?" Susan muttered, reacting to the other man's behavior.

"Who is that?" Courtney wanted to know.

As usual, Courtney was late to the party.

"This looks like trouble," Dex interjected, "and I can guarantee she's in the middle of it."

Gwen's date swung her around and the two strutted away from Pratt. Malice was written all over Pratt's face. After taking another drink from his glass, Pratt started back toward us. We must have looked like a small herd of deer caught in the headlights. Pratt was not happy and the closer he got, the more we could feel his internal struggle. He was feeling something more caustic than jealousy.

Pratt never made it back to our small herd. His cell phone must have alerted him. He pulled it from his pocket, looked at the screen, and turned toward an exit door.

PRATT

"What do you mean, you've been detained?"

We were within a half hour of seating everyone for dinner, and my parents had not yet arrived. My father called to say that I would have to give the welcome speech and make the introductions because he and my mother were still at the Canal House. Agents Daly and Wilson were there, questioning them about flights the Learjet had made over the past three years.

"Well, this night is going to hell in a handbasket in a hurry," was my response.

"Son, it's nothing to worry about. I'm making arrangements for the Feds to receive all of our flight information and manifests for the past three years, and then we'll leave. We'll probably arrive before dinner is over."

"I can't understand why those guys are wasting their time questioning you. I don't see how you and Mom are connected to their investigation."

I was clearly annoyed.

"Tom, you know about this investigation?"

"If it's about an illegal adoption ring, then yes, I know about it. I unknowingly stumbled upon it when I was investigating someone for embezzlement and drug related offenses."

"Look, Tom, let's not discuss this around your mother. She's already distraught enough as it is."

"OK. Get Daly and Wilson out of there, and I'll see you soon."

I stood behind the podium and looked out across the sea of guests: fifteen hundred people, smiling and waiting for me to speak. I wondered what secrets each of them were keeping. I wondered if they were truly as happy as they all appeared to be. I wondered if they could sense the amount of stress that I had willingly heaped upon my back in the last half-hour. In the meantime, I knew it was my duty to Courtney's cause, The Sable-Carter Women's Shelter, to stand tall, put on a happy face, welcome and thank everyone on behalf of my detained parents, and introduce a short opening video.

SUSAN

Pratt took the stage with a somber stroll in his step. He stood behind the podium, looked down at the floor, and frowned. Lifting his head, he appeared to have matured ten years. Not "aged." "Matured." There is a difference, and indeed, something was different. Slowly scanning the crowd, Pratt unknowingly took control of his audience. The room quieted as everyone waited for the charismatic man with a commanding presence to begin speaking.

Looking out over the tables circled with seated guests and surrounded by waiters preparing to clear salad plates, Pratt's eyes met mine. He smiled, and I blushed. His gaze reduced me to a schoolgirl, and I knew then that I wanted him to be mine.

Just that quick, as soon as I was ready to become vulnerable, my guard went up.

Is there sincerity in his smile, or is he using me as a pawn to regain the attention of his very captivating ex-wife. Maybe she's seated somewhere behind me, and he was smiling at her.

My heart sank. I looked down into my lap and closed my eyes.

God, please don't let me get hurt. Not again.

I thought of Zoe. The dating world would be much different for me, now. Would Pratt even be able to comprehend that? In some strange way, I thought he could.

Pratt began speaking to the crowd. His voice was strong as the microphone picked up his rich, soothing timbre. He cracked a joke about his tardy parents, and the crowd responded with a laugh. The atmosphere of the room lifted, and Pratt had found his rhythm. I saw him in a different light, then. He was a statesman, a leader, and a person with an enormous compassion for others.

Soon, the lights were dimmed and a video began. "Home," performed by Phillip Phillips, played softly in the background while vignettes of women and their children were featured. Some photographs provided glimpses of the scars left by the abuse they had endured. Others photos showed glimpses of happiness that could be found in a place offering a safe haven. At some time during the video, Courtney left the table where she had been seated between Dylan and her father, and Pratt emerged from the darkness and took his seat next to me. He leaned over and whispered in my ear.

"Thanks for being here."

Sweet and simple. That was the Pratt that I thought I was getting to know. Not the one who was caught up in some complicated relationship with a provocative vixen. His attraction to his ex-wife made no sense to me. She seemed to represent everything he tried to avoid, at least when he was with me. That made her all the more vexing and dangerous, and I was not sure that I possessed enough self-confidence, determination, and endurance to survive in the throes of her shadow.

When the video ended, the lights came up slowly, and Courtney was already standing behind the podium. After the applause ended, she spoke.

"Good evening. My name is Courtney Sable-Carter."

Her voice carried from the podium microphone, through several large speakers that were mounted in strategic locations, and bounced around the silent walls of the large room with a split second delay, creating an echoed reverberation.

That was all she said. The room burst into applause and the audience was on its feet. I looked over at Dylan. Overwhelmed, tears escaped his eyes. He was so proud of his new bride. Together, they had been through so much, which had led them to this place, this moment. Dex reached over and patted Dylan's shoulder in a sign of solidarity. Standing beside me, Pratt clapped and nodded. Ginny was smiling ear-to-ear. At the table beside us, Mr. Sable looked around the room, casually taking in all who had attended and were now expressing their adoration for his youngest daughter. Courtney's sisters were bouncing as they applauded their youngest sibling.

Mr. and Mrs. Pratt entered the hall and covertly slid into their seats that were on reserve at our table. As the applause began to diminish and people were taking their seats, Pratt quietly introduced me to his breathless parents. They smiled and took my hand as if they had been anticipating our meeting. At least I wanted to believe they were happy to meet me.

As Courtney spoke of her cause, my mind wandered. I was distracted by the presence of Pratt's parents only a few feet away from where I was sitting.

Do they really know who I am?
What has Pratt told them about me, if anything?
Do they know that I have a daughter?
Do they know that the three of us picnicked on their lawn by the Canal?
Do they know that their former daughter-in-law is seated somewhere in the hall with an employee of mine?
What about Marco? Why is he here, and how does he know Pratt's ex-wife?

Why is it that Marco has never mentioned her? Not that we talk all that often, and never about his love life or romantic escapades, whatever the case may be.

No one laughed when Courtney spoke. Her speech was meant to transport her audience into the terror of living a life dominated by fear while trying to protect and provide for your loved ones. She accomplished her mission. The room remained silent as she spoke. Just when she took everyone to rock bottom, she brought them out of the pit by thanking them for "showing up." She praised them for not taking a backseat while the weak and helpless were being beaten down verbally and physically abused at the hands of those who would find satisfaction and pleasure in their brutal power and ability to control others.

"Power misused for one's gain is abuse. Power exercised for the protection, preservation, and advancement of others is right and good. Tonight, we are here to provide a sanctuary for those who need a way out and a new start. You can, and will, make a difference with your generous pledges and contributions. I thank you for joining this worthy and honorable cause. Let the Delmarva Peninsula become known as a region that finds its strength in sacrifice for all that is good and right. By providing a way for one person to overcome evil, we all become a stronger and better community. Thank you."

Courtney received another standing ovation. Mr. and Mrs. Pratt nodded to each other and their son, signaling that Courtney had knocked it out of the park. Dylan and Mr. Sable were beaming with pride.

Dex leaned over and whispered in my ear, "That's the Courtney I know."

Indeed, Courtney had inspired her audience and was finding strength in her commitment to help the helpless. Even I was moved by her sincerity and sheer determination.

COURTNEY

After dinner and dessert, the audience heard from a "survivor" who shared her story and thanked the audience for their support and donations to a great and worthy cause. Mr. Pratt Sr. closed the dinner portion of the evening, and then the casino and dance floors reopened. I was exhausted and in desperate need of a second wind.

I excused myself from the table and headed for the ladies' room. When I returned to the table, a certain city councilwoman was sitting in my seat.

"Good evening, Mrs. Merck." I looked down my nose and greeted her.

Marien Merck, who was about 50+ and a divorcee, was always campaigning for votes or vying for the attention of wealthy men, especially those that were divorced or widowed. My father, whose status had recently changed due to the death of my mother, was now on her radar screen.

"Courtney, dear, that was a marvelous speech. You're a very gifted young woman. Your father should be very proud of you."

Don't tell me what my father should or should not be. What he should be is not around you and all of your phony hyperbole!

"Indeed, I am very proud of all three of my girls," my father boasted.

Marien was greatly pleased because her compliment had elicited a positive comment and a smile from my father. She had hit her latest target.

Please, don't flirt with my dad while I am standing here and you're sitting in my seat. I am not your little pawn.

Apparently, my claws were out, because Dylan felt the need to disarm me and rescue me from myself.

"Court, will you dance with me, please?"

Dylan took my arm and gently escorted me to the dance floor. The band was playing a fast set, so I took the opportunity to work out some of my mounting irritation with that totally exasperating woman.

See, she even causes me to use excessive hyperbole, except mine are no exaggeration.

"Court, I know what you're thinking. Your dad can handle himself. Let it go," Dylan called out over the music.

I didn't answer him. I knew he was right, but I didn't want to talk about it, either. Before the first dance was over, none of it mattered, anyway. Mr. Pratt Sr. had interrupted Marien and was now leading my father outside. I breathed a sigh of relief. I later learned that Mr. Pratt Sr. needed my father's advice about retaining some high-powered, well-connected legal services.

PRATT

I was relieved to see that my parents were able to make it in time for dinner. My father apologized for their late arrival, and I introduced my mother and him to everyone seated around our table. Susan asked my mother about their trip to the Cape. Susan's kind question launched my mother to a happier place. Susan certainly possessed the social graces that would help my mother relax and enjoy the evening.

After dessert and the final speaker, my father asked me to join him at the bar, except we didn't go to the bar. We walked outside.

"Dad, what happened? Why were Daly and Wilson at the Canal House?"

"It seems a very young child, who entered the country last week, died suddenly. She and another young girl were flown in under the pretense that they were going to receive medical attention at Children's Hospital. Except they were never admitted, nor did the hospital have any information about their cases. It has been determined that the children were smuggled into the country and illegally sold for adoption," my father quietly explained.

"What's that got to do with Mom and you?"

"The plane she came in on was our Learjet."

"What? Are they sure?"

"Yes. She was one of the two children flown back with Dylan and Courtney."

"Dear. God. How did they get onboard the Learjet?"

"It appears that your mother arranged for their transport."

"She did what? How did she get mixed up in this?"

"We have legitimately brought children into this country for medical treatment through Healing Wings, reputable medical agencies, and charities for years. We didn't realize that someone had contacted Javier and the crew and provided them with falsified records and documents."

"So, Mom didn't make that call?"

"Of course not!" my father's voice was raised, rankled by all of the accusations aimed at my mother.

"How many times has this happened?"

"We don't know. Your friends are looking into it."

"Dad, I think you'd better get a good lawyer. Please, don't breathe a word of this to Courtney or Dylan, not here, not tonight."

My first inclination was to call Daly and Wilson and tell them to back off. However, I realized that I needed to let my parents' attorney handle that message. I also wanted to tell those two to leave Courtney and Dylan out of it. I feared if Courtney knew that she had flown home with two children who were being "sold" and that one had not survived, it would throw her over the edge. However, I knew it was not a request that I could make, either.

I only had one option. I waited until Courtney and Dylan had left the dance floor and several large benefactors had corralled Courtney.

"Dylan, may I have a word with you?"

We made our way into a quiet hallway.

Unaware of my planned forewarning, Dylan began rambling with words of sincere gratitude.

"This has been a terrific evening. Please thank your parents, again, for making all of the arrangements and their generous contributions to the shelter. They have been so kind to us."

"I'll pass along your sentiments. Now, regarding my parent's generous contributions ..."

I proceeded to tell Dylan how my parents had been donating the Learjet and its crew to bring seriously ill children into the country for medical treatment that they would not otherwise receive in their native countries or be able to afford in the States. I told him of the illegal adoption ring that had used the name of one of the medical agencies as a front to use the Learjet and Healing Wings for its own purposes. My parents had been scammed on a large scale, possibly more than once.

"So, Dylan, were there two children on your return flight home?" I asked.

"Yes, there were. Two very young girls."

"Well, one of them died last week, and she was brought in for an illegal adoption, not for medical treatment."

Dylan closed his eyes and rubbed his forehead. "Oh, my God . . ." he murmured.

"As you can imagine, my mother is very shaken. My parents arrived late tonight because two FBI agents had detained them at the Canal House for questioning. Dylan, what you need to know is that the Feds will probably want to talk to you and Courtney in the very near future."

Dylan leaned back against the wall. He bent over at the waist and put his head down like he was going to be ill. When he finally stood back up, he looked pale and lightheaded.

"Pratt, how do these things happen? How could we not have known that something wasn't right? When I think back on it, now, it was all very hush-hush. They asked us not to disturb the children. We never really *saw* the girls. When they boarded in Bolivia and disembarked in Wilmington, they were strapped down on gurneys and I assumed they were asleep. We flew with them for twelve hours, and we didn't hear a peep out of them. How could we not have known?"

"If you *had* figured it out, it could have been far worse. I don't know how dangerous these people are. They could have been armed. It was best that you didn't know."

"What, and let an innocent child die? This is going to kill Courtney."

"I just thought you should know. I'm sorry you got mixed up in this."

GINNY

After dessert, Dex took me out onto the dance floor. He said he had a few calories to burn off and could not think of a better way to do it than to impress me with his new moves.

"New moves? I think you'd better perfect the old ones first, don't you?" I teased.

I loved Dex's sense of humor and the way he always made me the center of his world when we were out together. However, on that particular night, I could tell that underneath all of his cajoling throughout the evening, there was an unusual disturbance.

Finally, a slow set. Time to snuggle up to my handsome beau.

"Are you doing OK, Dex?"

Dex held me back at arm's length so he could read my face.

"Yes. Why do you ask?"

"Oh, I can tell when you're a little off, or worried about something."

"I'm not worried. It's nothing, really."

I could not have timed my question any better. The infamous Gwen walked up to us and actually asked if she could cut in on our dance.

Really?

My intuition told me that she had had far too much to drink, and was up to no good.

Knowing I could count on comfort in Susan's company, I looked for her, but she was off having a heated conversation with Gwen's date.

What's that all about?

Dylan and Pratt were nowhere to be seen, and Courtney was entertaining some high rollers.

Sheesh!

I was on my own. I walked casually back to the table and sat down at my seat. Marien Merck had disappeared. Then again, so had Courtney's dad and Pratt's dad. With nothing better to do, I glanced out at the dance floor. Gwen was all over Dex. I could feel my blood pressure rising. First, her hand was in his hair. Then, she moved it down his neck and across his chest. When she started pressing up against his leg, I jumped out of my chair and marched toward the dance floor. Fortunately, Dex pushed her away and left her standing alone. He saw me and shook his head.

"She is one unfortunate piece of work. Let's not ever let her cut in like that again. Where's her date, anyway?"

"Susan is giving him an earful, I think."

"Really? How does Susan know him? Did he do something inappropriate? I'll beat the . . ." Dex stopped mid-sentence. The last time he had tried to protect one of us, he nearly wound up with an assault charge.

"Dex, do you think you could calmly go over there and see if Susan is OK without decking the guy? I think it would be a good exercise for you, if you can pull it off."

"Ah, no! There you go, again, putting me up to one of your little schemes. The last time you did this, I got slapped in the face by Courtney."

"And rightfully so!"

"What? I was only following your instructions."

"And quite well, I might add."

"Oh, wait until I get you home, young lady!"

"And just what are your intentions, old man?"

Dex raised a playful eyebrow.

"Oh, you could definitely take me home, now!" I exclaimed, reading his very active mind.

Dex took a step toward me. I straight-armed him.

"Just one thing, how do you know Pratt's ex-wife? She is obviously very attracted to you and thought she could take liberties."

"Liberties? Believe me, she's attracted to anything that could give her a thrill, and she's used to having her way, too."

"How do you know all of this about her?"

"I'll tell you on the way home. Things seem to be winding down, so we should be able to leave soon."

SUSAN

Marco had to know that I would be attending the fundraiser. I could not understand why he had never mentioned it, and why he was there with Pratt's ex-wife. Did Marco realize that Gwen was only using him to get to Pratt? That still did not explain how Marco knew Gwen in the first place.

When Gwen cut in on Ginny and Dex, I decided to take advantage of Marco's free time and warn him.

"Marco, what a surprise to see you! I had no idea you'd be here tonight. How's everything going on the Main Line in Pennsylvania?"

"Hi, Susan! I thought I might see you here. You're looking well. By the way, Derek sends his regards."

"What? You've heard from him?"

"I try to stop by the prison and see him about once a month, or so."

"Shhhhh . . ."

I did not want Marco using the word "prison" anywhere near me.

"Why didn't you tell me?" I jeered.

"I never had reason to, and quite frankly, I don't want to get in the middle of whatever you two have going on."

"Going on? Marco, we're divorced. You know that. There's nothing going on."

I paused to let my emotions simmer down a little.

"How is Derek?" I asked quietly and much calmer.

"How do you think he is? He's in prison. His wife divorced him. Then she had his fucking baby and changed their last names. How the FUCK do you THINK he's doing?" Marco accentuated sardonically, getting up in my face. He reeked of whiskey.

I slapped him.

Shit! I slapped Marco right across his face! In front of all these people, most of whom I don't know. I slapped him in front of all the people that Courtney and Pratt want to impress. I actually slapped him across his face! SHIT!

I pointed a finger at Marco and leaned into him.

"You are never to breathe a word about my daughter, ever. Not to Derek, or anyone else. Do I make myself clear?"

I got within inches of his nose and repeatedly jabbed my finger into his puffed out chest.

"You have no right to spread rumors about her. You have no clue, and you are dead wrong," I snarled, identifying the actual source of my anger.

"Then, I guess that makes you someone's whore? Or, maybe she belongs to Tom Pratt? Which is it, Susan?" Marco snapped back.

My hand went up again, when someone from behind grabbed my wrist and stopped me.

"Mr. Corelli, I suggest you leave, or I'll escort you out myself."

Pratt had stepped in. I don't know how much he had heard, but he saved me from making another embarrassing mistake.

It was not long before Dylan and Dex were standing right behind Pratt. Rubbing out the sting on the side of his face, Marco turned and never looked back. Much to my great disappointment, he left without taking the inebriated

Gwen with him. That meant she was without a ride. I feared that Pratt would be the one elected to drive her home. No doubt, he would feel responsible to take care of her. He was that kind of chivalrous gentleman.

"I'll call a cab for Gwen and see to it that she gets in. That's as far as I'm going to go," Pratt stated before turning his full attention toward me.

"Are you OK?" Pratt softly brushed a tendril of my hair out of my eyes, taking some of my rage and shame with it.

"Yes. I'm so sorry."

I lowered my head.

"There's no need to apologize, Susan. He had it coming," Pratt consoled as he lifted my chin.

"Do you think we could take you Carters out just once without one of you hauling off and hitting someone?" he smirked.

Courtney walked over to see what all of the commotion was about as Pratt had us all laughing at the humor in the situation. After we had settled down, Pratt got serious.

"Susan, you need to lock that guy out of your company's network right now, and then fire him before he can do any damage."

"Oh, my God, you're right. I'll call our I.T. contractor right away and have it taken care of."

I also knew that I should notify Derek to make sure Marco's termination stuck.

I was not ready for what happened next.

PRATT

The evening was deemed a huge success. The event raised over 2.3 million in cash and pledges for The Sable-Carter Women's Shelter. Other major events took place that evening, as well. Susan fired Marco, but was first able to lock him out of their corporate network, Gwen made it home safely in a cab, and my parents had finally met Susan. Unfortunately, I had not escaped the evening unscathed.

After I had managed to get Gwen into a cab and gave the driver her address, fare, and a generous tip, I returned to Susan and my parents. Dex and Ginny were gathering up their belongings and preparing for the drive home.

"Susan, may I give you a lift home?" I offered, full of hope.

"Well, I came with Dex and Ginny, and I have a sitter that I have to . . . "

Ginny jumped in.

"Why don't you two ride together? Dex and I are ready to go. We'll leave now, pay the sitter, and make sure she gets home OK. We'll see you when you get in."

SUSAN

It was after midnight when Courtney and Dylan, Mr. and Mrs. Pratt Sr., and Tom and I were walking out the door. Pratt kissed his mother on her cheek and told her that he loved her. It was a very sweet gesture, which I could tell she cherished greatly. Pratt gave his father a manly father-son hug and said he would call. I hugged Pratt's mother and received a gentle embrace from his father. Courtney and Dylan thanked Pratt's parents and promised to stay in touch, keeping them apprised of the construction and the anticipated opening of the center.

Finally, it was time to leave. Pratt escorted me to his car. I was looking for the black Corvette that he had driven the night he had taken me to the Arrest Pediatric Cancer fundraiser. That night seemed like decades ago. The car whose headlights winked at him was a sweet red Lotus Elise.

Seriously?

"So, Pratt, who is it that you were trying to impress tonight? Certainly, you had no clue that you would be driving me home."

Pratt opened my door for me.

"My dear, I had every intention of driving you home tonight."

Pratt's confident smile was sexy as hell.

Keep your wits about you, Susan.

The car was so low to the ground that it was no easy feat for me to slide in gracefully as Pratt held the door open. He took my hand, and I carefully sat my butt down on the leather seat, and then I swung my legs in.

During the drive back to Lewes, Pratt and I shared our thoughts about the success of the evening, how impressed we were with Courtney, how impressed I was with him, and how nice it was to meet his parents.

Pratt also confirmed that he was going to officially throw his hat into the ring. He was in the process of garnering support and wanted to know if I would still be on board.

"Of course."

"Just one thing I ask of you," Pratt continued, "no more public brawls! I can't have the people that I'm close to picking fights with my future constituents while I'm on the campaign trail. After I'm elected, you can slap whomever your pretty hand pleases."

I laughed at his sarcasm, and then I corrected him.

"We are not that close. This," I waved in the space between the two of us, "is not close. We are not close."

"OK. You made your point: three times to be exact. We'll keep it simple, Susan. Just the way I like it!" he winked.

"It has to stay simple, Pratt. There are too many complicated obstacles between us."

"Things are only complicated when we allow them to be."

I knew he was right. I just didn't know how to untangle what I had already knotted up.

Then, as we zipped down Route 1 with virtually no other traffic in either direction, the topic of conversation turned unpleasant: what to do about Marco.

I told Pratt that I had successfully contacted our I.T. contractor and that he had called back within the half hour to assure me that Marco was locked out and had not been on the network since earlier that morning. I was relieved to hear it, and so was Pratt.

"Now, I have to find a way to tell Derek," I pondered aloud.

"Do you want me to go with you?"

"No, it would be a waste of your time. He probably won't see me, anyway. I suppose I could write it down in a letter and hope that he reads it."

"I could deliver it to make sure that he does," Pratt suggested.

"You would do that? What if he refuses to see you?"

"I don't think he will. He never has before."

"You've seen him? You've visited with him?"

"Yes, Susan, I have."

I could not speak. My mouth went dry.

Who is this man? What is his connection to Derek? Why is it that everyone sees Derek, except me?

"Wait a minute, how long have you been visiting him?"

Keep it simple? How do I keep something like Derek's imprisonment, and his refusal to see me while he lets everyone else in, simple?

Pratt did not answer right away. He kept his eyes on the road as we traveled well over the speed limit in his Lotus. Then he suddenly geared down and whipped over into the lot of a closed roadside farm market. He put the car in neutral and let the purring engine idle.

Pratt took a deep breath, and turned toward me.

"Susan, I knew Derek when we were teenagers. Occasionally, we'd all hang out together when we were down in Lewes during the summer. We weren't close friends, more like acquaintances. Fast forward many years, and I was there when they brought Derek in on hijacking and attempted murder charges. Several weeks after his incarceration, I received a phone call from Marco, whom I didn't know at the time. He said that Derek had a favor to ask of me. I went to visit Derek to confirm his request. That was it. I have visited with him a total of three times."

"Then you knew who I was all along?"

"Not exactly. The night you placed the 911 call and I was dispatched, I suspected that Ms. Susan McCabe was indeed Mrs. Derek Carter, or should I say the former Mrs. Carter."

"Thank you for that. So, you knew who I was when you had asked me out the first time?"

"Yes, by then, I had done my homework."

I was not able to fully comprehend everything he was confessing in just those few words.

"What was Derek's request?"

"His first request . . . "

"Wait! There was more than one request?"

"Yes. His first request was to keep an eye on you. Once you moved to Lewes and away from Valley Forge, Derek felt he needed someone here to look after you."

"He did?"

"Yes, Susan. He did. You were his world. While Derek could never undo what he had done, he wanted to make sure that you would be OK."

"The second request?" I was eager to hear it all.

Pratt swallowed hard and cleared his throat, clenching the steering wheel of his idling car. He knew it was not going to be good, and I was still waiting.

"When Derek found out that you had had a baby, he wanted to know who the baby belonged to, so he blatantly indicated that he would pay a handsome price for DNA evidence."

PRATT

Her eyes filled with tears.

"Who are you? How could you do such a thing?" Susan chastised.

She dropped her face into her hands, afraid to look at me.

"Susan, it wasn't me. I emphatically turned down his request and gave him a sharp warning. Then, you placed the 911 call. Even though there were no signs or evidence of anything being stolen or broken into, I still had my strong suspicions. Why do you think I staked out the Carter beach house all that night and the following week? I thought sure the perp would return. I was also inclined to believe that the person I was looking for was Marco. I visited Derek one more time to try to get a solid bead on who was doing his dirty work and to tell him to call it off. By then, Derek already knew that Zoe was his."

Susan lost it. I was sure she was not mad at me, but she sure took it out on me. I let her yell, and cry, and hit the dash of my car. But when she bolted and started running down Route 1, I had no choice but to go after her.

Do you know how difficult it is for a tall person to bolt out of a Lotus?

Susan was agile and fast. Even in bare feet, she was fast. I did not want to tackle her to the ground like I would an ordinary suspect. I did not want to hurt her or ruin her dress, so I caught up to her and ran with her. Once she stopped yelling at me to go away, we ran together in silence. She just needed to run. We must have run a good quarter mile before the Lotus went flying by at a high rate of speed, followed by an old Jeep some distance behind.

"Was that . . .?" Susan sputtered out of breath. She had finally come to a stop and was leaning over her knees.

"It sure was!"

We laughed. Susan laughed so hard she cried, again. I offered her a seat on a nearby random guardrail. Carefully, I put my arm around her, then laid her head on my shoulder, and just let her cry it out.

"It's OK, Susan. It's going to be OK."

"No one was supposed to know. I didn't want Zoe to ever know," she sobbed.

"You have plenty of time to figure it out. Right now, she's too young to understand."

"I don't think Dylan or Dex know. I've never told them, and I think Ginny has kept it quiet, too."

"There you go. Your secret is probably safe, for now. You'll know when it's time to tell them."

"What about Marco?" Susan asked.

"Well, he could be a loose cannon, especially now that you've terminated him and locked him out."

Susan pounded the heel of her bare foot into the sandy dirt that formed the shoulder of the deserted highway. It was true. There was not much she could do about Marco.

"What about your car?" she whimpered.

"Yeah, now that's a problem. I'll call the station and put an APB out on it. They'll have fun chasing it down. That I can almost guarantee!"

"I'll call Dex and ask him to pick us up . . . Shit, my purse is still in your car!"

"Not to worry, we'll get it back."

DEX

We were not in the car for more than two seconds, before Ginny started.

"OK, Dex, spill it. I've been waiting all night to hear about your connection to the infamous Gwen Pratt," Ginny demanded of me.

I had never seen her quite so anxious about another woman—other than Ava Sable—since I had known her.

"I know what you're thinking, and I am not jealous. I'm just curious," Ginny went on to defend her eager thirst for knowledge. "OK, so maybe this once I was a little jealous, but she was all over you like jellyfish tentacles," she confessed.

"That's a pretty accurate analogy."

"Well, how would you like it if some guy came on to me like that?"

"Ginny, if that ever happened and you looked distressed about it, I would probably take more than just one swing at him." I went on to further explain. "It would all hinge on your response, not his action. If you appeared to be in trouble, I would definitely step in. If you were inviting him in, then I would have to walk away."

"You'd walk away?"

"Probably. Yes. Brokenhearted, but I would have to walk away."

"Yet, you defended Courtney when Max Black got too close."

"Yes, I did."

"Did she look like she was in trouble?" Ginny protested.

"Not yet, but she had always been more like a sister to me, and brothers don't let other guys like that get near their sisters."

"How do you know that? You've never had a sister," Ginny countered.

"True, but Courtney and Susan have always been like sisters to me. I will always defend them."

"And me? Was I ever a sister to you?"

"I guess there was a time when you were, when Dan was alive and you two were inseparable. I thought Dan was the luckiest man in the world. I never believed that I would ever find someone like you. I also knew that I would never settle for anyone less."

"That's very sweet, Dex."

Ginny reached across and rubbed my thigh.

"Somewhere along the way, you became less of a sister and more of someone that I was beginning to dream about in a very sensual way. The night you kissed me . . ."

"I kissed you?" Ginny challenged the accuracy of my recollection.

"Yes. I was telling you how I felt, and you assaulted me with a kiss."

"I assaulted you?"

"Yes. It changed me forever. I was never the same after that kiss. And when you left for Darien, it nearly killed me. But then I realized that you weren't running away from me. You were running away from the past. You had to make that violent break before you and I could ever move forward."

"Come on, Dex. You're not that much of a romantic."

"Yes. Yes, I am. When you called and said that you were back on the Right Tackle, waiting for me, I knew our relationship was free to cross over and enter new territory."

" 'Territory?' That's an interesting choice of words. Am I 'territory' to you, now?"

"Quite the opposite. If I love you, then I can't 'own' you. That's why my reactions are so tied to your actions. If someone is fondling you at your request or permission, I have no power against them. Because I love you, I have no power over you, either. Everything is built on faith and trust. However, if someone is touching you or speaking to you in a way that upsets you or is against your will, then I will make sure that they never consider getting that close to you again."

"Dex, you really are quite the romantic. Pull the truck over. I want to show you my will, right now."

Ginny and I had never made love in a vehicle of any kind before. We were climbing into the backseat of my truck when my cell phone lit up. It was Pratt.

"Don't answer that," Ginny pleaded.

I rolled in beside her, pulling her under me. The cell phone pinged, indicating that Pratt had left a message.

Good.

Then, my cell lit up, again. It was Pratt, again.
"It must be important."
I took his call.

PRATT

Sitting on the guardrail, in the pitch dark, with no streetlights, no car, all dressed up, and Susan with no shoes on her feet, I could only laugh at our predicament. I could not believe that I was so calm about watching my car speed by with who-knows-who behind the wheel. I called the station, and it sounded like my buddies hoped that the Lotus would make its way back into their jurisdiction just so they would have the opportunity to chase it down.

At least their dream came true. Mine was sitting on the side of Route 1, and as usual, things were getting a little messy.

"Are you cold?" I asked, after I had finally reached Dex on his cell phone.

"A little," Susan murmured.

Removing my jacket, I placed it over Susan's shoulders and moved closer so I could put an arm around her to help ward off the chill that was settling in with the very early morning air. She shifted nervously. We sat in silence until I finally broke it.

"Why do I get the feeling that you would prefer I keep my distance?" I asked.

"Huh?"

Susan looked over at me.

That got her attention. I went on to explain myself.

"Let's see, you ran out of my car, you left me no choice but to chase after you, you continued to run for another mile *(a slight exaggeration)* in bare feet, I've given you my jacket to help keep you warm, and still you remain incorrigibly cold toward me. Am I that offensive?"

"No, not at all. It's just that I'm completely baffled by you and your ex-wife. I just cannot fathom why you would ever marry her. I don't know how to process all of that and keep it simple."

"Looking back, I can't believe I married her, either. But, I did."

The real truth: I always found it hard to believe that Gwen would ever marry a guy like me. But, she did. I guess I should have known that I would never be enough for her.

"Do you still love her?"

"No."

I had answered too quickly. I was afraid to ponder the truth. Gwen had some sort of hold on me that was impossible to explain. I began to wonder if Gwen had made it home OK. I had an urge to call her and ask.

Let her go. She brings you nothing but heartache.

Silence fell between us, again. I could feel Susan's curiosity resurfacing.

"How did you meet her?"

"We met in Lewes. We were both windsurfing in the Bay, just up from the public beach."

"Oh, so you had the privilege of staring at her half-naked body all day?"

"Not exactly."

"You know you did, all healthy young men stare at beautiful women."

"Susan, what do you want me say? That I was sexually attracted to her? That it was all about the sex? OK. I'll do it. I pounced on her like she was a dog in heat, and then I married her."

"What? You did not. Really? Is that all it took?"

"No. I really believed we were in love. At least, I was. I really believed we were going to live together forever, start a family, and spend the rest of our lives in total bliss."

"You believed in that fairy tale, too, huh?"

"Yes, I guess I did. How about you?"

"Hook, line, and sinker. When I met Derek, I fell fast. He was handsome and charming and promised me the world. And he gave me the world, even when I didn't ask for it. Even after we were married, Derek continued to court me with everything he had."

"What happened?"

Susan stared off into the dark as she answered.

"We couldn't have children. We tried for years. It was exhausting," she sighed.

We both guffawed at her accidental innuendo, before she continued.

"Derek would not consider any other options. Then, his father died and everything collapsed as quickly as it had started. I never saw it coming. Derek just fell apart."

After a slight pause she turned to me.

"And now, I have Zoe. Go figure."

"It's an all too familiar story. Gwen and I could never have children, though she never told me until after we were married."

"She knew?"

"It's not my story to tell, but let's just say that she was not forthcoming with information before we were married."

"Oh . . . I'm so sorry, Pratt."

"It's OK. I would have stayed with her, with or without children. She didn't see it that way. Confessing to her condition sent her over the edge. I forgave her, but she was too far gone."

Dex finally arrived. Susan and I climbed into the backseat of his truck and sat quietly during the ride back to Lewes. Our roadside topic of conversation was not meant to be shared with others, not even friends as close as Dex and Ginny.

Susan stared out her window as we bounced along in Dex's truck. All the while, Dex and I carried on a conversation about the guys that drove away in my Lotus. I glanced over at Susan from time to time to make sure she was OK. She was so quiet and still. I wanted to take her hand to let her know that I was thinking of her, but refrained from doing so. I didn't want to risk upsetting her further.

As we approached the Lewes cut-off, I received word that my car had been recovered and was waiting for me back at the station, along with the thieves who had been apprehended. Dex dropped me off to retrieve my car, before taking Susan home to the Carter beach house.

It had not taken long for my buddies to find the Lotus. However, it took a little longer for them to chase it down! Apparently, the car was too tempting for a group of young guys to pass up. Small world, it turned out to be the same guys who had taunted Courtney in her Porsche several summers ago. When I met them at the station, they remembered me, too, and nearly fell over.

"Fancy meeting you here! So, what have you been up to these days?" was all I could think of to say.

I did not press charges. They were a couple of young bucks who had found a Lotus idling in a small dirt parking lot in front of a farm stand with no one around. They had hit the lottery jackpot! They claimed that they had waited several minutes before they decided that they should drive it back to the police station—before someone else could actually steal it, of course.

They were not all that different from me when I was their age.

The arresting officer, Jared Murray, just shook his head and laughed.

"Then do you mind telling me why I had to chase you down Route 9 until you decided to pull over?" Murray challenged.

They had no answer. They had only done what any red-blooded American boy would have done.

"They did stop by their own volition when they reached Cape Henlopen Drive," Murray willingly acknowledged when he addressed me.

"Any damage to my car?" I asked.

"None that I could see."

"OK, I'll have it inspected tomorrow. Then I'll decide if I'm going to press charges. Before you let them go, let me check and make sure my girlfriend's purse and shoes are still in the car and intact."

I had actually referred to Susan as my "girlfriend." Huh, imagine that . . .

Everything seemed to be in order *(except my head and my heart)*, and the inspection showed that no damage had been done to the car. Charged only with speeding, reckless driving, and resisting arrest, the gentlemen were off the hook for car theft. It was my gift for "bringing the Lotus back." The driver did lose his license. It was a fair sentence and a lenient one, enough to send a message and teach a lesson. For some strange reason, I thought I would miss seeing them on the road, for a while, anyway.

DEX

Ginny had to wait until we returned home and were alone in bed before I could tell her about my fundamental non-involvement with Gwen. As soon as the lights were out and we were snuggled together, she asked again. Ginny's impatience was rising like a tar bubble on hot macadam. It was obvious that this mattered to her greatly.

"The first thing you need to know, Ginny, is that nothing ever happened between Gwen and me. Nothing happened that had any meaning, anyway. Got it?"

"Got it. Now, spill it."

Ginny sat up, withdrawing her naked body from mine. She pulled the sheets up over her breasts, a sure sign that I would be denied all access until she was completely satisfied that I had provided all the necessary and vital details about whatever it was that never happened.

Taking a deep breath before I entered the minefield of my past, I sat up on my elbow and proceeded to fill in the blanks.

"Gwen was quite the news story around town that summer. She was a lifeguard on the public beach, and while I rarely, as in never, went to the public beach, we had heard about this new sexy lifeguard. Keep in mind: to teenage boys, anything with boobs is sexy. But Derek had to go and check her out for himself.

"So he dragged you along? Derek made you go and gawk against your will? Yeah, right."

Ginny was not convinced of my innocence, and justly so.

"No. I was quite happy to tag along."

Ginny took a swipe at my bicep. It was her way of punishing my adolescent behavior, albeit almost a decade and a half ago.

"Go on with your very sorry story, your tale of great self-sacrifice for a friend," she muttered.

She was not going to let me off the hook without sinking it first and then watching me wiggle my way out of a snare that Derek's curiosity and drive to conquer had created in the first place. I continued.

"So, we went down to the beach the next day, and there she was. Derek was spellbound. Now I had seen him handily chase and flirt with girls before, but this was different. He was stupefied. He had no clue what to do. So, we left."

"He didn't talk to her, or anything?"

"Nothing. I don't even think she saw us. Anyway, I had a job at the gas dock that summer, and on my days off, Charles would sometimes ask me to help out with his charters, so I didn't get to hang out on the beach everyday like the Carter boys did. As the story goes, I believe Derek started visiting the public beach more often and worked harder each day to attract her attention, which I think he succeeded in doing to some degree. He really had it bad for her.

"Long story short, one night after Charles and I had returned from a fishing trip and scrubbed down the Morning Starr, Charles treated me to dinner out on the deck of Irish Eyes. When I was walking home—we lived with my grandmother at the time—I ran into Gwen near the drawbridge at the end of Angler's Road. She stopped me and asked my name, stating that she had seen me around town and at the marina. I could tell that she had been drinking. I had had a beer, too, with Charles, so I was in no position to judge her underage behavior. Anyway, she began describing this boat, something I guess she thought I would find enticing."

"I'm sure you were already 'enticed' enough," Ginny assessed accurately.

I continued, not wanting to dawdle in dangerous territory.

"Gwen said the boat was a beautiful relic that I would appreciate, but it was having some engine problems and asked if I thought I could get it running again. Well, I couldn't make any guarantees without seeing it."

"You fell for that old trick? Come on, Dex, you want me to believe that you had no idea what her motives were?"

"Actually, yes. I really believed it was about the boat."

"Dex, you are so hopeless."

Whew!

But, in my defense, I really did believe that Gwen wanted me to look at the boat. After we got into the boathouse, Gwen showed me the "boatload" she wanted me to see, but Ginny did not need to know about that.

"Gwen took me down to the boathouse. She made all the moves, Ginny. When we got inside and I boarded the boat to look inside the engine box, she followed me and pulled me down on top of her. I don't know how far it would have gone because it wasn't long after that that the boathouse went up in flames. It was obvious to me, right away, that the fire had been ignited by an accelerant. I thought I smelled gas just before the fire started, but attributed it to being in an enclosed area where gas tanks were stored for a nearby dinghy. I grabbed Gwen and pulled her out. After she was safe, I went back in and tried to get the boat out. I thought if I could untie it and push it out into the canal, at least it could be saved."

I laughed.

"What's so funny?" Ginny asked.

"I guess the boat *was* more enticing to me than Gwen was. After all, I had gone back for the boat! I had forgotten about Gwen. The cops arrested me and I was charged with arson, and thanks to my dad and Mr. Sable, I was later acquitted."

"So, Gwen was the girl in the boathouse?"

"Yes. I had no idea that Pratt had married her much later. I had moved away shortly after my acquittal. Seeing her tonight was a shock for me, too."

"Well, I can't blame her for trying to catch you. I'll have to remember to use a boat for bait if you ever try to get away from me."

"Believe me, Baby, you do not need any such bait to get my attention. You have landed me already."

"Well, I need your attention right now."

I pulled her back down under the covers with me.

"Let's see. Where did we leave off?"

"As I remember, we were in the back seat of your truck."

"Oh, yeah, maybe we should bait and sink this hook right now."

CHAPTER SEVEN

DYLAN

When the FBI feels the need to come knocking on your door, it doesn't matter that it's Sunday morning and you and your new bride are trying to sleep in after a long exhausting honeymoon. I threw on a pair of shorts and answered the door. The agents flashed their badges and introduced themselves.

"Come on in. Pratt said I might hear from you soon."

I offered them a cup of coffee, but they declined.

"Listen, I'm going to wake up my wife, but do me a favor, she doesn't know anything about this, and when she finds out that one of those two little girls died, it is going to break her heart. So take it easy, OK? Break it to her gently."

I woke Court. She got dressed quickly while I poured us each a cup of coffee. We sat side by side on the sofa and the agents sat opposite us on two chairs.

Thankfully, they did as I had requested. They explained the circumstances cautiously, allowing Court time to absorb what they were saying. When they told her that one of the girls had died, Court did something that I had not anticipated: she went into her professional persona and distanced herself emotionally from the victims. The agents showed us a picture of the girl who had died and another picture of a girl who they believed was also on the flight, but had not been found. Because we were never close enough to the girls when they were awake or asleep, neither one of us could positively identify either one, nor could we identify the nurse who accompanied them. Ashamedly, we had ignored everything around us, just as we had been asked to do.

Why didn't we know something was wrong with that whole scenario?

Regrettably, we *were* able to positively identify the pictures of Javier, the customs agent in Atlanta, our pilot, co-pilot, our flight attendant, and Mr. and Mrs. Pratt Sr.

The only time Court showed any emotion was when they asked us to identify Anna Pratt and Tom Pratt Sr. It all made sense to Court, then. That explained why Mr. Pratt had sought the private counsel of Court's father.

Is it really possible that the Pratts are involved?

The agents assured us that Court and I were not suspects or persons of interest. They thanked us for our cooperation, and then they were gone.

After closing the door, Court called her father.

COURTNEY

"Please tell me the Pratts had nothing to do with this. Did Tom Pratt set us up?"

"To my knowledge, Tom Pratt is not a suspect. His parents have been implicated because their jet and their employees were used to bring the girls into this country. That's about all I can tell you."

"Do you believe they actively participated in this?"

"No, not for a second. However, they could be considered accessories to the crime. We need to prove beyond the shadow of a doubt that they had no knowledge that the Learjet was being used for illegal transport."

"Are you representing them?"

"No. On my advice, they retained a law firm in DC, and that firm has recommended a private investigator. Both have experience with international crimes and illegal adoptions. These are serious charges, as you well know. We need to get the Pratts out from under this immediately."

"Good. I hope whoever is responsible is caught and brought to justice with the maximum sentence levied on their heads. I can't believe this happened right under our noses."

The rest of the day was lost in a fog. Dylan, sensing that I needed space to "work it out of my system," went out to work on the barn while I pored over the plans for the Sable-Carter Women's Shelter. Dex stopped by later in the morning and spent the day helping his brother.

I no longer referred to Dex as Dylan's half-brother and never called him my "half-brother-in-law." Besides, the two of them had become more like brothers than most brothers I had represented in my legal experience.

The Sable-Carter Women's Shelter was due to break ground that week. The builders, Dex included, wanted to get it under roof before winter hit. After I stared at the plans longer than any normal person should, I realized that not even work was going to be able to pull me out of my tailspin. I needed a bigger distraction and called my father, again.

"Dad, let's take the QE II out for a sail. I need to clear my head."

My father had the QE II put back into the water after the weather broke earlier that spring, but to my knowledge, he had not taken her out.

"I don't know about that."

"Come on, Dad. I need to be on the water."

"You sound just like your mother."

His words were a beautiful compliment.

I knew Dylan would be game, but when I asked Dex if he and Ginny would like to join us, I learned that Ginny was babysitting Zoe, and Susan had left in a big hurry for Valley Forge that morning. To make matters worse, Dylan, who was usually the last to know, was already in the loop about Susan's departure. It meant that I was now at the end of the family information chain.

*What does it matter, I was never in the loop where
Ginny and Susan were concerned, anyway.*

"It's not so bad," Dylan later quipped, "sometimes
you're better off not knowing."
He had made a good point.

SUSAN

I had terminated Marco, and our I.T. contractor had
successfully locked him out of our systems and the offices.
What I had failed to do was to make sure that Marco was
locked out of Derek's home office.

Before moving to Lewes, I had given Marco a key to
Derek's home office so he could have access to documents
and work that remained there. I called my renters, and
they confirmed that Marco had indeed been there that
morning and removed a container. I asked them to please
call the police if Marco returned before the locksmith
arrived to change the locks.

I needed to go home to see for myself that nothing
had been destroyed and then try to determine what had
been removed. Before I left, Pratt stopped by to deliver my
purse and my shoes that I had left behind in his car. Much
to his surprise, and satisfaction, the door to the beach
house was locked and he had to be buzzed in.

"Come on up!" I heard Ginny say into the monitor. I
was on the second floor with Zoe. As soon as I heard Pratt
come through the door and begin his ascent, I put my
toddling Zoe down and walked out into the hallway to
intercept him. As he was rounding the second floor
landing, we made eye contact and a smile spread across his
face. Seemingly relieved that I had stepped out to welcome
him, he never let go of my gaze. He walked right up to me
and took me into his arms, not because we were on the

dance floor, and not because it had become a customary greeting. He took me into his arms because he knew that I needed his strength.

"Hi . . ." he whispered into my hair. "Are you doing OK?"

"I think so. Marco has keys to Derek's home office. According to my renters, he used them very early this morning and removed a container of some sort."

"That can't be good," Pratt acknowledged.

"I know, right? Ginny's going to babysit Zoe, and I'm going to go up to see what's been taken, if I can even make that determination. Derek's office was his private space, so it was always somewhat of a mystery to me. Plus, Marco has been in and out numerous times since I've moved here, so I'm not even sure what I'm looking for."

"Wait until tomorrow and I'll go with you."

"No. I need to do this today. I called a locksmith, so the lock should be changed within an hour or two. I want to pick up my new key, make sure the renters are squared away, and take inventory of what's there, or not."

"Susan, I don't like your going up there alone, especially knowing that Marco is in the area, too. I don't know what he is capable of."

"I'm not sure, either, but I'm fairly certain he would never hurt me. Listen, could you do me a huge favor? If and when you visit Derek next, please tell him that it is imperative that I speak with him. Tell him it would be a 'business only' meeting. He needs to know about Marco."

"Are you sure you're up for seeing him?"

"No. I'm not, but I have no choice."

"When will you be back?"

"I'm hoping this will not take long. I'm packing for two days, but if all goes well, I'll be back tonight and everything else can be handled online.

Pratt held me close, rubbing my back for reassurance. He let out a heavy sigh before releasing me.

"Call me if you need anything. Don't be a hero. Zoe needs her mommy, and I need to know that you're OK."

Pratt's sincere dark brown eyes held mine. For a brief moment, we were the only two people in the world.

What? He actually . . . Dare I think it?

I arrived in Valley Forge two and a half hours later. First, I greeted the family that was renting my house and reassured them that everything was OK. It felt strange to knock on my own front door. They, in turn, handed me my new key to Derek's old office. They also said they were relieved to know that Marco was now locked out of it. They let me know that he had always made them feel uncomfortable when he had stopped by in the past.

Why was I always the last one to figure these things out?

I went back to Derek's office. I used my new key to unlock the door to the outside entrance and slowly opened it, as if I might startle someone on the other side.

Are the ghosts of our past here, hovering in wait for me?

I stepped quietly into the dark space and was immediately flooded with memories, like the time he had made love to me on the sofa on the far side of the room. Or the time Derek and I celebrated with champagne the night he came home and announced that he had signed a big contract with a major retailer. We made love on his desktop that night, and again in our bed. His office still smelled like him. I closed my eyes and breathed in a reflection that was happy and secure at one time. As I inhaled deeper, the air turned sour. It hurt to remember our final days.

I remembered the day he had opened his desk drawer, and I first saw the gun. He had promised me that he only wanted it for self-defense and that it would never leave the house. I shuddered when I thought about the phone call I had received from Ginny and how I had found his cell phone and her purse, and yet his gun went missing. I recalled Dylan's voice on the phone as he calmly tried to convey that Dex had been shot and that Derek was in police custody. I remembered wanting to shoot myself. Little did I know, at the time, that little zygote Zoe had already been conceived and was taking rapid shape in my womb.

How I loved my little girl. How I had loved my husband. And now, it was over, and I was standing in the middle of a room that had held so much promise and birthed so much pain.

I carefully sifted through the drawers of Derek's desk and file cabinets. Then it hit me, Derek's laptop was gone. It had been removed just recently because there was dust everywhere, except for where the laptop had once resided, its outline still visible. I approached his safe on the opposite wall. Pulling down on the handle, it opened without the need of a correct combination. Inside was an empty compartment that had been cleaned out.

Marco must have known the combination. Derek must have given it to him.

Panic overcame me as I thought about the safe in our bedroom containing our personal belongings. I locked up Derek's office and went back into the main house.

"I am terribly sorry to bother you again, but I need to collect a few things from the safe in the master suite."

If anything is missing, I am going to die a thousand deaths, and I am not talking about the jewelry.

Thankfully, my renters had no reservations about allowing me to enter what was now their bedroom. It was uncomfortable thinking about them sleeping in my bed, using my shower, and brushing their teeth in my sink. It no longer felt like "my" room, even though my furniture was still there. All of the pictures on my dresser were of people

I didn't know, like the people in a picture frame one buys in a department store.

Beautiful people, but I don't know any of them.

The room smelled different, too. They used different laundry detergent, soaps, shampoos, and candles than I did. I liked Vanilla. They liked Cedar, or was it Sandalwood?

I carefully opened the safe. I used to hate when combination locks did not open on the first try. It created all kinds of self-doubts. To this day, I still have nightmares about not being able to find my high school locker or being able to dial up the correct combination. High school had marred me for life in so many ways.

I successfully opened the safe on my first attempt. When I looked inside, a huge weight was lifted from my shoulders. The pictures were still there. Oh, and so was the jewelry. I left the jewels and gathered up the photos to take with me until they could be properly destroyed. They were not from your ordinary family photograph album.

My cell phone rang.

"Hi, Pratt! I'm here, safe and sound."

I was sure I sounded relieved to hear from him, but he had no idea just how relieved I was.

"Good. I'm on my way to see Derek. I'll call you later and let you know how it goes."

"Thanks, Pratt. I owe you."

"Big time! Susan, be careful. Watch your back and come home quickly."

Home . . .

CHAPTER EIGHT

DEREK

When the guard informed me that my visitor was Tom Pratt, I knew I was in for a good time. I strongly suspected that Pratt saw Gwen with Corelli at the fundraiser the night before. It probably pushed him over the edge, so he came to see me to demand that I call off Corelli. Fat chance. I knew what went on beyond the walls of this hellhole. He was supposed to keep an eye on Susan, not try to sleep with her.

"Pratt, what a pleasure! And to what do I owe the honor of your unexpected visit? What did my errant wife do now? Get you all worked up and then turn you down? Yeah, that's right. I heard you've been chasing her tail."

"Your EX-wife, Derek. And believe me, nothing pleases me more than to spend my day visiting with you on the other side of this glass wall while your little toady is screwing up and screwing you, too. And royally, I might add. You should know that he got himself fired last night."

"How's that even possible? He works for me, asshole."

"He may *work* for you, but he was *employed* by your EX-wife. Susan terminated him last night. He's been shut down and locked out."

"I'll rehire him."

"From here? Right. I don't think you'll want to do that, anyway. He's been siphoning money from your company to the tune of a cool half million a year.

"Really. And you know this because?"

"I can smell a thief, and Corelli reeks. He's got you coming and going, Derek. You're paying him to do your dirty work, and he's cleaning out your house while he's at it."

"Yeah, and he's taking care of your insatiable ex-wife, too! At least someone is getting their job done."

I had reason to believe that Pratt didn't see that coming.

"Well then, aren't we the pair? So, Derek, if you know so much, do you want to tell me how Marco and Gwen know each other?"

"Come on, Pratt, they've been at it for years."

Pratt did not respond. He just sat there.

"What's the matter, Pratt? Didn't sniff that one out?"

I got a good laugh out of that! I continued my verbal assault. I was on a roll.

"In fact, I bet they're banging away, right now, while we're here having this nice little chat. Ironic, isn't it? Now look who's getting fucked!"

I could see red and purple starting to craw up Pratt's neck like a stowaway tick or a spider that fell out of a tree onto the back of his collar.

"Just answer the question, Derek. How do they know each other?"

"It's a small world, Pratt, and she'll have every man sucked dry before the apocalypse at the rate she goes through men."

I could have imagined it, but smoke was spewing from Pratt's nostrils like a relief valve about to blow wide open. If there had not been a glass wall between us, I was certain that he would have tried to strangle or beat the shit out of me. He sure looked like he was going to lunge for the glass. Best of all, it certainly would have been out of character for the usually calm Tom Pratt.

"I'm not here to defend Gwen or get into her escapades or motives," Pratt said, backing off.

Well, that's disappointing.

"Well, maybe you should. She and Corelli have been sharing benefits for as long as I've known him. You know they joined the Mile High Club on that little Learjet of yours, right?"

I had made another attempt at rattling him at the expense of his ex-wife's indiscretions.

"The Learjet? How is that even possible?"

OK, now that was entertaining. Once again, I had a great laugh at the expense of his misery. I knew that imagining Marco with his ex-wife at 30,000 feet in his parents' Learjet would drive him crazy as hell. Even I knew that Pratt would never get over Gwen. She was not a woman you could casually walk away from. That much, even I understood.

COURTNEY

Boarding the QE II was like stepping onto holy ground. She represented all that our mother had loved: the water, the wind, and her family. Today, it would be just Dad and me. In the end, Dylan and Dex decided that it would be best if they stayed behind and continued the progress they were making on the old battered barn.

Dad and I went about quietly stowing away our gear as we prepared to leave port. There was a steady breeze out of the southwest and the sky was full of mare's tails. I just needed time on the water to clear my head. The pictures of the two little girls were haunting me. I somehow felt responsible, even though my therapist would have disagreed and try to convince me otherwise.

Finally underway and out beyond the breakwater, we remarked how well the QE II had wintered under her cover. Dad complimented the great work the upholsterer had done on the cushions and how they looked like new. I made no comment. Secretly, I hated that upholsterer.

After a few adjustments, the power winches raised the sails, which filled out nicely. Dad killed the engine and the QE II flew with the wind and rolled against the waves. I took a deep breath and brought the salt air into my expanding lungs that had been tightly restricted under the pressures of the latest developments. Sea spray made its way into the cockpit as the QE II listed about twenty degrees on her first long tack. We were quiet for the first league when I finally had the courage to break our silence.

"Dad, how on earth did they, whoever "they" are, manage to get two little girls onto a private jet and fly them into the U.S. without raising one red flag?"

"Depends on how many people were involved and what positions they had covered," my dad answered with a steady hand on the helm, making small adjustments with the shifting wind. "What's mind boggling is that everyone who was involved on your flight has been cleared, except for the Pratts. The Learjet has been grounded and impounded, and the Pratts have been told not to leave the country."

My dad took a new tack in our conversation.

"Courtney, you and Dylan need to think about the unified message you will need to give to the press when the story breaks," my dad wisely advised.

"Great. I can see the headlines now: 'Founders of Women's Shelter Turn Blind Eye to Illegal Adoption.'" I mockingly declared, sweeping my arm across as if I were following the flow of a headline in print.

"Yes, this is not going to look good for you two, or the Pratts. You may lose some of the pledges you all worked so hard to earn," my father grimly prophesied.

It was true. The shelter would likely take a hit.

I looked back at the coastline. The town of Lewes looked so peaceful and quiet, unlike the scandal that had just rocked our world. Colorful umbrellas dotted the public beach like a Seurat painting. Children were probably running in and out of the water, enjoying a planned beach day. It was something one little passenger aboard our flight home from Bariloche would never know. I wondered who her birth mother was and if she even knew what had happened to her baby girl. Tears formed in my eyes, already damp because of the piercing wind. Even though I was wearing dark sunglasses, my dad could tell that I was struggling.

"Let's craft your sound bites," he suggested, knowing that I needed to work on something, anything.

Who could have done this and without remorse? How did they get those children, and perhaps others, on the Pratts' Learjet without someone knowing about it, or questioning it? Where is that poor little girl?

PRATT

Shortly after I had verified that Susan had made it safely to her home in Valley Forge, I received a call from Marien Merck. Why she thought it was so urgent that we meet was beyond me.

Perhaps, it's because I put her daughter into a cab and sent her home last night.

If Marien was so worried about her daughter, then she should have stayed and taken Gwen home herself. Marien should have been grateful that I at least saw to it that Gwen had made it home safely, unlike Gwen's vulgar date. And, by the way, I did call Gwen before I left for the prison to make sure that she had arrived home safely. I strongly doubted that Marco gave Gwen's wellbeing a second thought.

"Tom, how nice of you to stuff me into a cab last night and leave me in the care of someone you know nothing about," Gwen snarled over the phone.

"Me? The person who abandoned you was that insolent boyfriend of yours."

"He's not my boyfriend."

"That's not what I'm hearing. Apparently, you two have been seeing each other for years."

"I see a lot of people, Tom."

It was true. Gwen was the Executive Vice President of an international human resource corporation that had offices in six of the seven continents and managed an impressive client list.

"True. But to my knowledge, you haven't been sleeping with any of them."

I was searching. Gwen did not immediately reply.

"Who I choose to sleep with is no longer any of your business, Tom."

"It is when the guy you're sleeping with is dangerous."

"I assure you, Marco is not dangerous," she scoffed.

I had every reason to believe differently, including two agents who had discreetly shared with me that they suspected Marco was involved with an illegal adoption ring.

"I assure you, Gwen, that man is not safe for you to be around. The guy apparently has no morals, or scruples."

"Why do you care?"

"Gwen, I will always care."

"Then show me."

"Show you?"

"Yes. Stop seeing that pathetic blond with the illegitimate carpet rat."

"Now you're just being rude. Susan is a good person and her daughter . . ."

"Oh, she has a name? Susan. . . . Isn't that charming. She must be an old soul, just like you."

"Gwen, be nice."

Gwen could be such a bratty child, sometimes.

"Tell me this, Tom, since when do you entertain good friends with a private picnic by the Canal? We used to take private picnics. Remember?"

"Oh, so you're having me followed?"

"The Canal is a public waterway, and you should know that very little is private in this small town."

"Then, you also know that she's only a very good friend."

"Oh, so now she's a *very* good friend. If we keep this up, you'll finally admit that you're sleeping with her, too."

"GWEN!"

She had crossed a line. A lie is a lie and hurtful when casually cast out. She was digging, and rumors were going to be hatched and given wings. It was a game she understood and played like a pro.

"Tom, if you still care for me, and you really want me to stop seeing Marco, then you need to stop spending time with *Suuu-san*, and start spending time with me. Let's stop playing hide and seek and admit that we should get back together."

"I don't play silly games, Gwen."

"Then let's play for keeps."

Simple just went out the window.

* * *

When Gwen and I were first married, everything was easy. She had her high-powered job, and I was a local cop. We were young and childless, no serious responsibilities: not even a dog. We worked hard and played harder. Gwen pretty much made her own schedule. I, on the other hand, worked rotating shifts. It was an adjustment, at first. We tried to remedy our scheduling challenges with short jaunts and romantic getaways when I had days off. When I had vacation time, we would globetrot to places neither of us had visited before. With Gwen's salary and bonuses, my pay, and my parents' trusts, we were never short on cash. Though it may sound like it, we were not total spendthrifts, either. Following in both our parents' footsteps, we also made sure that we gave back to our communities and supported several large charities. Gwen's favorite was Save The Children, and mine was Arrest Pediatric Cancer.

* * *

Now, with Gwen's recent affiliation, plus her latest suggestion, there was nothing simple remaining. Gwen's involvement with Marco just took everything and twisted it into knots. She needed to get away from him, and I could not tell her why for fear of blowing open the investigation into Marco's criminal activity and putting the lives of more innocent children at risk.

I was about to enter into a tangled mess.

However, because getting back together sounded like something she wanted to do, perhaps one last attempt might work. Not known for keeping her word, I knew that I would be the one taking all the risks. Though I had some doubts and reservations that it could work, I agreed to stay away from Susan, which I was already commanded to do because of the ongoing investigation, and Gwen agreed to stay away from Marco. At the very least, it had the potential to separate Gwen from the walking time bomb to which she had attached her wagon. As much as I enjoyed Susan's company and would miss Zoe's smiles and giggles, it was the best I could do for everyone involved. I recognized that Gwen's suggestion was blackmail in its finest cloaked form; however, it would keep her away from Marco, and innocent children could potentially be saved from being stolen from their unknowing families. The stakes were high, and the price was steep. At the time, I didn't realize the high price I was about to pay.

Fortunately, my meeting with Marien was short and sweet. We sat at the back of the bar at Jerry's Seafood on Second Street. It was between their lunch and dinner crowd, so the restaurant was fairly quiet.

"Tom, thank you for meeting me on such short notice."

"It's always a pleasure, Marien," I politely exaggerated.

"I guess you're wondering why I asked you to meet me here."

"Well, it's not my birthday. So yes, I was caught a little off guard."

"I understand Mayor Felts has put a bug in your ear about running for his office."

"I prefer not to use the term 'bug' on the campaign trail," I joked.

Marien half-smiled at my little jest.

"So, you're considering a run?" Marien asked with her eyebrows raised.

"Yes, I'm giving it strong consideration."

"I'm here to tell you that you're making a big mistake."

"Really? Why would you think that?"

"Because, I will be your worst nightmare."

COURTNEY

Before returning to the dock, there was one more thing I needed to discuss with my father.

"Why Marien Merck? Of all people to take an interest in, why her?"

"Interest? In what way?" my father requested further clarification, which I believed was unnecessary.

Please don't make me go into detail. This is comparable to having the "sex talk," except I'm about to ask you about yours.

"Interested in romantic ways."

Yuck, just the thought makes me want to puke.

"Who says I'm interested? Where is this coming from?" my dad sneered.

"Because, at my wedding and more recently the fundraiser, Marien was all about you, and you tolerated her," I accused.

My dad stared at me. Actually, it was more of a warning glare. I had obviously offended him in some way and had made a great miscalculation on how he would receive my indictment of his behavior, or lack thereof.

"Young lady, I don't appreciate what you're insinuating. For your information, Marien is seriously contemplating throwing her hat into the ring for the mayoral election next spring. She has asked me for advice and support."

"Really?"

"Yes. So get off your high horse about Marien Merck."

I thought about my dad's response. It was fair. I had misjudged the circumstances; however, I had not misjudged Marien Merck's ulterior motives. I had discerning eyes, and I recognized the glint in hers when she spoke with my father. Not to mention, there was the one damning testimony of my older sister.

"Dad, you need to know that Marien Merck asked Bridget if you were ready to start dating. Now, what does that tell you?"

My father did not answer me right away. Instead he changed course, literally.

"PREPARE TO COME ABOUT!" he shouted out as if he had a whole crew on board.

"What?"

"We're returning home. HARD-A-LEE!"

Dad swung the QE II hard across the wind, preparing for her new course. The QE II's jib thrashed wildly, making a loud racket until it filled out on the opposite side. Its controlled chaos was the personification of my dad's spirit. I had hurt him with my suggestive remarks. He was running from my questions and comments.

My father put the wind directly at the QE II's stern and let her sails fill out on opposite sides of the boat, setting her on a dead run with the wind directly behind us. He would have to mind the helm, maintaining the "wing on wing" position of the sails so that an accidental jibe would not cause the main boom to come flying back across amidships, potentially taking out one or both of us. The stiff wind was steady at 12 knots, and the QE II was surfing and then sliding off the back of the faster moving rollers. The QE II heaved heavily and creaked loudly as it maneuvered fore and aft the energy of each wave. Likewise, my Dad was working off some of his frustration with his youngest daughter. He and the QE II were so in tune that it left me feeling like an intruder. I had touched a raw nerve.

SUSAN

I was looking forward to returning to Lewes. It was beginning to feel more like home each day, especially because Zoe was there waiting for me. I was happy to begin my drive back to Slower Lower Delaware. I was also anxious to hear from Pratt. He had called earlier in the day to make sure that I had arrived in Valley Forge safely and to let me know that he had planned on visiting with Derek. That was the last I had heard from him.

Before leaving Pennsylvania to head south, I called Pratt to tell him that I was returning sooner, rather than later. He seemed pleased to hear that my trip went well and that I had not run into Marco. At the time of my call, Pratt was in the middle of something important and said that we would talk later. I called Ginny to let her know that I was on my way.

With the large envelope containing my photos on the passenger seat and my new keys tucked away in my purse, I made one stop to fill up the Explorer before heading for Route 1 South. It was an interesting drive. Different. First, I was alone. Second, my thoughts kept drifting toward Pratt.

I was allowing myself to fall for him. He was a true gentleman, and I felt safe when I was with him. He made me feel like I mattered. Even his earlier phone call led me to believe that everything was going to work out. The fact that he enjoyed being around Zoe was an extra special added plus. He seemed to genuinely care about both of us.

I turned on the radio and allowed my thoughts to wonder what could be.

When I had finally reached the Lewes cut-off, I made the decision to take a short detour before reaching the drawbridge. I would turn right onto Franklin Avenue and drive by Pratt's house.

A white Mercedes C-Class convertible was parked in front of Pratt's Lotus. With its tan soft top down, the Mercedes looked like a sweet ride.

It probably belongs to one or both of his parents.

I knocked on the front door. It was very quiet inside. I waited a few seconds and knocked again. I could hear footsteps approaching the door. They certainly didn't sound like Pratt's, unless he took to wearing heels.

"Well, well, who do we have here?" Gwen asked very sarcastically.

She was definitely the last person I had expected to see at Pratt's. I clutched.

"I'm sorry, is Pratt, . . . uh, Tom home?" I asked sheepishly, intimidated by the fact that she was inside his house and I was standing outside on the small stoop.

"Does it look like he's here?"

"Well, I saw his car out front, and . . . "

"Right, 'out front' just like mine. See that car over there, Sweetie? That one belongs to me, and it's going to be here for a while. In the meantime, Tom has walked uptown for a meeting. Official business. So, is there something I can help you with before I get back to my unpacking?"

Unpacking? Did she just fucking say that she was unpacking? I've been played for a fool and used as his pawn! I was led to believe that Pratt might actually care about me. What kind of man does that? I was being deliberately used for the purpose of bringing back his ex. He said it himself that whenever he takes an interest in another woman, she shows up. He was even willing to bet that she would. And this time, he played the game so well that she's now in the process of moving back in, all at my expense.

I never did hear what had transpired between Pratt and Derek. As soon as fucking Gwen went back inside to finish her fucking unpacking, I turned on my heels, returned to my car, and drove off, kicking up gravel and spraying it all over her goddamn car.

YOU TWO SORRY ASSES DESERVE EACH OTHER.

I cried from Pratt's house to the Carter beach house. I needed Zoe. I needed to hold my baby. I needed to be near someone as pure and as innocent as she. I needed to be where it was safe, free of all the entanglements of adult game playing and cruel relationships.

Pratt and his goddamn "keep it simple" shit. I could still hear him, "Keep it simple, Susan. Are you looking for complicated?" Asshole.

I ran up the stairs. Ginny and Zoe were playing on the floor. Dex had just gotten back from Dylan's and was knocking back a beer. Ginny rushed over and threw her arms around me. She knew immediately that something was wrong. She probably heard it in my footsteps. We were that in tune to one another.

God, I am so blessed to have her as my best friend.

"Susan, you don't look so good. I thought you said everything went really well?"

"Everything did go well up north. It was when I got back here that everything went to shit."

I threw my hands over my mouth. Zoe was old enough then to make attempts at mimicking what she had heard.

Little Zoe ran over to me, and I scooped her up into my arms.

"Mommy missed you SO much!" I gave her a big hug and a kiss.

"What happened?" Dex wanted to know.

"I was an idiot. That's what happened. I allowed myself to believe that Pratt might actually care about me, when all along he was using me to get his ex-wife back home."

"What makes you think that?" Ginny asked, not wanting to believe it was true.

"Because, I stopped by his house on my way home, and SHE was there, unpacking."

I hugged Zoe a little tighter. Bless her heart, she kissed my face and laid her head on my shoulder.

"I can't believe it!" Dex raked a hand back through his hair in frustration. "That makes no sense. I know for a fact that he's into you. I can't believe he's still running after that bi ... " Dex caught himself, too. "She is nothing but trouble, and Pratt should be smart enough to know better.

"I don't get it, either," Ginny jumped in. "Just the other night, he put Gwen into a cab and chose to drive you home. Well, he almost got you home, until you bolted, and his car was stolen."

"Yeah, there is that. But I talked to him earlier today, and everything seemed fine. I just don't get it. I just can't take getting hurt again. Not now. Not ever."

PRATT

When I returned home, Gwen was there, waiting for me.

I have got to change these locks. I'll call the locksmith first thing in the morning.

"What are you doing here, Gwen? You really need to stop letting yourself in."

"You know you love it, Tom. How was your little meeting with my mother?"

"Short and sweet. Let me ask you again. Why are you here?"

"Oh, I misplaced something and thought I may have left it here."

"What are you missing?"

"You . . ." Gwen stepped toward me and looked up into my eyes.

You have to understand, Gwen has these inescapable turquoise eyes. I get lost in them every time.

"Don't do this, Gwen." I stepped back and away from her.

"Don't you miss me?" she pouted.

"I missed you every minute of every day for years, Gwen. It took me a long time to get over your leaving me."

"I missed you, too, Tom."

"That's a load of crap. How could you possibly miss me from someone else's bed?"

"I did miss you. That's why it happened. I traveled so much; we never saw each other. I was on the road, and I was lonely."

"Didn't you think I was lonely, too? The worst part is that you never stopped. I asked you to stop seeing that guy, and you chose not to. You made your choice."

"He was my boss! It wasn't like I could just stop without consequences."

"And that's why there are laws about superiors dating their subordinates, and he was an idiot for letting it happen."

"I could be your subordinate," Gwen teased with a salacious grin, stepping up to me.

I held her off.

"GWEN, stop!"

"You're just mad and jealous."

"You're damn straight I'm mad, and jealous. If you really missed me, you would have resigned that job."

"He's gone. Your parents saw to that. I never loved him, anyway. It was all a big mistake."

"Yes, a very hurtful mistake. Did you ever think about what you were doing to me? I loved you with every part of my being. I have never loved anyone or anything more than you."

"Do you still love me, Tom?"

"Gwen, I will always love you."

I knew it to be true. Years ago, she had stolen my heart and locked it away.

"We could try again, couldn't we?" she pleaded.

If I had pressed myself hard for answers, I knew deep down inside that she would eventually leave me, again. It would only be a matter of time. I wanted my heart returned to me.

Can patterns be broken as easily as hearts?

SUSAN

He broke my heart. I had begun to daydream about what a life with Pratt would mean for Zoe and me. He was a good man, and I thought he would be a good role model for my sweet little girl. Then, he broke my heart.

"Don't worry, Susan," Ginny tried to console me that night as we sat out on the top deck, commiserating over a bottle of wine. "There are a gazillion Pratts in the world."

"There are not a gazillion Pratts who would be able to accept who I am and care about Zoe as if she was their own," I corrected her.

"Susan, since when did you become such a pessimist? Are you going to let one little bump in the road get you down?"

"This is not just a little bump in the road. This is a big sinkhole. I didn't realize how deep I had fallen until he was gone."

"Listen, he was your first love interest since Derek. The first one is always going to be tough. Think of him as your rebound crush. Trust me, there will be plenty more."

"Crush." ... Yep, that succinctly describes how I feel: crushed.

"Right. And where and how am I going to meet these 'plenty more' guys? Who's to say I even want to meet a guy, or that I need a guy? Pratt just happened to come along when I wasn't looking. I think that is one of the reasons it's so hard to let go. He just sneaked up on me and into my life, and now I can't deny his significance. He *was* significant. And now he's gone. In a flash, he's just gone."

"I know about that 'in a flash' thing. It's a risk we all have to take."

"I'm sorry, Ginny. I didn't mean to trivialize what you've been through."

I was afraid I had inserted myself into territory that belonged solely to her.

"Not at all. We all experience losses that occur 'in a flash,' and none of them can be minimalized by another. For example, 'in a flash,' your life and dreams with Derek ended. Whether it was the moment he shot Dex or the moment you found out. 'In a flash,' that chapter in your life ended. 'In a flash,' I lost my baby on the stairway of the original Carter beach house, and in another 'flash' I lost my adoring husband on the side of Interstate 95."

Tears filled Ginny's eyes as she made her poignant point. She swallowed the lump in her throat before she continued.

" 'In a flash,' our lives can change and it usually transpires with circumstances that are totally out of our control. So, we have to decide if we are going to accept what happened and move forward with it; or stand still, allowing rigor mortis to set in, causing us to live imprisoned by it, like being encased in concrete."

Ginny always had a way of clarifying things for me. Whether it was over a late night hot chocolate, a glass of wine in the hot tub, a good cry in Courtney's powder room, or a bottle of wine on a starry night. Together, Ginny and I could solve the problems of the world.

DEX

The month of June was departing on a hot, steamy note. The sun rose up each morning and began its daily assault where the humidity left off the night before. Once the morning sun had cleared the horizon, and if the Bay was calm, you could sit and watch the steam rise from the water as the air heated rapidly. It was a sure sign that the day was going to be a miserable one to work outside. If there had been a thunderstorm the night before, of which there were many, then the Bay would have been churned up and the sun would rise without notice, hiding behind the thick clouds that would try to stall over the area with hopes of delaying their departure. It seemed everyone and everything wanted to extend their stays in Lewes. Unfortunately, the storms and their lingering cloud cover provided little relief from the oppressive heat.

With July on the horizon, there came an unexpected hurricane that blew into our lives, ripping our canvases and banners to shreds. I heard about it the day Courtney had gone sailing with her dad while Dylan and I stayed behind to work on his barn. During a much-needed break, Dylan and I talked over cold beers. Dylan nervously told me about the FBI agents that had visited Courtney and him that Sunday morning. He tried to describe the flight back from Bariloche and how shaken he and Courtney were to later learn that the two children who were flying with them had actually been illegally smuggled onto their flight. Much to their horror, one of the girls had died shortly after she had reached her new family in the States. Dylan explained that the Pratts were being investigated for their possible involvement.

Later that day, I shared the news with Ginny and Susan. Susan realized, then, that breaking off any possible relationship with Pratt might have been for the best. Perhaps, in some twisted way, Gwen had done her a favor.

"You don't think Zoe is in any danger, do you?" she asked, making no effort to conceal her paranoia.

"I don't believe so. It sounds as though all of the children involved were from outside the U.S. with little to no paper trail left behind."

"Who would do such a thing?" Ginny pondered out loud.

Then Susan slipped and dropped a bomb about an unofficial announcement.

"How does Pratt expect to run for mayor if his family is accused and potentially convicted of any involvement with an illegal child adoption ring?"

"PRATT'S RUNNING FOR MAYOR?" Ginny and I blurted out together.

"You did not hear that from me." Susan tried to cover her tracks.

CHAPTER NINE

GWEN

My name is Gwen Marysa Merck Pratt. You know *of* me. However, you have not heard *from* me. You may not like me right now, and that is understandable because you have already heard several sides of my story, none of which were mine. You should hear from me before you pass judgment. Do you really believe that I am all that different from you?

I was a little crazy in my youth. I got away with it because my parents were absent most of the time. So, I largely blame them. More on that will come later.

Anyway, when I met Tom Pratt, I knew that he was someone who could potentially find me amidst the wreckage left behind by my parents' misguidance. I knew he would be able to repair what was left of me. I also believed that he would derive great satisfaction and pleasure in his mission to do so.

Tom Pratt was well grounded. He was not about bars and cheap drinks. He was all about dinner and a show, a day of wine tasting, a weekend ski trip to Vail with separate rooms, concerts and limousines, and Ravens games with a private skybox for me and a few of his buddies from the station and their wives. With Tom, everything was first class and aboveboard.

Did my "separate rooms" clarification surprise you? It did not surprise me. I knew immediately that Tom was an honorable man. He was like a breath of fresh air and the Prince Charming little girls read about in fairy tales. He was never in a hurry, and everything with Tom was black or white, right or wrong.

It took me two years to get Tom to the altar. My father and stepmother adored him, so they were very excited and happy for me. My mother was skeptical and said that the marriage would never last because I lacked perseverance and gratitude. Served on a silver platter, she said I would never recognize a good thing when I had it.

I was my parents' "oops" baby. No one had to tell me, the math made it pretty clear. They had only been married for five months when I was born. My father was having an extramarital affair with my mother when I happened, and my father wanted to do the right thing. I have two older half-brothers. There are twelve years between my older half-brother and me. My oldest half-brother is fourteen years my senior. In reality, they are a generation ahead of me, and I really don't know them all that well. "Family" was just not our thing.

When I was in elementary school, my mother became a state senator. Her campaigns and civic duties never left much time for me, or my dad. My parents divorced when I was twelve. My half-brothers were married and long gone by then. My mother received full custody of me, and my father was left to beg for weekends and holidays whenever he could. I cried for days. I loved my dad and knew that my time with him would become scarce. My father, however, later corroborated the story my mother had given me for their breakup: my father was having another affair.

When my father was gallivanting (as my mother described it), I had no clue. His love and time spent with me had never wavered or waned. My mother was rarely home, and my dad was lonely. Being a preteen, I never noticed that anything was different in our household. Like every young girl, my world was all about me. When I would return home after a weekend sleepover with friends, I had no clue, nor did I care, about what had happened during my absence from the house. In fact, I don't believe that I had ever met "that other woman," before my parents separated. My mother had several names and very unkind words for my Dad's "disgusting little tramp."

The divorce proceedings became very ugly, and my mother sued for full custody, which she obtained. I never understood why she refused my father's pleas for shared custody. It made no sense to me. It was obvious that she avoided the duties of motherhood whenever she could. As the arguments continued, it became clear: she wanted my father to be denied anything or anyone that he desired or needed, and I was the something or someone he wanted most. The divorce attorneys played dirty, and the atmosphere surrounding my parents became vile. While the attorneys' coffers expanded exponentially and I became more distressed, my parents nearly came to blows. My mother's language expanded, as well.

My father married "that shameless whore" when I was fourteen. It turned out that she was actually a very nice person. During the rare times that I did get to spend with them before I turned eighteen, I could tell that she adored my father. They never fought like my parents used to. They laughed and smiled, a lot. It was comforting to see my father so happy. Regardless, I learned very quickly that I should never speak about "that fucking bitch" around my mother.

Despite our differences, which actually there were not all that many, my mother managed to raise me. Later in life, I began to understand that she and I were actually very much alike. That was perhaps the biggest reason we fought as much as we did, and the also the biggest reason we were so close. The reality was that I loved my mother very much. I would have done anything for her.

I try not to think about it.

As a young teen, I needed affirmation as I struggled to define myself in the middle of all the carnage that surrounded me. I had my first sexual encounter when I was seventeen. He was a young man from Wilmington who spent his summers in Lewes. He was sixteen, a year younger than I was, and owned a Mustang convertible. As an impressionable teenager, I put an over-valued importance on the ownership of, or access to, hot cars. *(Perhaps, I still do as an adult.)* At the time, we were both virgins and curious. Once we had our first taste, we were like rabbits. My mother never noticed. She was too preoccupied. His parents were very kind to me, and I was sure they never realized that we were playmates whose favorite toys were each other. We were never where we said we would be. If you named a secluded place between Lewes and Rehoboth, we had been there. Looking back, I'm surprised that we were never found out. That winter, we lost touch, and he never returned to Lewes. I can't tell you if he is dead or alive.

Sad, I try not to think about it.

Just prior to my departure for college, my mother lost her state senate seat in a failed re-election bid. "Returning home," she ran a successful campaign to become a city councilwoman in the town of Lewes, Delaware. That fall, I left for school. How ironic: she returns, and I leave.

When I was nineteen and home on winter break, I was diagnosed with ovarian cancer.

"It is rare for a woman of your young age to develop this type of cancer, but it happens. You are the third woman under twenty years of age that I have treated with ovarian cancer in my twelve years of practice," my doctor proudly boasted.

"Young woman, my ass!" I wanted to scream. *"I'm still a teenager, God dammit! And now you're telling me that I will never have children? Eat shit and die, you moron!"*

My mother sat by staring at her watch. She had an important meeting to attend to that afternoon. We never talked about it. She never asked how I was handling the diagnosis, the prescribed eradication, or its future implications, at least not that I can remember.

A hysterectomy was ordered, and I fell into a deep depression after it was over. Therapy sessions and drugs were prescribed. I tried them all. I missed my spring semester and stayed with my father and stepmother during my recovery and recuperation so I would not be left at home alone.

It was easy to talk with my stepmother. She cared, but she was careful never to pass judgment as I opened up more and more to her. She was also resolute in pointing out that it was easier for her to be so accepting *because* she was not my biological mother. For reasons I never understood, she always defended my mother and my mother's actions. In many ways, she was more like a grandmother to me than a stepmother.

In the fall, when I did return to school, my behavior became more erratic. I had stopped seeing my therapist, and because of their side effects, I stopped taking the drugs, too. Outside of sexually transmitted diseases, I figured because I couldn't get pregnant, I could hook up without fear and I felt that I had a right to do so, if I wanted. Even today, I would like to believe that my promiscuous behavior had been justifiable. The truth: it was not that black and white. I was not looking for sex, or redemption. I was looking for something deeper. I needed to feel loved. I needed to be touched, real physical contact, if only for an hour or two. If I went home alone after a night at the bars or a big party, I considered myself a failure, and rarely did I accept failing at anything. I hated failure, so rarely did it occur.

Ironically, the harder I tried to be loved, the more elusive love became. At the time, it made no sense to me. It seemed that I could land any man I desired; yet by sun up, they were on their way out the door.

I try not to think back on that time in my life. I was so horribly alone.

After graduation, I became fed up with watching my girlfriends marry and begin families while maintaining their dream jobs. I decided to prove to the world that I didn't need to take the same highway that everyone else was on. I worked tirelessly on my career path and rose quickly through the ranks, surpassing everyone on the corporate ladder to success. With excess cash in my pockets, I took up expensive hobbies like scuba diving, skydiving, snow skiing, water skiing, sailboarding, sail racing, and earned my pilot's license. That was how I met Tom Pratt. In an ironic twist of fate, our paths collided in Lewes.

It was quite accidental, literally. I was windsurfing on the Delaware Bay, just off the Lewes beach where I used to lifeguard many summers before. The wind and the Bay were still kicked up after a heavy nor'easter that had taken two days to push through. There had to have been at least eight of us crazies out there windsurfing. One of the eight was Tom Pratt. I was captivated by his strength and command of the wind and sail as his strong back, muscular arms and legs sent him flying through the peaks and troughs of the heavy seas. Watching him catch air was like watching a rocket blast off. Everything about Tom Pratt was intense.

I was holding my own until Tom got close, and I decided to show off. I grabbed some air and went flying off the peak of a wave. It was awesome, until I landed. I hit something that was partially submerged just below the water's surface. The impact jarred my body, and I hit my head when I went sailing off my board. Fortunately, I was successful in grabbing Tom's attention. He watched it all unfold before his eyes. He got to me immediately and saved me from drowning.

Tom released his sail, dove in, and raised me out of the water, lifting me onto his board. In very rough water, he paddled both of us back to shore, riding a wave whenever he could and fighting to catch another until we reached the sand. A witness on the beach called for an ambulance. Other witnesses said that it was an incredible rescue because Tom had managed to keep me on the board and my head out of the water while fighting the rough seas.

Tom later said that I had hit a submerged piling and the impact left me unconscious and face down in the water. He also informed my father that my board and both sails were rescued by a couple of teenage boys who wanted to be "a part of the action."

Tom followed the ambulance, with me in it, to the hospital. He knew everyone on the ambulance crew, and I later learned that he was an off-duty Lewes police officer. I was very disoriented, so he stayed with me at Beebe Hospital until my father and stepmother arrived.

The very next day, Tom was back at Beebe, waiting around until I was discharged. He asked my father for a phone number so he "could check up on me and make sure that I was going to be OK." He also told my father that my board and sail were dropped off at his house and he would like to return them. Apparently, everyone in Sussex County knew and liked Tom Pratt.

My father, with my permission, gave Tom my number, and as they say, "The rest is history."

Tom, as I quickly discovered, loved a good chase. So, I gladly gave him one. I soon realized that the faster I ran, the closer we got to the altar. I also did something else that was very much out of character for me: I remained chaste as we abstained for the first several months. Actually, it was Tom who never, in any way, forced himself upon me, which served to prolong our eventual copulation.

I hate that word. However, it was fun to use around Tom, because he loathed it, too. "Cop-u-lation," I used to tease him after our first night together, which was absolutely mind-blowing for both of us.

For the first time in my life, I had finally felt what it was like to have someone "make love" to me. Tom was not looking for a good time. He was looking for something long lasting and meaningful. He was not going to leave me.

After our huge Roman Catholic Wedding Mass, thanks to my mother's wishes and my parents' fat bank accounts, I moved into Tom's very small house on Franklin Avenue. I was hoping that we would find ourselves in need of more space and subsequently move into the Pratt Canal House, as his mother had invited us to do. Or perhaps we would build or buy a bigger house somewhere within the town limits, preferably in Shipcarpenter Square or on Bay Avenue. We certainly had the means. Regardless, Tom felt that we should save our money and once children arrived, then we could think about putting down some new, more permanent roots.

There would never be any children. I knew that, but I never had the courage to tell Tom. We had talked about having children many times, and I always thought we would be able explore other options when the time came. However, when the time did come, I could not even begin to fathom it. If they were not "mine," I did not want them. I was too afraid that I would not be able to love them like they were my own. I was afraid that an adopted child might bring with them traits that I would not be able to tolerate or understand. I was becoming acutely aware of just how selfish I was. I knew that if I discovered that I didn't love the child, I would abandon it mentally and spiritually. I also knew that if that did happen, Tom would have enough love for both of us. That didn't matter to me, because deep down inside, I knew that I would never be able to share him with anyone else outside of me and mine. I could not begin to think about other options; I loved him too much to share.

When the truth finally came out, Tom was understandably hurt. I had not been honest with him. My mother had to tell him what I never could. It was a horrible time in our marriage.

Our relationship changed after that revelation, and I committed another more regrettable transgression that very night. My reaction to the truth, once revealed, is not one that I am proud of. I drove off, eventually landing at my boss's townhouse. I proceeded to get drunk, and broke my wedding vows to Tom. When I arrived home at 3:00 the next morning, it did not take Tom long to figure out where I had been and what I had done.

Within several weeks, my boss was transferred to our offices in London. That was when I fully comprehended the power of money and influence, both of which there was no shortage of in the Pratt family. To this day, I believe the Pratts had pulled their well-connected strings to make for my boss's swift disappearance.

Still, Tom never gave up on us. Regardless of the mistake I had made, he was persistent in trying to convince me that he wanted our marriage to work. I believed him; however, I could not rid myself of the guilt and let down. I was angry with the Pratts for interfering, but I wanted Tom to be angry with me for what I had done. I deserved to be punished. His overwhelming kindness and consolation became an annoyance to me. I wanted him to lash out at me. I wanted him to commit a crime greater than my own.

I started arguing, yet Tom would never yell back. I was shouting at a kind-hearted wall. It quickly became apparent that he was not up to a good fight, at least not one that I had seen my parents execute with such exacted malicious hostility. Tom would have to punish me by other coerced means.

Tom was a true gentleman; though, once we got behind closed doors, I soon discovered that he could be persuaded to try just about anything, as long as he believed it would bring me pleasure and no harm would come to either one of us. Tom had one hard limit: "no cameras or videography of any kind." I could live with that.

In accordance with my demands, our lovemaking became very rough. I had to beg him at first, asking him to be more brutally forceful each time. Our first breakthrough came with bindings. Somehow, I managed to find ways to make it all about my pleasure rather than any deserved harsh punishment. Finally, I had the opportunity to demonstrate how a leather belt at his hand would send me over the top quickly. Two birds killed with one stone: great sex and my punishment served up by my very handsome, almost deviant, husband. After I had reached several intense orgasms and lay spent on our bed, Tom abruptly stopped. He was not at all happy, or turned on. He was pissed. He quickly cut me loose and left the house. When he finally returned home, hours later, he could not look at me.

We never gave the belt an encore performance. He would not even consider talking about what had happened. Needless to say, the belt vanished, never to be seen around his contoured waist again, even though it had been his favorite for many years.

I think about that night, a lot.

So, why did I leave such a wonderful man? I ask myself that very question many times a day. What did guys like Cal Koppelman, Marco Corelli, and others, have that could draw me away from a man as kind and as caring as Tom Pratt?

CHAPTER TEN

GINNY

When Marco Corelli was first taken into custody, Pratt immediately called Susan. Because Susan was Corelli's former employer, Pratt suspected that investigative reporters would dig into Corelli's history and find her there. Pratt was certain that if they discovered Susan had terminated Corelli shortly before his arrest, it would make for juicy gossip and supposition. In his estimation, it was highly likely that the same reporters would begin hounding her in the very near future about her association with suspect Marco Corelli.

Personally, Dex never liked Corelli. Marco was always telling Susan that everything was fine with Valley Forge Graphic Design while providing excuses for why he was habitually late in sending her the closing reports and statements. Though I disagreed with Dex early on, it was not long before I, too, felt that Susan had placed an unhealthy trust in Corelli. When I met him at the fundraiser, escorting the infamous Gwen Pratt, it was then that I knew I definitely did not like the guy. To top it off, he ended the night by abandoning Gwen, leaving her without a ride home. What guy with any decorum ditches his date miles away from home? Admittedly, with a sick sense of humor, I did appreciate that it was Gwen whom he had deserted!

"Corelli's involved in this?" we overheard Susan ask. "At what level?"

It was impossible for Dex and me not to eavesdrop on their conversation, especially when the shouting and tears started.

"Do you mean to tell me that you knew all along that he was being investigated and you never told me?" Susan asked with ferocity.

"I couldn't tell you. First, I was under strict orders not to tell you. Second, it could have potentially jeopardized the case. I kept telling myself that innocent children had to come first. You and I, being adults, could work it out later," we overheard Pratt try to explain.

"Later? There is no later, Pratt. You've hurt me for the last time."

"WAIT! DON'T HANG UP!" we heard Pratt shout through her cell phone. Then he continued.

"Technically, I shouldn't be calling you now, except I know how vicious the press can be, and I can't leave you to the wolves like that."

"Pratt, how could you? The way I see it, you left me *for* a wolf: a bitch in heat, to be exact. So don't pretend to care now."

"Susan, that's harsh. Where's that coming from?"

"I'm not blind and stupid, Pratt."

Susan hung up and ran down to her room for a good cry. I was lost. For the first time, I didn't know how to help my best friend, nor did we have a clue as to what was about to happen to our quiet waterfront home on a one-way pothole disaster of a road that had kept us fairly isolated from the rest of the world.

If and when the story about Corelli's arrest, the potential charges, the Pratts' involvement, and Susan's association broke on national news, we knew our quiet beach town located in Slower Lower Delaware would be in for a rocky summer.

PRATT

When the story broke on national news, my mother became physically ill. Unsubstantiated reports claimed that she had given Javier and the crew of the Learjet orders to pick up the two little girls in Bolivia. A flight plan had been filed and the order was carried out. My mother questioned every move and conversation she had had regarding the Learjet in the last three months just to be certain that she had not said or signed anything that could have been misconstrued as a directive to do so.

My father, their DC attorney, and their private investigator spoke by phone with Javier and the Learjet pilot. Each clearly stated that a woman identifying herself as Mrs. Pratt and "sure as hell sounded like her" had called hours before take off and directed them to pick up the children in Bolivia, a stop they had made before on behalf of my parents. The paperwork that accompanied the children and their nurse looked legit. No one questioned the whereabouts of the children's parents because "Mrs. Pratt" had made it clear that the parents were not able to make the flight and a private nurse would attend to the children. Javier and the pilot were told that the patients were being sponsored by "Healing Wings," an organization that my parents had founded.

"Healing Wings" is a consortium of private jet and helicopter owners who volunteer their equipment, crew, and services to help transport sick children who would otherwise not survive if not given treatment in hospitals beyond their reach. Their charter states that a parent or a legal guardian must accompany the patient and stay with them until they are returned to their native country. The consortium also uses its connections and influence to expedite the necessary visas and provide accommodations during the family's stay.

As we suspected, once the story broke, news vans were parked up and down Gills Neck Road, waiting for anyone who would come out and talk to them. My father requested that Kirk and Janice stay out of sight and that I not step foot on the property. They did not want me to be brought into their mess.

My parents' attorney arrived within hours and issued a statement on their behalf, proclaiming that my mother never, under any circumstance, authorized the flight in question to and from Bolivia. Yes, in the past, my parents had sent the Learjet to pick up seriously ill children and deliver them and their families to the United States for medical treatment, but under no circumstance had they ever authorized flights without at least one of the parents being on board with their child. He further made clear that under no circumstance did my parents ever authorize a flight for the purposes of abetting illegal adoptions. In fact, all of the flights that my parents had authorized were for children who eventually returned home once they were well enough to travel.

Mr. Sable, representing Healing Wings, gave a similar statement, adding that there was no record of the Bolivian flight that was under investigation being ordered by or filed with their organization. Likewise, the spokesperson for Children's Hospital stated that they had no records regarding the pending or subsequent arrival of either child.

The next afternoon, I received a call from Daly and Wilson. Marco had come up clean. They could not connect him to the flight or the falsified documents that accompanied it. They had to release him.

COURTNEY

It was the perfect summer storm, and our office and the shelter were sucked right into its vortex.

First, the arrest and subsequent release of Corelli sent a tsunami of reporters to Lewes. The Pratts had been implicated in the smuggling of innocent children into the United States only to be sold as orphans in part of an illegal adoption scheme making millions in their "quest to find homes for less fortunate children."

Second, the Pratts had hired my father years ago to draw up the charter for Healing Wings and was on retainer for any legal matters regarding the foundation. Needless to say, our office was suddenly flooded with calls and demands for interviews and statements. The media smelled wealth and politically connected blood, and a feeding frenzy was birthed.

Third, the demand for housing in Lewes skyrocketed overnight as investigative reporters and their crews searched for long-term accommodations, as well as all of the curiosity seekers that were coming out of the woodwork. Summer tenants were looking to sublet their vacation rentals for higher rents, which most rental contracts did not allow. Homeowners were looking to break leases and in many cases, lease their private residences for the fortunes they were being offered. The real estate world had gone mad.

Fourth, when the news broke, we lost several large pledges made to the Sable-Carter Women's Shelter. I had to quickly assemble a team to make visits and phone calls to salvage what we could. I personally made a visit to the Pratt Canal House. I drove slowly through the parked media parade on either side of Gills Neck Road. I pulled up to the gate where a hired guard was anticipating my arrival and allowed me to drive through, announcing to the house that I was making my approach. Knowing the capability of the high-powered camera lenses focused on the house, I parked as close to the front entrance as I could and ran through the front door as Kirk held it open for me.

"Welcome, Mrs. Carter. I hope they weren't too rude to you out there."

"Thank you, Kirk. I just took my time and tried not to draw too much attention."

At the insistence of my Personal Assistant, I had borrowed her car. She said that driving my Porsche into the media zoo would give the appearance that I was part of the legal team and begging for attention. Carla drove an old Toyota Camry with at least 200,000 miles logged on the odometer.

Note to self: I really need to give Carla a raise.

"Janice has prepared some sweet tea and sandwiches. You'll find Mrs. Pratt in the sun room," Kirk directed after hurrying me inside.

"Thank you, Kirk, for everything. I know this quarantine is no picnic for you and Janice."

I found Anna Pratt seated in a lush sunroom filled with exotic plants and flowers. I noticed that the glass wall facing Gills Neck Road was now covered with greenery that had been moved in place to provide a cover. As soon as I entered, Mrs. Pratt rose from her chair and greeted me.

"Courtney, it's so good to have a visitor from a friendly camp," Mrs. Carter remarked with much candor.

I took her hands into mine. She seemed frailer than had I remembered.

"Mrs. Pratt, the honor is all mine. I know this must be a very difficult time for you. Thank you for seeing me."

"Yes, the world has turned upside-down in the blink of an eye. I thought that what we were doing for children was a good thing."

"It is a good and noble thing that you're doing. It's just that someone took advantage of your name and foundation. The truth will come to light, soon, and hopefully those responsible will receive maximum sentences.

"Yes, we are praying for that. I hope this gets cleared up soon."

We took our seats and Mrs. Carter offered me a choice of sandwiches that were beautifully prepared by Janice and served on fine Lenox china. I politely accepted one and placed it on my plate. Our sweet tea had been poured into Steuben crystal glassware. Mrs. Pratt loved to entertain in high fashion. It was therapy for her troubled soul; I was sure.

"Mrs. Pratt, the reason for my visit has to do with the women's shelter. Since the news broke, we have had several large pledges withdrawn. Being one of our major benefactors, I wanted to know if you had any intentions of following suit?"

Mrs. Pratt looked saddened and distraught.

"Will you excuse me, dear?" she asked before leaving the room.

I heard her exit the hallway and enter another room on the same floor.

Oh, no. I've upset her. How thoughtless of me.

Mrs. Pratt soon returned and handed me a slip of paper.

"I don't know what you have lost in contributions, but the work you are doing is so very important. We hope this check will help recover some of the losses."

I was speechless. The Pratts were in the middle of a fight to keep their family out of prison, and yet, she still had the heart to give more. I had no words, and never will, for the amount of gratitude that filled my heart that afternoon.

Ginny spoke with her father, a pediatric surgeon in Darien, Connecticut, who had also made a substantially large pledge. He had no intention of withdrawing and offered his support. Dex visited with Mrs. Pollock who had already made a large cash contribution and pledged an escalating amount to follow each year. For an elderly woman whom we believed lived on a fixed income, she surprised all of us with her sudden financial determination.

Dex, Dylan, Ginny, and Susan made several other calls that day, and through our combined efforts, we learned that the hemorrhaging had stopped.

I surprised Dylan by praising a god I did not believe in.

"Huh . . ." Dylan smirked.

DEX

The Sable-Carter Women's Shelter was well underway, and just as Mr. Sable had predicted, once the story broke about Courtney and Dylan being on board the private flight that smuggled the children into the country, several large pledges for the shelter were withdrawn. The Pratt family had made a second large donation before the storm kicked up in the media, and a third after the story broke. Courtney decided that one of the wings of the shelter was to be named in their honor, regardless of what the media might portray.

Tom Pratt became scarce with the exception of a few calls he had made to me. Though the Pratts were a very influential family and strong supporters of the Sable-Carter Women's Shelter, I was not going to sugarcoat the way I felt about how he had treated Susan.

"How's she doing?" Pratt wanted to know.

"What the fuck do you care? You broke her heart, Pratt. She won't admit it, but you hurt her. She was beginning to believe that maybe the two of you could make a go of it. Then you let her walk in on Gwen?"

"It wasn't exactly like that."

"Then how was it? The bitch was at your house!"

"Listen, Dex, she *was* my wife! She still had a key and stopped by to look for something she thought she had left behind."

"Right, you fell for that? I would not have led Susan to believe that you were developing feelings for her if Gwen had easy access to you and your house. How is that fair? How is that even healthy for you?"

"It wasn't."

I could hear Pratt's exasperation through the phone.

"Dex, I *was* developing feelings for Susan. I would be lying if I said I was not falling for her. In fact, I did fall for her. She has every right to be disgusted with me. It is killing me that I can't see her, or Zoe, or spend time with them. But that is the way it has to be while this whole investigation is going on. And right now, I need to keep Gwen away from Corelli. She *was* my wife at one time. I can't just shut my feelings off like a water faucet."

"Why not? You expected Susan to shut it down, like flipping a switch. And do you honestly believe that what you had with Gwen was a marriage?

"What do you know about marriage, Dex? Have you ever been married? No. Ginny is a wonderful woman, and yet you can't get yourself down on one knee to propose to her, now can you?"

"It's different with Ginny. I don't know that she could ever go through it again. Of course, I've thought about it. If I was ever going to propose to someone, it would be Ginny."

"Then what's stopping you?"

"I can't take her to that place again. Not yet."

There was a lot to what Pratt was saying. He *was* married to Gwen at one time. I guess he did owe her some semblance of respect and duty. Everyone deserves that. And poor Pratt, he always felt like he had to save the world.

Pratt had raised a good point about my reluctance to propose to Ginny. She did deserve a second chance at marriage. She just didn't deserve to go through the fear and memories that it would trigger. For Ginny and me, we would probably end up going through life as a happy cohabitating couple. Hell, after seven years, I think we would be considered legally married, anyway—without the ceremony and honeymoon, fear and memories.

"Listen, Dex, do me a huge favor."

"You called to ask me for a favor? What is it? You want my vote? Is that it?"

"No. I see Susan spilled the beans."

Pratt sounded annoyed.

"She didn't mean to. It slipped," I explained on Susan's behalf.

I knew Pratt always appreciated a straight shooter, so I added a shot of reality.

"But, fat chance you'll get elected in this town. That's not going to happen. Not now."

"Right. My request has nothing to do with any of that. I wanted you to know that Corelli was released this afternoon. They didn't have enough evidence to hold him. He came up clean."

"Jeez, Pratt. Where is the scumbag?"

"In Pennsylvania, but I don't trust him."

"You have the best chance of knowing his whereabouts and keeping tabs on him."

"How's that?"

"Use your ex-wife for bait," I crudely suggested.

Did I really just say that?

"Sorry, Pratt, that was uncalled for, I know. But maybe Gwen could provide some information about Corelli's favorite haunts and habits."

Pratt went on to explain that Gwen had promised him that she would cut all ties with Corelli. I argued that Pratt should exploit her connection and use it for the sake of justice.

Pratt was hemming and hawing. There was something that he was not telling me.

Pratt, what have you gotten yourself into?

After I got off the phone, I thought about Pratt's messed up relationship with Gwen. Part of me thought it was somehow noble of him to try to protect her, yet stupid. I thought of how brokenhearted Susan was and how unfair life could be, especially for truly good people.

I thought about Ginny and me. I knew that we might never marry. However, I promised myself that I would give her a million honeymoons between now and "until death do us part." I loved her that much.

GWEN

I had struck gold.

Marco left me a parting gift before he was arrested: two laptops. One was his, and the other belonged to Derek Carter. Marco wanted me to copy specific files and folders onto Derek's hard drive and then permanently delete them from his. Marco was smart enough to do it for himself, but he knew the Feds were moving in fast. I was more than happy to take care of it because it would also give me the access I needed to wipe away any records connecting me to either one of the men.

I took both laptops to Tom's house and worked away while he was at Jerry's Seafood, meeting with my mother. I was interrupted only once by Susan Carter. Or was she McCabe? Whatever. The look of surprise on her face was priceless.

Back to the laptops. Now, if you really want to know what people are up to, where do you go? Right. You go to their search engine history and their photo library.

JACKPOT!

There she was in Derek's photos, in all her glory. Susan "Whomever-She-Was," was going to become the person that I wanted her to be. She now belonged to me. If Tom decided to file his candidacy, I now possessed the means to play a tricky game of "Connect the Dots" to obliterate any chance he had of winning the election while providing me with anything I could possibly want from him.

Yum!

CHAPTER ELEVEN

SUSAN

The days were hot and humid and long. The media had not pursued me as Pratt had predicted they would, and the Carter beach house tried to fall back into its normal routine. Dex went to work as soon as the sun was up and landed back home between six and seven o'clock at night. I don't think I have ever known a man that worked as hard as Dex Lassiter. During the week, Ginny taught piano lessons between three and seven o'clock. Some days, it was difficult to stay in the house while her students were there. I knew her schedule as well as she did. I did not know her students' names, but I knew which ones routinely practiced and which ones were there because their parents were forcing them to be there.

I knew that Wednesday was a particularly good day to disappear; otherwise, Zoe and I would be subjected to listening to the same four measures over and over again. On that day, I thought Ginny was, in actuality, a glorified babysitter while mom and dad were out running errands or getting their supermarket shopping done.

On the other hand, I rarely missed a Thursday at the Carter beach house. On Thursdays, Ginny had a line-up of students that were advanced and their playing made me wish I had stuck with my own piano lessons when I was their age. One student in particular reminded me of Pratt. Listening to him play caused me to reminisce back to Courtney and Dylan's wedding when Pratt played and sang to Courtney. If I had been the bride, it very well may have been the highlight of my day. It was almost painful to hear Ginny's student play, but I could not tear myself away from the music. Happily, Zoe seemed to appreciate Thursdays, as well.

On Wednesdays, the awful piano day, I usually wandered up to Mrs. Pollock's. Dex and Ginny tried to look in on her daily, or call her when they were away. Adding me to the visitation schedule helped everyone. Plus, Mrs. Pollock loved Zoe, and Zoe adored Mrs. Pollock and her homemade cookies. Gilda always tagged along. Once Zoe started walking, she could not go anywhere without Gilda. If we had to leave Gilda behind, Gilda would lie by the downstairs door and would still be there when we returned. Zoe and Gilda had become the best of friends.

Mrs. Pollock was everyone's grandmother. She knew us well and listened attentively as we tried to sort out the challenges of our daily lives. She had a sixth sense when it came to our wellbeing and knew how to extract our confessions when we were not exactly forthcoming. My visit that day was no different.

Mrs. Pollock opened the door to the squeals of Zoe's delight. Gilda sat at my feet, panting because she knew a treat was due at any moment. The heavenly aroma of fresh baked Toll House chocolate chip cookies was overwhelming as it wafted out the door and surrounded us.

Mrs. Pollock, though in her eighties and living alone, took immaculate care of herself and her home. Her healthy hair was a beautiful luminous silver. She claimed that she had never dyed it in her entire life. I could not tell you how long or short it was, because she always wore it tied up on her head. Also, Mrs. Pollock always wore dresses, never pants. When she greeted us at the door, she was still wearing an apron over her dress. It proudly displayed the evidence of her morning activities in preparation for our visit.

"Oh, it must be Wednesday! My little troop is here for their weekly escape from purgatory!" she exclaimed, clasping her hands together.

I put Zoe down, and she immediately toddled across the kitchen and over to the counter where Mrs. Pollock had a rack of cookies cooling. Mrs. Pollock extracted a dog treat from the pocket of her soiled apron and handed it down to Gilda who very gingerly took it from her arthritic fingers.

"I baked some extra cookies for you to take back to Dex. They're his favorite," Mrs. Pollock instructed.

"Oh, he'll love that!"

Mrs. Pollock hobbled over to the counter where Zoe was now gazing up longingly at the array of warm sugar, vanilla, flour, and chocolate chip lumps of joy.

"May she have one?" Mrs. Pollock asked with a cookie in her hand, ready to be offered.

She knew my answer before she asked, but God bless her, she always asked permission before spoiling my daughter.

"Of course, but only if I can have one, too!"

It was the compliment Mrs. Pollock always looked forward to hearing, and it always made her day.

The teapot on her old gas stove began whistling, and Gilda let out a half-baked howl. Startled, Zoe ran back to me as best as she could, smearing chocolate goo up and down my pant leg.

Oh the joys of motherhood! I figure I'll be able to wear one outfit for an entire day when she enters pre-school.

Mrs. Pollock placed two hot cups of tea and an apple juice pouch on a large tray with a plate of cookies and several cloth napkins.

"Would you mind carrying this out to the deck for us, dear?" Mrs. Pollock asked of me.

At a snail's pace, we made our way outside. Our progress was solely dependent on who was moving slower that day: Zoe or Mrs. Pollock.

Sitting down in the shade of her retractable awning, I inhaled the hot, humid salt air. The heat did not seem to bother Mrs. Pollock, even with the various layers that she was wearing. Mrs. Pollock had a small child size rocker for Zoe. Gilda lay down on the warm boards and kept one eye open at all times so she would not lose track of Zoe, or any crumbs that might make their way to the deck. Zoe rocked happily in her little rocker and drank her juice pouch. I picked up my cup of tea and blew across the top, hoping it would cool quickly. I chuckled to myself, thinking how funny and cute it was that Mrs. Pollock and Dex were so much alike. They both enjoyed hot beverages in the summer declaring, "a hot water pipe never sweats!" Dex was the apple of Mrs. Pollock's eye, the son she never had.

"So, Susan, I understand your latest romantic interest, Mr. Tom Pratt, has gotten himself into a bit of a spot," Mrs. Pollock noted as she placed her teacup back onto its saucer.

Mrs. Pollock never danced around a topic. She said her old age gave her the right to be as direct and as indiscreet as she pleased.

"Not exactly. From what I gather, it's his mother that has been implicated, not Tom Pratt. And what, pray tell, made you believe that he's my latest interest?"

Being around the very proper Mrs. Pollock made me say things like "pray tell." She had the strangest effect on me.

"Darling, this is a small town and most everyone adores Tom. Why, when he finally divorced Marien Merck's daughter, we just about threw a party in his honor."

"Well, if the Mercks are so disliked, then why did you all vote Marien into office?"

"Because she's connected, and she knows how to work the system. Plus, she's a staunch conservative. The retirees who have taken up residency down here like that about her. They do not want some left wing liberal to come in here and rock the boat. Our political sea legs are not what they used to be."

"Now that surprises me. I imagined you would enjoy a good political fight."

"Oh, I do! And I tend to lean left of center, which always leaves me in opposition with the general population on the Delmarva Peninsula. Believe me, Marien Merck did not receive my vote. That is for sure. I keep an eagle's eye and a sharp ear to the ground on that one."

Mrs. Pollock was such a sketch.

"So, Susan, how is the handsome Tom Pratt managing the scandal surrounding his family?" she asked.

"I don't really know. Apparently, the Lewes grapevine is a little behind on the latest pop news."

"Oh? What are we missing?"

"Gwen has moved back in with Tom Pratt."

"No! That's impossible. He is far too smart to make that mistake twice. I may have to call him and give him a piece of my mind. Does his mother know about this?"

"I have no clue. I've only met his mother once."

"My dear, if Anna finds out about this, she is going to put that boy over her knee!"

The vision of petite Mrs. Pratt putting her tall rugged son over her knee and paddling his backside made me laugh. I had to put my hand over my mouth so I would not spew tea.

"Oh, Mrs. Pollock, that would be a sight to see!"

PRATT

Several days later, I followed Dex's suggestion and stopped by Gwen's townhouse after I got off duty. Gwen was seated in her kitchen, enjoying a glass of wine while she waited for me.

"Hi, Tom!" she greeted as I strolled up to her front door. "Come in. Can I offer you a beer?"

"No. Thanks. I'm fine."

"I don't think you've been here before, have you?"

Gwen had moved back into the area about year ago, settling into a new townhouse near the Breakwater Trail and on the other end of Gills Neck Road. It was the first time I had stepped foot into her new home. I followed her into the kitchen. The contemporary upscale design and furnishings matched her to a tee.

'Would you like a tour?"

"No. That won't be necessary. I can't stay that long. I'm here on business."

"Oh ... So, darling, do you think running for mayor is still a viable option for you?" Gwen asked as she sat down at her kitchen bar reunited with her glass of wine.

I leaned back against the counter, knowing her commentary was not over.

"I don't know. I haven't given it much thought in the last twenty-four hours. What do you think?"

I already knew what Gwen thought. I knew that she was looking forward to the soon-to-be relentless campaign battle between her mother and me.

"Your family is all over the news and the media is parked outside your parents' canal house right this minute," Gwen mused.

* * *

The Pratts and the Wagman's (Marien's maiden name) had been at odds over many decades. It basically boiled down to their views over the literal "views" of the area.

The Wagman's had a stake in several hotels up and down the Atlantic coast and saw the coastline as an opportunity to bring in revenues for the "betterment of the communities they serve." On the other side of the debate, the Pratts have always believed that the Delmarva coastline needed to be preserved in its natural state as much as possible. To discredit the Pratt platform, the Wagman's repeatedly pointed to my parents' sprawling estate along the Canal as "hypocriticism." I know. There is no such word. In a public forum, my father tried to politely correct Marien.

"You mean 'hypocritical,' don't you?" my father offered, presenting her with the opportunity to correct her error.

Marien decided she could make up a word if she wanted. Other larger campaigns had succeeded in doing so.

* * *

"I think that you may want to reconsider. I don't see the investigation and its fallout blowing over anytime soon. And it will come up whenever the Pratt name is mentioned," Gwen continued in making her point.

I turned so I could speak directly to her. It was difficult for me to maintain focus. She was scantily dressed and her body was a definite distraction.

"Yes. Your mother would certainly find a way to turn my parents' acquittal into campaign mud, now wouldn't she?"

Gwen would love to see her mother and me in a good dogfight. It would be such a turn-on for her.

"Acquittal, huh? You are in for the fight of your life if you file for candidacy," she sneered playfully.

"And you'd like that, wouldn't you?"

I studied her face to see if she was taking the bait. She looked interested.

Wrong kind of fight, Gwen.

"I need you to do something for me," I decided to get to the point.

Gwen stood up from the kitchen bar and approached me in her usual playful style. One foot in front of the other and in slow motion, she walked right into me, her firm breasts against my chest. She slid her delicate fingers up to my shoulders. I took her slender wrists into my hands and halted their ascent. Their next stop would have been my face and her lips would have possessed mine.

"What's the matter, Baby? I'm sure I can give you whatever it is that you need. You're not due to report back to duty until tomorrow, so we have all day, and all night."

"Listen Gwen, that's not why I'm here. I need some information, and you have the means to obtain it."

"Ah, so you do want to play a new game?"

"This is serious, this is not a bedroom game."

"Serious? I can be serious."

Gwen raised a leg and wrapped it around my waist, pulling her body tight into my groin. I was losing the fight.

"GWEN! For once in your life, focus on something other than sex! What is it with you? I am asking you for your help."

"I can help . . ." Gwen began a slow rhythmic assault.

"I don't need that kind of help."

I grabbed her hips and held her still.

"Oh, but you do! When was the last time you made love to a woman, especially one like me? Or any woman, for that matter? You know you need this . . . we both know how good this would be. You shouldn't deny yourself; it's not healthy."

"I assure you, my health is more than fine," I insinuated that other things were happening in my life with hopes of redirecting her energy and need to please me.

"Oh, Tom, you're no fun anymore," Gwen whined and pouted as she lowered her leg, stood back, and smoothed out the fabric of her shorts.

There was a time when I found her mischievous behavior quite the turn-on. Now, her actions had become an annoyance. I decided to just state what needed to be done, and hopefully she would stop with the cheesy seduction.

"I need to know how Corelli got those girls on to my parents' Learjet in Bolivia, and how he falsified the documents. If anyone is clever and cunning enough to get that out of him, it's you."

"You need to know because your parents are in a lot of hot water, huh?"

"Yes, they are. But they're innocent, Gwen. You of all people should know that my mother would never authorize or participate in any activity involving harm to children or their families."

"Harm? Try death, Tom. One of them died."

Good. Now she's focusing. If she cares about what happened, perhaps she'll cooperate.

"Corelli's involved, Gwen."

"He was released. They found nothing that connected him."

"I know different," I stated emphatically, beginning to lose my patience.

"Are you withholding evidence?" she charged.

"No! You know me better than that."

"And what if I did help you? What's in it for me?"

GWEN

He wanted me to save his mother, but I had my own skin to think about. Cozying back up to Corelli did not seem like a sensible thing for me to do.

"I'm not going near Corelli. A deal's a deal. I promised to stay away from Corelli, and you promised to stay away from Susan McCabe who, by the way, is really Susan Carter, as in Derek Carter's ex-wife. She and her little lovechild would not be good for your soon-to-be unremarkable campaign."

"Gwen, you really need to leave Susan and Zoe out of this."

"So the little one has a name, too? Zoe. Isn't that cute?"

"Leave them alone, Gwen. They're no threat to you. Leave them be."

I had struck a nerve. Tom had feelings for them, and she had something I could not compete with: a child, albeit Derek's. I had to take care of the "Susan and Zoe" obstacle and then win back Tom's heart. Too much was at stake to lose him now.

"Tom, please, you need to relax. Come to bed with me. Come play with me, like we used to," I beckoned.

PRATT

Fighting off Gwen's advances was no easy task for me. She had a hold on my heart and my body that was difficult to understand. Making love to her was like becoming a heroin addict after your first hit. She always left you needing another fix, especially if she was offering it up. I had realized after our second year of marriage that I was on a one-way street with her. In many ways, I had become painfully aware that our lovemaking was pure sex to her, and she had taken me down a path that did not come naturally to me. Gwen was not good for me. Yet, for the longest time, I believed that I could not live without her.

My body screamed at me, *"One more time! What could it hurt to have one more roll with her? Make it your last hurrah. You know you want it. You deserve it. Just think about how good it will feel. You know how good she feels. Go for it. She'll take us to that sweet place of pain and pleasure mixed with a dollop of heaven. You want that, don't you?"*

My heart was crying, *"She's going to drown us! We can't go on pretending that what we know doesn't matter. We will cease to breathe if you don't stop this. She is sucking the life out of you. She already broke me into pieces, why do you continue to allow her to stomp all over the debris she leaves behind each time we do this? What will become of me when she finally leaves you for good?"*

My head stepped in. *"Tom, where is your self-respect? Who do you want to be: the person she controls with sex, or a man with principles? What would you tell your own son to do?"*

I backed away.

"Gwen, I can't. I promised a dear, sweet old lady that I would pay her a visit today. She said she had something very important that needed to be addressed, immediately."

"Who is this 'dear, sweet old lady,' if you don't mind my asking?"

Gwen looked concerned.

"Mrs. Marjory Pollock."

"You've got to be kidding me. What does she want? You haven't filed for candidacy yet, have you?"

"No, not yet. But news travels fast in this town. Mayor Felts may be circling the wagons."

I needed to leave, but decided to give it one more try before I went out the door.

"What do you say, Gwen? We team up and bring Corelli to justice?"

I could see she was mulling it over.

"I'll give it some thought," she sighed as she poured another glass of wine.

I departed for Mrs. Pollock's house.

I walked up the several steps to Mrs. Pollock's door and knocked lightly. I could hear her moving around inside, making her way to the door.

"Com-ing!" she called out in a sing-songy two-note tune.

When she opened the door, she sounded surprised to see me, which was funny because I was there at her invitation.

"Oh! Come in, Tom! I'm so glad to see you!"

Her aged smile and eyes were like the rings of a majestic tree trunk, and I mean that in a complimentary way. Each line and crease around her lips and eyes deepened with her expression, displaying the joy and pain of her many years, an outward sign of her wisdom.

"I know your time is limited," she continued, "so let's get down to business. Would you like a cup of tea or coffee before we sit?"

"Actually, a glass of water would be fine."

She was moving as fast as she could, and I knew she wanted to be the perfect hostess, but it was difficult for me to stand still in her kitchen as she hobbled around to get my glass of water and a cup of tea for herself.

This is why patience is considered such a highly rated virtue.

"Let's go into the parlor where we can sit and talk," Mrs. Pollock directed.

Her teacup rattled on its saucer as she teetered by me.

"Here, let me carry that for you," I politely offered.

I took the teacup and saucer from her hands and followed behind her.

We finally arrived in her parlor and sat down on two dark green velvet Victorian chairs with a small tea table between us.

"How can I help you, Mrs. Pollock?" I asked as I took a sip of cool water. The ice cubes shifted in the glass and a drip of condensation fell onto my pant leg.

"Mr. Pratt, I thank you for your kind consideration and concern; however, I am not the one in need of help. You, on the other hand, could certainly benefit from my advice."

Mrs. Pollock was a wise woman. She did not mince words, so she had my full attention. She continued.

"Word has it that you have allowed Gwen Merck to move back into your house? Is there any truth to that particular rumor?"

"With all due respect, Mrs. Pollock, her legal name is Gwen Merck Pratt. And no, I have not allowed her to move back in with me. Has she visited me recently? Yes. She has spent some time in my home in recent weeks."

I tried to be as straightforward as I could without getting into the sordid details.

"And do you intend to throw your hat into the ring for the upcoming mayoral election next spring?"

"Yes, I do."

"Do you think any good can come from your reconnection to Ms. Gwen Merck Pratt, especially if you are running against her mother?"

"I . . ."

"Because I strongly advise against sleeping with the enemy's daughter."

I nearly spit water into her lap. I had not expected Mrs. Pollock to be that blunt. She raised her hand at me before I could defend myself.

"And don't tell me, son, that you are not sleeping with her. Frankly, I don't care if you bang her into the next county . . ."

I almost fell over.

"If people believe you are sleeping with her without being married, or that you foolishly remarried her, then you are wasting everyone's time and money trying to launch your campaign into the win column. Do I make myself clear?"

"Yes."

"And another thing, how dare you break Susan McCabe's heart? I know, I know. She was married to Derek Carter; however, I do respect her wish to be known as McCabe."

"Mrs. Pollock, I never meant to hurt Susan. Once everything clears, I hope I can patch up whatever damage I've done."

"What? Do you think a woman's heart can be patched like the potholes out there on Bay Avenue?" Mrs. Pollock shook a crooked arthritic finger toward the road. "How much do you think that poor girl's heart can take? Those wounds will keep reopening if you don't put a stop to this at once. You cannot resurface someone's heart like some forgotten road. Mark my words, Tom Pratt. You need to make immediate repairs. Keep Gwen out of your house, and make right by Susan McCabe . . . and Zoe. I pray God will protect that sweet little girl."

A tear formed in Mrs. Pollock's old post-cataract eyes. Her words were direct, but her eyes were telling.

Mrs. Pollock wanted to insure that Zoe would be safe from the wounds created by adults at war.

Mrs. Pollock was being tough on me, but they were the words I needed to hear. Having made her point, I thanked her for her wise advice. Thinking our conversation was a wrap, I stood to leave.

"I'm not finished yet, young man. Sit down."

I did as I was told.

"What about your dear mother? How is she surviving?"

"Not well. There are news vans parked up and down their road, and she is afraid to leave the house. Actually, my parents are not allowed to leave the area."

"Poor Anna," Mrs. Pollock sympathized.

"I have not been able to visit them. My parents have banned me from setting foot on their property. They're concerned that I might become entangled in their mess."

"It will happen anyway, Tom. Soon enough, the scavengers will be camped out in front of your house, too. You have to keep Gwen away. You need to help your mother. The campaign can wait until this is over and hopefully your good reputation will still be intact."

"And Susan?" I asked, hoping Mrs. Pollock would tell me how I should proceed to make the necessary repairs she advocated.

"What about Susan?" she asked, throwing my responsibility back at me.

Mrs. Pollock was a smart woman.

When I returned home, I had every intention of calling Susan to try to straighten out whatever misconceptions she may have had about my current relationship with Gwen. I parked the car, gathered the mail from the box, picked up a package that had been left on the stoop, unlocked the door, and entered my empty, quiet house.

Have you ever noticed how a UPS or Federal Express package demands your immediate attention? This one was no different. It was a plain manila business envelope with a label addressed to me. It was clearly marked "DO NOT BEND."

I pulled up the clasp, opened the envelope, and carefully pulled out the 8X10 photos. At first, I could not breathe. I was not prepared to see her and in such compromising poses.

How and when did this happen? Why would she do this?

The enclosed note read:

"See what you're missing!
There are plenty more where these came from."

I studied the photos, looking for clues that would tell me where, when, and who had taken them. More importantly, I needed to know who had access to them. When I thought I had found the answers, I carefully stuffed the photos back into the envelope.

Susan, answer the phone.
Voicemail.
"Susan, please call me. I need to see you."

Five times with the same result: voicemail and no call back.

I called Courtney Sable-Carter, hoping she might be able to make my appeal.

"Courtney, thanks for taking my call."

"Sure, why wouldn't I?"

"Well, it's good to hear that there is at least one person out there who has not been tainted."

"What's up, Pratt?"

"I need to speak with Susan and no one over at the Carter beach house is willing to take my call. Would you be able to go over there and intercede for me?"

"Now?"

"Yes, immediately."

I went on to explain how Susan, for some reason, believed that Gwen was back living with me, which was not true.

"I knew it!" Courtney yelled into the phone, jolting my ear. "You really do have a thing for her, don't you?"

"It's not like that."

Unfortunately, to make sure Courtney understood the urgency of the matter, I had to tell her about the envelope and its contents left on my stoop.

About a half hour later, Dex called and said that I should meet everyone at the beach house. The sun was setting, and it was turning dark.

Everyone?

As I approached the Carter beach house, I could see Courtney's Porsche, Dylan's truck, Dex's truck, Ginny's Jeep, and Susan's Explorer all parked in the drive. "Everyone" was accounted for. I had to park on East Canal Street. It was confirmed: the Carter clan was a tight-knit group. I rang the intercom and Dex met me on the lower landing.

"You hurt her and I'll bring this town down around your head. I don't care who you are," he growled two inches from my face.

"Are you threatening me?"

"You're damn straight I'm threatening you."

"That's very admirable. But believe me, the last thing I want to do is hurt her. May I see her in private, please?"

"You'll have to ask her."

Susan left Zoe in Ginny's care and escorted me down to the den on the second floor. Courtney had not shared the reason for my visit, only that it would be for Susan's best interest and safety. I was grateful for her non-disclosure.

"Susan, please, sit down. This is not going to be easy."

The look on her face was one of great pain and suspicion. I figured it would be best to get it over with quickly, like getting a shot in the doctor's office or pulling a waterproof Band-Aid off of one's hairy chest.

"Susan, I visited with Mrs. Pollock today. She's informed me that you suspect that I have allowed Gwen to move back in with me."

"Suspect? No, Gwen told me that she was unpacking. What would you think?"

"When was this?"

"When I returned from Valley Forge. I stopped by your house. She was there, and she clearly said that she was unpacking."

"Susan, I can guarantee you that she has not moved back in, nor will she ever move back in. In fact, the locks have been changed."

Susan did not react.

"Do you have any questions about that?"

"No."

"Good."

I inhaled deeply. The next item on my agenda was not going to be easy.

"Susan, this envelope was left on my stoop with the mail today. I thought you should know that someone out there thinks I needed to see these, which I didn't—need to see them, that is." I was stammering uncomfortably. "What I do care about is that someone obviously means to do you harm in some form or another."

I cautiously handed the envelope to her and watched her pull out the contents. When she turned them over and looked, she screamed. Her shriek was filled with horror and disgust, and it traveled upstairs. I could hear Zoe calling for her mommy as Dex and Dylan came flying down the stairs.

"NO! STOP!" Susan screeched, anticipating their reaction. "I need you to leave, he's not hurting me. This is a private matter."

"Are you sure you're all right, Susan? You don't have to put up with him," Dex snarled.

"Yes, Dex, I'm fine. Go back upstairs."

As soon as they left, Susan lowered her head into her hands and softly cried out.

"How is this possible? These were private. There were no other copies. I thought I had the only copies. Why would he do this to me? I am so embarrassed. I have never been so humiliated. Did you look at these?"

"Yes, I did. Not to gawk at them, Susan. I looked for clues as to who took them, where they were taken, when they were taken, and who might have had access to them."

"I can tell you who took them, and I believe he is the only one with access."

"Derek?"

Susan looked down and whispered ashamedly, "Yes."

After a brief pause, she bravely lifted her face, but still avoided eye contact with me.

"Derek and I were married when these were taken."

I took one of her hands in mine.

"Susan, you don't owe me an explanation, and believe me, I've done some things in my life that I would consider very private, too. I certainly have no right to pass judgment."

Susan nodded her head. She was obviously ashamed.

"I'll head over to the prison tomorrow to find out how Derek was able to get these to land on my stoop today. OK?"

"Yes. And I want to know why he would do this to me?"

Susan laid her head on my shoulder and softly cried. Her past had resurfaced and entered the present new life she was trying so desperately to make for herself and her daughter.

I understood, all too well.

CHAPTER TWELVE

DEREK

"Children, Pratt? Really? Your family is trafficking children? That's about as low as you can go. And your mother is at the center of it? If either one of them is convicted they will never survive prison with that charge on their heads. What is wrong with you people?"

Juicy headlines from the outside world travel fast in prison.

"Don't flatter yourself by defaming my family, Derek."

"I don't have to, the news media has already done a good job of that for me. Listen, every bastard locked up in here because of you is having a field day, just hoping you get yours. They're all lining up to be a back door guest at your welcoming party."

Good one!

"That's very thoughtful, but the Guest of Honor has no plans of showing up."

"Why are you here, Pratt?"

"It has to do with Susan."

"I've already told you, stay away from her. And keep your hands off my daughter. If your family goes anywhere near her, I'll have you strung up by your fucking nuts."

"Nice, Derek. So, now you care about what happens to them? Why the sudden interest?"

"You know better. I've always cared about Susan. There isn't a day that goes by that I don't think about her and what's happened."

"And Zoe?"

I knew Pratt's tricks. He was trying to get me all sappy about my wife ... er, ex-wife, ... and my daughter.

"Listen, Pratt, stop with the bullshit and cut to the chase."

"Pictures of Susan were delivered in an envelope to my front stoop. She was naked—as in fully exposed."

That's all he said. I was not about to take the bait. "So?"

"So, I want to know how they got there and why you would even think about distributing them."

"I don't know what you're talking about."

"Are you sure? Because I have them right here."

Pratt raised a large business envelope from his lap and opened the flap.

"Do I need to show you these?" Pratt asked with the resonance of a threat in his voice.

There is no way this scumbag has what he's suggesting he has. Those photos were locked away. Not unless Susan turned them over to him. Why would she do that?

I recalled how beautiful Susan looked in some of the poses I had caught, and how embarrassed she was to look at them. She made me promise to keep them locked up and never show them to anyone. Yes, over the years I had broken several promises I had made to her, but never that one. She had trusted me.

Yes, there was a day when Susan trusted me with her life ...

"Pratt, don't play games with me. I'll expose you and your family. You know as well as I do that the media would eat up anything that shows an ugly side of your family's seemingly spotless reputation. Especially now that your mother is raping children and their families."

Pratt nearly flew out of his chair. Yep, the boy had a soft spot for momma. The guard watched closely as Pratt instantaneously caught himself and promptly replanted his ass. After a short-lived stare down, Pratt slid an 8X10 photo out of the envelope. I recognized it immediately. At least he had the decency to cover everything from her beautiful collarbone down.

It was a picture I had taken of Susan on our one-year anniversary. We had taken a trip to Spain to see the real running of the bulls.

* * *

When we were still dating, I had taken Susan to the "Running of the Bull" at Dewey Beach. It was insane. We spent the day with thousands of other totally inebriated people and ended up having to stay on the beach until we were sober enough to drive back to the beach house. As we lay on the beach, it was the first time we had ever entertained the possibility of a future together. (One of several uncharacteristically impulsive things I had done that day.) The following day, my dad gave me a whale of a lecture about how one should treat a lady.

Anyway, for our first wedding anniversary, I surprised Susan with a trip to see the real running in Spain. That night in our hotel room and as her gift to me, she had allowed me to do something I had always wanted to do: photograph her in the nude. Susan had the most amazing body. Though she never flaunted it, her body was that of a pin-up girl. The fact that she was shy about her nakedness and saved it all for me, made her even more tantalizing when she released her inner seductress.

She struck various provocative poses for what seemed like an hour while I snapped off dozens of pictures and tried to control my erection at the same time. Susan later confessed that being able to observe her effect on me made her work the camera even harder to challenge the extent of my limitations. When I could no longer hold off, I reached out and touched her. Once our lips met, we quickly made our way to the bed. It was a night that neither one of us would ever forget. For that reason, neither of us wanted the photos to be destroyed, and quite honestly, even if she destroyed her copies, I was not about to destroy the files. They were doubtless works of art.

* * *

"What the hell are you doing with that? Where did you get that?"

Now, I was the one who was out of his seat. The guards approached me and were about to have me removed when Pratt begged them to wait, explaining that he was there as part of a criminal investigation. I shook myself loose and took my seat.

"Where did you get those, and what do you intend to do with them?" I growled with fierce determination, trying not to attract the unwanted attention of the guards, again.

"I intend to keep them out of the media and the hands of anyone who would mean to do harm to Susan and your daughter," Pratt snarled back.

"How did you get them?"

"I already told you. They were in an envelope and dropped on my front stoop. Someone deliberately planted them there. And, for your information, Susan is horrified, so now I am asking *you* how they got there."

For reasons unbeknownst to me, I believed he was genuinely trying to protect my dear ex-wife. She never deserved any of this.

"Susan had copies in her safe, in our bedroom. Those *were* the only printed copies, but these are not those. The ones that Susan had were printed on professional grade glossy photo stock. These are printed on high quality matte stock. The images must have come from my photo library on my laptop."

PRATT

My mind raced. It had to be Corelli. Susan had discovered that Derek's laptop went missing, and Corelli was the only one with easy access. Plus, in the wake of his termination, I had every reason to believe that Corelli had motive to hurt Susan.

I called my parents. They were immediately on board and began making arrangements for the arrival of their houseguests. My next call was to Dex.

"Dex, you need to pack up Susan and Zoe and move them to my parents' canal house, immediately."

"What? Are you nuts? Why would you want to put them in the center of that media circus over there?"

"Because that's where they'll be the safest."

"Pratt, you need to tell me what's going on before I do any such thing."

I explained as quickly and as accurately as I could the reasons I had for suspecting that Corelli was seeking revenge and how he might do it. I noted that if successful, Susan and Zoe were going to be harassed like nothing we had seen, yet. I also disclosed that despite Corelli's release, I still believed that he was connected to the ring that was trafficking children. The man was a loose cannon, now armed and loaded.

"Listen, Dex, both of them will be safer there. With the entire world parked outside of my parents' house on every side, waiting and watching for someone to move, Corelli won't be able to get near them without being caught on tape. The state and local police are already present and are keeping the media under control and at a safe distance. It's the safest place for them."

"So, how do you propose I get them in there?"

"Get Marty to take you down in the water-taxi."

When I arrived home, approximately an hour later, I was served with a search warrant.

What the fuck?

Rarely, if ever, did I swear.

GWEN

I called my lawyer and told her to get her ass over to my townhouse, immediately. The Feds were at my home with a search warrant. Two of the agents sat me down in my dining room and questioned me, ad nauseam, about my association with Cal Koppelman and Marco Corelli while a half dozen agents went through my personal belongings.

An hour later, the Feds left empty-handed, just as I had thought they would, and my attorney still had not shown up. In fact, I received a quicker response from Tom than I did from my overpaid legal counsel. I called Tom as soon as the Feds had pulled away. Tom returned my call within five minutes. I fired my attorney's ass. The least she could do was take my call so I could tell her so.

"Hey, are you OK?"

That was my ex-husband, always putting my concerns before his own.

"I just want you to know that I had nothing to do with whatever picture it is that they have of us. My house was searched, too," Tom empathized.

"What picture are you talking about?" I was totally confused.

"Someone came forth with a picture of you and me meeting up with your former boss when we made that stop in Paraguay years ago. Remember how strange that was?"

"Yes, I do remember."

"Well, apparently, your former boss has been linked to that illegal adoption ring," Tom announced as if vindicated for disliking the guy all along.

I gasped.

"Tom, you don't think they suspect us, do you?"

"What else could it be? Just continue to cooperate and give them everything they need. It will be over soon. For now, the Feds have to follow every lead."

Tom and I had taken a trip to Bariloche years before when we were trying to patch things up. I had requested that we make a stop in Paraguay on our way back, to visit an orphanage that I had heavily supported. At the time, I believed Tom thought it was a great idea and hoped that our visit might help me reconsider other options for eventually adopting a child of our own. Oddly enough, at the orphanage, we ran into my former boss, Cal Koppelman. It certainly was memorable. It took me the entire flight home to convince Tom that the meeting had not been pre-arranged.

Unbeknownst to us, someone had snapped a picture of the "three big American benefactors" and proudly displayed it in their office to commemorate the day.

Following the trail they were blazing to build the case against Marco and Cal, the picture was spotted and seized. I later learned that it was Javier and our pilot who identified me as the Mrs. Pratt who had directed them to land in Bolivia on the more recent flight.

His whereabouts unknown, Cal was considered a fugitive. It was only a matter of time for Corelli, too.

SUSAN

Despite Dex's calm composure, I was scared. He and Ginny helped me pack everything that I thought we would need into Mrs. Pollock's Oldsmobile. Dex thought it would be best to leave the Explorer at the beach house. Mrs. Pollock, loving intrigue, was thrilled to lend her car to the cause. In exchange, Dex promised to be Mrs. Pollock's private chauffeur until everything blew over. It was a deal we knew she would never refuse. Ginny promised me that if we had forgotten anything, she would find a way to get it to us.

In case we were spotted and harassed, Courtney traveled with us to take care of any overly aggressive media hounds. Mrs. Pollock's Oldsmobile glided up Savannah Road like we were riding on air. The car was a tank. When we turned onto Angler's Road, we could see that Marty was already on board the water taxi with the engine running. Pratt had taken care of everything. Marty graciously helped us load our luggage onto his boat and then gave us a very abridged version of his safety regulations.

"Your lifejackets are under your seats, and here's a life preserver for the little one."

That was it. We were on our way.

Everything was right out of a high stakes action movie. We got the call, scrambled and packed, dove into the getaway car, and slipped away. The boat and its pilot were waiting, ready to rock and roll as soon as we were on board.

Then we puttered down the canal.

Rather than the chase scene that I had imagined from the 1971 classic "Puppet on a Chain," we puttered like the one-stroke engine of the riverboat in "The African

Queen." Even Marty, in some strange laidback way, reminded me of Humphrey Bogart.

I could not help myself. Seated on the bench with Zoe in my lap, I just started laughing.

"What's so funny?" Courtney asked, wanting in on the joke.

"This. Us," I responded waving my free arm indicating the trip we were on.

Courtney caught on and laughed with me. It was the first time Courtney and I had actually shared a moment just between the two of us. I was truly grateful for her companionship that day. Knowing that these situations did not intimidate her and that she was with us, made me feel more confident and, obviously, relaxed.

When we rounded the bend and I got my first glimpse of the media frenzy surrounding the Pratt Canal House, nothing seemed funny anymore. I subconsciously covered Zoe with my shoulder. I especially wanted to make sure that none of the cameras zoomed in on her. Fortunately, there was a lot of land between the Canal and Gills Neck Road, so none of them could get near us. As soon as I saw Kirk and Janice standing on the dock behind the house, I felt infinitely better. Once we got within one hundred feet of the dock, the large home blocked the view of the camera lenses.

One small bump up against a wooden piling and we had landed. Zoe recognized Janice and started waving her arms and kicking her feet. I carefully handed her over the side of the boat and into Janice's waiting arms.

"Well, hello there!" Janice gushed. "You are just as pretty as ever."

Zoe appropriately smiled and giggled, smushing her face with her little hands.

"I think I'll move her up to solid ground before we both fall in!" Janice informed me nervously as she held tight to my little ball of energy.

Kirk helped us load our things into a dock cart and then escorted us up to the main house as he dragged the cart behind him.

Courtney already had a comfortable relationship with Anna Pratt, but I was thoroughly intimidated by the Pratt's wealth and community standing, locally, nationally and internationally. So, I was relieved that Marty was willing to wait at the dock for Courtney while she went up to the house with me.

"Keep it simple," echoed in my head.

Mr. and Mrs. Pratt greeted us inside their back entrance, which was just off the large kitchen where I had first met Janice in what seemed like a lifetime ago. In somewhat familiar territory, I began to let go of the stress invoked by setting up temporary residency in someone else's home.

The Pratts were very welcoming and begged me to make myself at home. Courtney had cordially said her hellos, reassured the Pratts that she and her father were at their disposal, and then asked Kirk if he would walk her back to the dock where Marty was patiently waiting.

"I should get back to the boat before Marty decides to stir up a little commotion with the photographers and reporters," Courtney kidded, although I could tell she was serious in her concern about Marty's notorious contrariness.

Courtney was gone that quick, leaving me to fend for myself.

Janice showed Zoe and me to the second floor where we would be staying. Kirk had already carried our things up to our suite and placed them in my room, so I was free to take in my new surroundings while carrying my oblivious Zoe. Up a beautiful wide and winding staircase, our quarters were off to the left. Mr. and Mrs. Pratt's master suite was on the opposite side of the second floor in a separate wing. Janice assured me that Zoe would not wake them in the middle of the night if she cried or fussed; however, everyone would be able to reach us in a moment's notice, if needed.

Our suite faced the canal and offered a bedroom, full private bath, and a sitting room where someone had graciously set up a crib for Zoe.

Janice then proceeded to give us a quick tour of the entire house and showed me how to operate the estate's elaborate security and intercom system. I was completely overwhelmed.

"Buck up," I told myself. *"This poor family is going through more hell than I would ever want to endure in my lifetime. I can manage this. Just keep it simple and don't overcomplicate matters."*

Over dinner, I learned that our suite on the second floor was Pratt's when the family stayed there during their summer vacations. That was before Pratt actually moved into his permanent residence in Lewes.

Over dinner, Anna Pratt shared stories of how "Tommy" used to fish in the Canal by the weeping willow tree. Janice laughed and joined in as they recalled the time Tommy had hooked a striper that was pound for pound his size. Kirk said the women greatly exaggerated the size of the aquatic animal in their story, but acknowledged that it looked more like a thrashing sea monster compared to the very young Pratt who was trying to reel it in from his post on the bank of the Canal.

As the story went, Pratt refused to let the fish take his fishing rod and reel, so he held on for dear life. The fish pulled the "hollering" Tommy off the bank and into the water. Kirk, already on his way, had to go in after Pratt and convince the young lad to let go of his fishing rod. Therefore, the fish became "the REALLY BIG ONE that got away!" Tommy decided that the fish, as with all champions in our lives, deserved a nickname. He immediately named it "Darth." Mrs. Pratt said they were not quite sure whether he meant "Dart," or if it was short for "Darth Vader."

"To this day, I swear he still goes down there to look for that fish!" Mr. Pratt Sr. laughed.

Zoe laughed, because everyone else at the table was laughing.

I found the Pratts to be so super sweet and accommodating. Even though Janice and Kirk were there as their employees, they were treated like family members.

There was a special bond between all of them, and they quickly made me feel a part of it.

After dinner, I walked Zoe around the first floor with hopes of tiring her after all of the over-stimulation during the day and dinner. Toward the front of the house, we came across the music room. There, in the far corner of the large room with a high ceiling, random width wood floor, and oriental rugs, was a beautiful Steinway piano. Imagining what the room would sound like if filled with the melodies of Pratt's playing, and better yet—singing. I stood and stared.

Without my notice, Anna Pratt sneaked up behind me and scooped up Zoe.

"I know I'm partial, so my opinion doesn't hold much weight, but Tom is a very gifted musician," she quietly commented.

"Oh, I know," I swooned.

"So, you've heard him play?"

"Yes, at Courtney and Dylan's wedding."

"Ah, yes. We heard all about that. We were so sorry we couldn't make the big event. We were grounded in the Netherlands, but Tommy told us all about it."

Anna Pratt stared at the piano with me and sighed.

"He was so happy here when he was growing up. Then he met Gwen Merck. Nothing has been the same since that day. His father and I tried to warn him, but he was too far gone."

Mrs. Pratt took another deep breath and turned to me.

"That was, until he told us about this incredible woman that danced with him at the Sable-Carter wedding. You put his landing gear down, Susan. He was finally returning to solid ground. And yet, his ex-wife keeps reappearing. She's a hellcat, that one. But she has nothing on you. You are the stabilizer that he needs and the horizon that he should look for."

"I can't save your son from himself, Mrs. Pratt."

"No, you can't. But you certainly have a way of drawing his attention away from danger. Please, don't give up on him."

That first night at the Pratt Canal House, it took Zoe a long time to fall asleep. The new bed in the new room threw her into overdrive. When she finally went down, I strolled over to the window and looked out across the long stretch of moonlit ground between Pratt's bedroom window and the Canal. The willow tree swayed gently in the light breeze. It was Pratt's safe haven, holding many of his secrets, like the diary of a young prince.

The Canal quietly made its way to Rehoboth in the dark. I wondered whatever happened to Darth and Tommy Pratt's fishing rod. Yes, Anna Pratt's little boy had grown up to be a noble young man, only to be side-tracked by a damsel who had created great distress within this very kind and generous family.

I crawled into Pratt's old bed and curled up into a fetal position beneath the sheets.

"Everything will be all right," whispered the willow.

CHAPTER THIRTEEN

PRATT

The following morning, as I was preparing to call and check-in on my parents and Susan, Daly and Wilson showed up on the small stoop of my house. I invited them in, and they got right down to business. The two laptops they had removed from my attic belonged to Derek Carter and Marco Corelli. They wanted to know why I was in possession of them and how they got there.

I was caught off guard and hesitated. I had no idea. Up to that point, I assumed the boxes they had removed contained my previous years' tax returns that I had kept stored in the attic. I silently tried to reconcile how those two laptops ended up hidden in my house without my knowledge. I could only come up with two possibilities: Susan or Gwen.

Susan discovered that Derek's laptop went missing from Derek's office. She claimed that Corelli removed it. Or, did he? Did Susan rush to Valley Forge so she could retrieve it herself?

If Corelli took Derek's laptop, then how did it end up in my attic? Perhaps he gave both laptops to Gwen. But, to what end?

Maybe he gave both of the laptops to Susan. But why would he do that? Maybe, as part of his termination from Valley Forge Graphic Design, he had to turn in his laptop, and Susan retrieved the other. But what would be her motive to make up a story about Corelli removing Derek's?

Both Susan and Gwen have been in my house recently. Is it possible that one of the two used my house to cover their tracks, putting me in the direct line of fire? It is the perfect set-up, including the involvement of my parents and their Learjet.

How did Courtney and Dylan's flight get so easily entangled in this mess? I made those arrangements.

Is it possible that Gwen and Susan are conspiring together?

SUSAN

The next afternoon, there was a large commotion downstairs. Janice was visibly shaken when she approached me in the upstairs sitting room.

"Susan, there are two investigators downstairs who are demanding to speak with you."

"Really?"

I looked over to Zoe who was ignoring her own toys and happily playing with some of Pratt's old trucks and action figures.

"May I watch Zoe for you?" Janice kindly offered.

I could not imagine why the investigators needed to speak with me.

"Of course."

Feeling very scared and insecure, I kissed Zoe on the cheek, left her with Janice, and made my way down the large staircase. Mr. and Mrs. Pratt were waiting for me at the foot of the stairs.

"It's all right, Susan," Mrs. Pratt whispered, as she took my hand, though she did not look all that confident, either. "These gentlemen need to ask you a few questions."

Mr. Pratt made the introductions.

"You may use the library," Mr. Pratt directed, reassuring me that he and Anna would be waiting in the front parlor when the gentlemen were through with their questioning.

Kirk escorted us back and closed the doors behind him as he left the room.

The library, being on the first floor, had a tall ceiling with six evenly spaced double French doors that had to be eight feet high, all leading to an outside brick patio that surrounded the room on three sides. A grove of conifers lined the property on the two sides perpendicular to the Canal, protecting the room from the media frenzy parked out front and leaving the Canal view unobstructed. Between the evenly spaced doors were ceiling to floor shelves filled with books and the occasional memorabilia or a family photograph. An eight to ten foot ladder was mounted onto a rail system that circled the room, making it possible for one to have access to any book desired. A large dark cherry desk was at the far end of the room with two burgundy leather wingback chairs facing it. I spun around and noticed a large family portrait mounted on an inside wall opposite the desk. It was easy to spot the young Tommy Pratt. All smiles, he was hugging what I guessed to be the family dog, a big yellow lab. Standing between Pratt's parents was an older girl, maybe two to three years older than he. She had curly blond hair tied up into two long pigtails. She was wearing a white dress that matched Anna Pratt's.

Pratt must have an older sister! Why has he never mentioned her?

Suddenly, and somewhere between the millions and millions of words on the pages of books swirling around me, and the portrait and more smaller photos of a girl who seemed to disappear somewhere near the age of nine, I found myself lost in a sea of the unknown.

"Susan, are you all right?" Agent Daly asked quietly.

"Yes. I'll be fine."

The room slowly stopped spinning.

"Please, have a seat," the other gentleman directed as he waved toward one of the chairs.

I sat down and hoped that the chair would swallow me up.

Wilson sat in the opposite chair. Daly leaned his haunches back on the desk and crossed his arms in front of his chest. Neither gentleman said anything right away. They appeared to be studying me, making me even more uncomfortable. Finally, Daly dropped his arms, leaned forward and braced himself on the edge of the desk with his large hands.

"Susan, do you know why we're here?" Daly asked.

"Not really."

I felt my adrenaline heated blood rushing to my face, and the room became very warm.

"During a search of Tom Pratt's house, we found two laptops. You do know Tom Pratt, correct?"

"Yes, sir, I do."

"Of course, you do. He brought you here. Is that correct?"

"He arranged for me to be here. Yes."

"Regarding the laptops that were confiscated from Tom Pratt's house, one belongs to a man by the name of Marco Corelli, and the other belongs to a man by the name of Derek Carter. Do you know either of those two men?"

My mouth went dry, but somehow I had managed to swallow saliva down my windpipe, causing me to gag.

"Are you sure you're all right, Ms. McCabe?" This time the agent named Wilson leaned over to ask.

My mind was racing with a million different reasons why I was being questioned about Derek and Marco, none of which made any sense. My body was shaking and my hands were sweating.

The photos. Does this have anything to do with the photos? What if these men have seen the photos?

I felt naked. My breath became shallow and accelerated. I was becoming lightheaded.

"I want my attorney."

I had no idea what I was saying. I had no attorney. I was simply overwhelmed.

"Keep it simple, Susan. Are you looking for complicated?" echoed in my ears.

"You are not a suspect, Susan. You are not being arrested, but you do have the right to have an attorney present if you feel you need one. If you wish to exercise your right, please make it quick," Wilson advised.

I blasted out through the door. Mr. Pratt heard my footsteps and came running.

"Susan, what's wrong?"

"I need an attorney. I need Courtney."

It took all of fifteen minutes for Courtney to arrive.

"Where is she?" I heard Courtney beg of Mr. Pratt as he and Kirk met her at the front door.

"She's in the parlor and the agents are waiting back in the library."

Courtney explained to the gentlemen that I was once married to Derek, ...

Big surprise, they already know that.

... and that Marco Corelli worked for a corporation owned by my ex-husband and me.

They already know that, too.

"Susan, we need to know how the laptops of Derek Carter and Marco Corelli ended up in Tom Pratt's attic."

Courtney remained as cool as a cucumber. Not I.

"I have no idea," my voice trembled.

"When was the last time you saw either of the men?"

"I have not seen my ex-husband since his arraignment. The last time I saw Marco Corelli was at the fundraiser for the Carter-Sable Women's Shelter, the night I fired him."

Courtney filled in the details about the dates, times, and places.

"Susan, have you ever had either laptop in your personal possession?"

"I can't remember the last time I saw Marco with his laptop. Probably more than a year ago, but I have never been in possession of it, even though it is property of Valley Forge Graphic Design. Derek's laptop went missing..." I stopped suddenly.

"Courtney, may I speak with you in private?" I asked.

"Gentlemen, would you mind stepping out of the room, please?" Courtney excused the agents.

Both men acquiesced and left the room.

"Courtney, you don't suppose that's how Pratt got ahold of those pictures of me, do you? Did he have Derek's laptop all along?"

"It could be, but that doesn't sound like something Pratt would do or set-up? What good would it do him to print out your photos and pretend he found them on his stoop? It would only serve to tie him to Derek's laptop. Why would he want to do that?"

"Of course, then Corelli must be the one that removed it from Derek's office. What if he supplied it to Pratt at Pratt's request? Pratt has been visiting Derek. What if they've been...?"

My head was spinning.

"Susan," Courtney grabbed my arms, "look at me. The Feds are here in connection with the trafficking and illegal adoption of children. You want this resolved, right?"

"Yes."

"This is not about you and those pictures. Even if the pictures connected you to Derek's laptop, this is not about you, or the photos. This is solely about whoever smuggled those children into the States and sold them. You want the perpetrators caught no matter who they are, don't you?"

"Yes. Absolutely."

"Then we go back in there and answer their questions directly. They haven't asked about your pictures, so don't even mention them. If they do, I will answer. Got it?"

"Yes."

Thank God, the photos of me were never mentioned. However, I was sure if someone at the agency searched Derek's laptop, they must have found them. Though, Courtney was right, they had the decency not to mention them to me.

There was, however, one picture that was of particular interest. It was one that I had never seen before. Daly showed me a photo taken of three people and asked if I could identify any of them. I pointed out Tom Pratt and Gwen. I had no idea who the third gentleman was, and they didn't tell me.

It seemed like hours, but Courtney said their questioning only lasted about thirty minutes, tops, and she said I had done well.

I watched the agents leave and become swamped by a sea of reporters. Courtney waited, walked quietly out to her PA's car, and then slipped away.

PRATT

"It sure didn't take you long!" I joked when I answered her call.

"What the hell, Pratt?" Courtney barked. "Both laptops were found in your attic? You'd better get yourself a good attorney."

"I didn't put them there. They know that."

"If not you, then who?" Courtney acted like I should have known.

"There's only one person who would have had access to both laptops between the time Corelli was fired and they were found in my attic, and that's Corelli. And who had access to Corelli and me?"

"Gwen and Susan."

"Bingo."

"And they had access to your house?"

"Sadly, yes."

"Why would Corelli give either one of them both laptops?"

"Because he's no fool. He knew it was only a matter of time before the Feds closed in on him."

Someone was pounding on my door.

"I gotta go, Courtney. Film at eleven."

"What?"

I hung up abruptly and answered my door. No surprise. Wilson and Daly.

"I can't seem to shake you guys. Come in."

After things settled down, I called Gwen. I needed to see her, and she sounded relieved to hear my voice.

Ten minutes later, Gwen was at my door looking as delicious as ever.

"Where have you been, Gwen? I've been worried about you."

I pulled Gwen into my house, closed the door, and locked it immediately.

"Are you all right?" I asked, smoothing my hands down her terrified face.

"I am, now. Thank God you're here."

She fell into my arms and I held her securely in my embrace for as long as she needed.

"You're in a lot of trouble, aren't you?" I whispered into her hair. As before, it smelled of vanilla and coconut, triggering a recollection of past intimate entanglements.

"Yes, I think I am. And you are, too?"

"Yes. But I think I can get us out of here. First, I need to know if you're the one who put those pictures of Susan on my stoop."

"Susan? What's Susan got to do with this? Why is it always about Susan?" Gwen sniped, clearly annoyed.

"Because for once, I need to know if you're being honest with me before I stick my neck out for you."

"All right. Yes. I put her pictures on your stoop. I knew you would find her behavior repulsive, and I wanted you to see what a tramp she is."

"OK, then. Point well taken."

I pulled her into me and kissed her lightly.

"By the way, you should know that it has always been you, since the day I rescued you in the Bay, it has always been you," I whispered into her lips.

Gwen took a deep breath, laid her head on my chest, and sighed.

"Then rescue me now, Tom. I'm in over my head."

I caressed and rocked her gently as one does for a sleepless baby.

"I need to know the truth, Gwen, so I know exactly how to help."

I held her back so I could look into her weary eyes.

"Were you involved with Corelli and Koppelman's scheme to bring those children into this country?" I asked directly.

"Yes, but you have to understand, at first I thought they were transporting them here for medical reasons, for a really good cause."

"How long have you been involved?"

"I don't know." She sounded exasperated and exhausted. "The first flight I made was from Wilmington to Boston. Remember that time you got really mad at me for chartering a flight up to Boston rather than flying with your family to the Cape?"

"Yes, I do. You said you had corporate business in Boston. It wasn't corporate business then, was it?"

"No."

"You flew with children from Wilmington to Boston?"

"Yes. But I thought we were doing a good thing, Tom. Cal needed three children delivered to a hospital in Boston, or so I thought. Marco met me in Wilmington, and Cal met me in Boston where the children were whisked off. Cal was the one who chartered the plane. He explained to me how the children could not wait for the slow and tedious bureaucracy of this country and how much the children and the families would benefit from what I had done. And then you sent the Learjet to retrieve me from Boston and bring me to the Cape to be with you and your family. That was the first time Cal saw the Learjet and how accessible it was to me."

Gwen began sobbing. She was finally able to admit her guilt. She was finding freedom in the truth. I held her tighter and kissed her head. Gwen sighed heavily and continued.

"Then he gave me my share and asked me join the team."

"Cal paid you for making the delivery, saw the Learjet, and then asked you to join his team?"

"Yes."

"The fact that he paid you for making the delivery didn't tell you that something was wrong?" I asked, laced with sympathy.

"I don't know what I was thinking. I guess I chose to ignore the obvious. I was making a lot of bad choices in those days."

"That's an understatement. When did Cal start involving my parents' Learjet and the crew?"

Gwen stared up at me quizzically. Then she dropped her head and spoke to the floor at my feet.

"After our trip to Paraguay," Gwen answered ashamedly.

To make her apology clear, she raised her head and looked into my searching eyes. She knew that I needed to know every raw, hurtful detail.

"Listen, Tom, I messed up. I was half crazy after admitting that I could never give you children. This was my opportunity to do something right for other people who were just like me."

"So, you got into bed with Koppelman—in every conceivable way, I might add—including his child abduction scheme?"

"Tom, I never meant to hurt you."

"Gwen, please, let's not revisit your romantic escapades. Not now. We'll try to repair those roads once we leave here."

I kissed her ever so softly and reassuringly, again. I needed more answers. Gwen needed more reassurance and leaned her body into mine so I could feel the ache in her abdomen. I carefully pushed her back far enough to continue without distraction. I had to get my answers before we could move on.

"So, tell me, how many flights are we trying to cover?"

"With the Learjet? Only three."

"How many have you been involved in?"

"I don't know."

She began rubbing her one hand up and down my chest.

"More than twenty?"

"Yes."

"More than fifty?"

"Perhaps."

She was becoming nervous and evasive.

"Don't be flippant about this. This is serious."

I grabbed her hand and stopped her assault on my body.

"Don't you think I know that?" she snapped back.

"If you want me to cover for this whole mess, I need to know, and then we can leave here."

"More than fifty, Tom. I am so sorry. I thought I was doing the right thing," she pleaded.

I actually felt sorry for her. My heart had been shattered into a million pieces, and it was time to let it all wash out to sea.

Having heard enough, two shadows emerged from the kitchen. I blocked the front door and Gwen screamed.

"NO! Tom, how could you?"

Daly read Gwen her charges and her rights.

"You have the right to remain silent. Anything you say can and will be used against you in a court of law. You have the right . . . "

As Daly put her in handcuffs and continued, I pulled Wilson aside.

"How'd we do?"

"We got enough, plus we have the print paper that matched the paper she used to print Susan's photos, tying her to both laptops, the data transfers, and the falsified documents. It's a closed case."

"Remember, the photos stay out of the press and the courtroom. They are to be destroyed, got it?"

"I'll see to it myself. Whoops, bad choice of words. I'll take care of it, not to worry," Wilson smirked.

I've learned that anytime someone says, "not to worry" or "trust me," that's when you should become very concerned.

"Do me a favor, pull the front door shut when you leave. I'm getting out of here before the news breaks. This street isn't big enough for that mess over at my parents' house."

"Yeah, but you've got this whole church parking lot next door to fill!" Wilson laughed. "Not to mention the police station across the street!"

"Exactly. I'm out of here. I'm going over to my parents to deliver the news."

I started for the front door and then turned back around quickly.

"I mean it, Wilson. If I see those pictures turn up anywhere, I'm coming after you, and you'll never look at another photo again in your lifetime."

Wilson dropped his head and chuckled.

"OK, Pratt, and thanks for your help."

"Thank you."

When I walked out my front door, Gwen was screaming for me like a baby being ripped from its mother's arms.

How appropriate . . .

I jumped into the Lotus and drove down to the dock. The Lewes-Rehoboth Water Taxi had just docked, and Marty was preparing for his next trip.

"Yo! Marty! Give me a lift down to my parents?" I shouted as I ran down the dock.

Marty chuckled. "You're a genius, Pratt. That's a real mess down there. I've had to add it to my little tour spiel. 'Off the starboard side, we have the Pratt Canal House. If you look to the far end of the property, you'll see the paparazzi lined up, waiting to snap a photo of the infinitely handsome Thomas Pratt Junior as he flips them the bird!' "

Marty "digitally" demonstrated his commentary.

"You're too much, Marty!"

"Yeah, I crack me up. Get on board, and I'll take you down."

Dropping me on the dock at the far end of my parents' property, I got out and thanked Marty profusely. He refused to accept any payment, saying it was his way of thanking the "Boys in Blue" for helping him over the years with the occasional rowdy drunk. (Actually, our uniforms in Lewes are gray.)

I ran up the lawn and into the house as voices on the far side of the lawn started yelling and pointing in my direction. The media had spotted me, but it no longer mattered. Soon, when the arrests of Marco and Gwen became the next big breaking story, they would be moving on.

As soon as I told my mother that Gwen's arrest had been made and that my mother was no longer a suspect, she breathed a deep sigh of relief, hugged me, and cried.

"Praise God, I can breathe again. Tomorrow, I am working in the garden all day. I need to get outside. How long before this foolishness gets off our lawn?" she asked waving her hands and pointing toward the front of the house as if she could make it all disappear like magic.

Susan stood in the background. I slowly approached her.

"I am so sorry. I hope you can forgive me and we can start over," I said to the most genuine woman I had ever met.

"Yes, and yes, I think I would like that."

I held her, and in front of Zoe and my parents, we shared our first kiss.

"I think I would like more of that later when the paparazzi and my family disappear," I whispered.

"We're standing right here, Thomas!" my mother jeered with a smile on her face.

My mother and Janice begged Susan to stay for dinner, which she did. It was good to see my mother finally smile and eat. She was finally at peace.

CHAPTER FOURTEEN

SUSAN

Things did not quiet down as quickly as we had hoped. As soon as the story broke, many of the news vans parked on Gills Neck Road left and divided their presence between Franklin Avenue on one side of the Canal, and Bay Avenue on the other. Every officer, except for Pratt, was called into service and the State Police arrived to assist. The vacationers had gotten more than they had bargained for that week. Some loved that they were in the middle of an international news event, while most were very put-out.

Pratt decided that it would be best if Zoe and I stayed at the Canal House for one more night. Lori Caruso, a dispatcher from the Lewes Police Station, told Pratt that his house on Franklin Avenue had been surrounded and that he would be crazy to show up there any time soon. We called Dex and Ginny. They confirmed that they were holed up in the Carter beach house with Gilda while police were outside clearing the news teams and their vehicles off Bay Avenue and away from the beach in front of their house. The frenzy of reporters and their equipment had blocked traffic on the very narrow road, making it impossible for any other vehicle to pass. Dex was one of the first to call and complain, stating that if Mrs. Pollock had a medical emergency, the gridlock on Bay Avenue would make it impossible for anyone to get to her.

I told Ginny that Zoe and I would try to return home the following day.

Needless to say, everyone was relieved to hear that the Pratts were cleared of any connection or wrongdoing. Gwen was taken into custody at Tom Pratt's house, and

Marco was taken into custody at his home in Malvern, Pennsylvania.

After dinner that evening, Mrs. Pratt suggested that she watch Zoe, allowing Tom and me to have some privacy to sort out everything that had taken place in the last several weeks.

It was twilight when Pratt and I strolled out to the willow tree. His large, strong hand felt so good wrapped tightly around mine.

"Thank you for bringing us here, Pratt. I'm almost sorry that we have to leave tomorrow. Your parents have been so supportive, and Janice and Kirk have been so gracious and helpful."

"I'm not surprised you feel that way, those are some of the many reasons I wanted you here. I have been blessed with a spectacular family, that's for sure," Pratt said as he chewed on a long piece of grass."

"Speaking of family, I was interrogated in the library, you know."

"The library, eh?"

"Yes. And I noticed several family pictures. Well, I presumed that they were family pictures."

"Yes, they probably were."

Pratt shifted, anticipating where my commentary was headed.

"In several of them, there was a young girl. She looked a year or two older than you. I also noticed that she doesn't show up in any of the more recent photos. May I ask who she is?"

"I think you just did."

"Yes. I guess I did."

"Of course, you may ask. For one under such harsh interrogation, you were pretty observant of your surroundings."

"Believe me, I was terrified."

"Yes, well, the girl in the photos was my older sister, Rachel."

"Was?"

"Yes. She died of leukemia when she was nine."

"Oh, I'm so sorry. I didn't know."

"It's all right. It was a long time ago. We were away on a mission trip in Uganda when she started having what we thought were flu like symptoms. By the time my parents realized that antibiotics weren't helping and that she was only getting worse, they went crazy trying to arrange a way to get her out and back to the States, but it was too late. She was gone within hours of landing in Dulles. We never took another trip like that again. It wasn't long after that that my father bought his first Learjet and later, the helicopter. I think he never wanted to feel that trapped again. I'll never forget it. It took my mother years to start living again. She mourned and convalesced right here on this canal. One day, when I was nine, I invited her to come out under the willow with me. We just sat here for what seemed like hours and watched the water go by."

"You have no other sisters or brothers?"

"No. It was just Rachel and me. When I lost my big sister, I instantly became an only child, a very lonely, only child."

"I'm so sorry, Pratt," I said, rubbing his arm.

We stood in silence. Pratt placed his arm around my shoulder, as the sun dropped behind a grove of trees on the west side of the property.

"What was she like?"

"I was only seven when she died, so I don't have many memories of her, only what my parents tell me. They say she used to help get me ready for school in the morning. Then, she made sure no one picked on me at school. She was always there for me. That's what I remember most. Mom said we would ride our bikes up and down the drive all day long, which was one of several reasons why they installed the gate. I kind of remember that. We both took piano lessons together, too. I do remember arguing when we were forced to play duets."

"And you kept playing even after she died?"

"Especially after she died. It was a way for me to cope."

"I would love to hear you play again. Sometime soon?"

"I think that could be arranged."

A gust of wind caught the boughs of the weeping willow as he took me confidently into his arms and kissed me as I had not been kissed in years. The shushing of the willow filled the air as Pratt's lips touched mine. A torrent of emotion laced with thrill ran through the core of my body like an drug induced high and settled in a place that had not been energized by the touch of a man since the last time Derek and I had made love. My legs were weakening, causing me to tilt my head back. I was in need of oxygen to rescue every nerve cell in my body that was wantonly crying out for more.

Finally, I was able to give the love that had been bottled up within me for years. Pratt had opened the gates, and my need to share my desire for this man surged beyond anything my adult wisdom could contain.

I moaned as Pratt's lips found my neck, and I reacted to the explosive sensations he was sending down my spine. I wanted him to take my body and lay it down beneath the weeping willow and claim it for himself.

"Hmmm . . . your kisses are so soft and tender, just like you," Pratt whispered into my neck.

He put his hand behind my head and brought my eyes to his. There was a look of fierceness in his face, one that I wanted to ravish and send beyond the point of no return. He was bringing out the temptress in me, and she wanted to be set free.

"Come with me," Pratt directed.

"What? Where are we going?"

In the dark, Pratt took my hand and we crossed the lawn to the frame of an old stone barn that sat on the estate and had long since lost its roof. Once we had entered the structure, I could see that it was also missing its fourth side, leaving the interior open to the Canal. Inside the three walls was a beautiful swimming pool. Pratt walked over to a wall and flipped a switch. The water lit up a turquoise blue, sending silver-white ribbons of reflections off the walls of stone and into the night sky. A hot tub came alive on the far end. The space provided seclusion and romantic intrigue.

Pratt strolled over to a long granite bar and pulled out a bottle of wine from the cooler beneath it.

"As I remember, you enjoyed the unoaked chardonnay?"

"Yes, you remembered correctly."

Pratt uncorked the bottle and pulled down two glasses from the rack above his head. Before pouring the wine, he did the strangest thing. He stopped and stared at me.

"You are simply amazing. I never thought this night would come, and here you are."

Pratt went back to work, pouring two glasses. Then, handing one to me, he raised his.

"Here's to a simpler life for you and me. Nothing complicated. Just us and a little girl named Zoe."

"That sounds complicated to me."

"Only if we choose to make it complicated," Pratt reassured me.

"OK then, I'm in."

Pratt and I sat poolside and celebrated with wine and, finally, some casual conversation.

"So, Pratt, do you mind that everyone in the Carter circle calls you Pratt?"

"No, not at all. As a matter of fact, I kind of like it".

"So what's with all of your hot cars? First it was the black Corvette, now it's a red Lotus."

"It's a hobby. One of my two guilty pleasures."

"Oh? What's the second one?"

"That will have to wait for another time, my dear," he smirked and leaned back on his chair.

"By the way, where is the Lotus? I didn't see it parked out front, or anywhere, for that matter?"

"I left it at the marina with Marty. He's going to hold on to it for a few days. He wouldn't take payment for jockeying us around under the cover of his boat, so I gave him the keys to my car to look after for a few days."

"You are a strange one, Pratt. So now you're without wheels?"

"No, not really. I have a Jeep Rubicon over in the other barn at the other end of the drive," he said pointing off in the distance, in some general direction.

I vaguely remembered seeing a newer barn on the opposite end of the property.

"Why is it that everyone down here has a Jeep?"

"You are so full of questions, Ms. McCabe!"

Yes, when I was around Pratt, my curiosity did seem to surface and throw a party at his expense. I recalled how I thought I had lost him after an evening at his house, due to my out of control meddling into his private life.

"I'm sorry, Pratt. I don't know why I do that. I really don't mean to offend you. I just find you . . . intriguing."

"That's quite all right. I enjoy answering your questions. Some of them are a little surprising at times, but I like knowing that you care enough to ask."

"Surprising, huh?"

"Sometimes, yes."

"Then you have the right to ask me a surprising question. How's that? Fair enough?"

"Fair enough."

"So what's your one surprising question?" I asked, bracing myself as I tried to imagine something he would not already know about me and would take me by surprise.

"Care to take a swim?"

"That's your surprise question? Sadly, I don't have a swimsuit with me," I pouted.

Are you wearing decent underwear?"

"I think so."

"Good, how's that for a surprising question?"

PRATT

I felt young again, like a teenager. Being with Susan was like returning to my youth and having all the years consumed by the locusts returned to me for a glorious do-over.

I had not realized how trapped I had been since the day I had rescued Gwen from the Bay. Looking back, I was beginning to realize how harmful that relationship had been.

On somewhat of a dare or "surprise question," call it what you want, Susan agreed to go swimming with me. It was beautifully innocent in some ways, and very sensuous in others. Susan was very shy about it and went into the bathhouse to remove her outer layers. I, on the other hand, stood poolside, stripped off my shirt and shorts, kicked my sandals onto the pool deck, and dove in wearing my boxer briefs.

The water was cool and refreshing, free of the chains that had held me for so long. When I surfaced, it was like being baptized into a new life. I knew that I was about to drown again, but I would willingly jump out of my lifeboat to join Susan in whatever fate had in store for us.

Being extra careful not to expose anything, Susan emerged from the bathhouse with a towel wrapped around her body and whatever she had on underneath.

"I don't know that I can do this," she spoke hesitantly.

"Wait right there, I've got this."

Planting the palm of one hand on the pool deck, I shot up out of the water, landing on both of my feet. (OK, I was showing off!) I gallantly (and proudly) strolled over to the board and turned off the pool lights. The water turned dark, assuring her that once she was in, her beautiful body would be cloaked and safe from my new, rambunctious schoolboy stares. With a mighty cannonball, I jumped back into the water next to where Susan was standing, sending water everywhere. (Another schoolboy move that I had perfected!)

Susan appropriately screamed.

Resurfacing, I shook my head, sending more water in her direction. She jumped back, again.

"Now you have to get in!" I yelled up to her. "You're soaking wet!"

"Turn around!" she commanded. "I'm not taking this drenched towel off until you turn around."

I did as I was told, and then I heard Susan slice through the water.

Good girl!

"Ah! It's cold!" she squealed as soon as she resurfaced as far from me as she could.

Have you ever noticed how all girls always think the water is cold? It does not matter whether you are in the ocean or a heated pool; to them the water is always cold.

I swam over to her, and we naturally held on to each other as we treaded water together. A light kiss and my body reacted. I did not want to scare her away or have her think I was trying to take advantage of her half-nakedness, so I did my best not to brush up against her.

Like a playful tease, Susan pushed away from me and took off swimming toward the far end. I swam after her. She was fast, but I was faster. When she caught up to me, we hung on to the side of the pool to catch our breaths.

"Come join me in the hot tub. We can talk and drink our wine," I suggested as I once again hopped out of the water.

Turning around, I extended my arm to help her out. Susan had covered her eyes.

"I can't. You have to get into the hot tub first."

"OK."

I walked back to the opposite end, thinking how cute Susan's genuine shyness was. Grabbing our wine glasses from the table as I walked by, I stepped down into the swirling hot water.

"OK, I'm underwater. Come on out, Shy One."

"No. Not until you look away and cover your eyes."

I did as I was told. As I waited, everything got very quiet. It seemed like minutes had past.

"OK, you can open your eyes now," Susan whispered.

Just the sound of her calmed voice sent a shock wave through my body.

I slowly opened my eyes and reveled at her beautiful face sitting opposite me.

Susan and I talked about many things, but mostly we shared how happy we were that we had been able to wait out the dark days and finally relax together, in private. I made my move and slid across the tub to her. Placing my hands around her bare waist, I pulled her in. No longer did I care if she felt what the nearness of her was doing to me. Our lips slowly met. Hers were wet, and warm, and soft, and delicious. My hands moved down across her hips to pull her in tight as she naturally straddled my body.

Dear God, she's wearing a thong.

The cheeks of her buttocks were smooth and firm, and there was no denying that I wanted all of her. Her heavy sigh and labored breathing let me know that she was filled with the same passionate desire for me. Sitting face to face, she lowered her weight onto me and pressed in. I was losing control. I was losing the battle. As she began lowering my boxer briefs, I reached around to release her bra, except I could not find the hooks. Susan aptly freed me from one of the final barriers between us while I had given up on the hooks and moved to her shoulder straps.

"Wait . . ." she whispered.

Wait? How can you possibly ask me to wait, now?

Susan slid back from my lap. Her hands came to the surface of the water and released the front closure of her bra. She pulled the cups apart, and the straps fell from her shoulders. Then she pushed her bra off and allowed it float away in the water while her breasts bobbed just below the water's turbulent surface.

Oh, my God . . .

"Whoa! Whoa!" I yelled and jumped across her body, knocking her completely off my lap and into the water. I snatched up her bra.

"What are you doing?" Susan laughed as she came back up out of the water.

"Saving it before it gets caught around the filter," I explained, throwing her bra over the side of the hot tub and onto the pool deck.

"Come here."

I grabbed her arm, pulled her across the swirling water and positioned her in front of me, again. I kissed her lips while I caressed and massaged her newly exposed skin with one hand. I laced the fingers of my free hand through her thong and lowered it over her thighs, down her legs, and slipped it off her toes, also throwing it onto the pool deck.

I pulled her in to me. There was no hiding my intention. I asked her permission to continue.

"Susan, are you OK with this?"

"Yes. Yes. A thousand times, yes!"

"I want to make love to you. Now."

"Are you asking me?" she pushed herself down farther.

"Yes," I growled, desperately trying to wait for her spoken answer.

"Yes . . . " she sucked in her breath as she lowered herself on to me, and I entered in.

I slept on the third floor that night. Susan and Zoe were occupying my quarters on the second floor. I would like to tell you that I drifted off to sleep in a state of complete peace, but that is not what happened. I was at peace knowing that we were finally able to restore and continue our relationship. I was very happy knowing that Zoe and Susan were safe under our roof. However, sleep evaded me. It was all too good to be true.

CHAPTER FIFTEEN

SUSAN

Zoe woke up at 7:00 AM.

"Momma! Momma!"

How I loved the sound of her sweet voice. I sneaked into the sitting room where she was bouncing up and down in the crib.

"Good morning, Baby Girl! Did you have a good sleep?"

I always asked her the same question every morning. Zoe continued jumping.

"Gee-a! Gee-a!" she proclaimed, slapping her hands on the top rail.

She was asking for Gilda, her best friend in the whole world, followed closely by her Uncle Dex.

"Soon, Zoe. We'll see Gilda soon."

Dressing Zoe was always an adventure. That morning, I dressed my little wiggle-worm in a yellow sundress with matching sunflower sandals. The ensemble was a one-year birthday present from Mrs. Pollock.

Working on a few hours of sleep, dressing myself was even more of a challenge. My hair was still damp from the night before, and my body was begging me to go back to bed. No such luck.

Zoe and I slowly made our way down to the kitchen where Janice was already at work brewing a pot of coffee and mixing a batch of pancake batter.

Hmmm . . .

The aroma of just fried crispy bacon hung boldly in the air. Janice was spoiling us just as Ginny so often does for Dex, Zoe, and me.

Mornings don't come much better than this!

"Good Morning!" Janice greeted us, scooping up Zoe and plopping her down on the countertop. "Let me see those shoes. Ooooo, they're beautiful!"

Zoe appropriately laughed and clapped. Janice gave her a big hug.

"I'm going to miss you two when you leave here."

"I'm going to miss you and Kirk, too," I confessed to Janice and admitted to myself.

"Well then, don't be a stranger. Come back whenever you want."

"We just might do that."

Janice put Zoe back down on her two little feet.

"Would you like some pancakes, eggs, and bacon?"

"Maybe we should wait for Pra ... uh, Tom."

"Oh no, you don't want to do that. You'll miss dinner before he gets out of bed!"

We both laughed. I would have to take her word for it.

"I think not!" a strong comforting voice came from the hallway. In strolled the very rugged looking Tom Pratt. My heart skipped a beat as my empty stomach did a somersault. It was a rush to see him so soon after our nighttime romp. He looked different to me now. I knew every inch of him, and he knew me. I had permission to touch him, and flirt with him, and tell him how much I loved him. He had asked permission, the previous night, and had granted the same to me. I recalled his words as he made love to me.

"Susan, I have waited so long for you, for us. I am so glad you are here, ... and I will always be here for you. It's that simple. I am yours."

Pratt's hair was a mess and he was still wearing what I presumed he had worn to bed the night before: pajama pants and a stretched out T-shirt. He sauntered over to me, or so I thought. He breezed right past me, picked up Zoe, swung her around, and gave her a kiss on the cheek. Living with her Uncle Dex, it was a morning ritual Zoe was all too familiar with and half expected.

How did he know to do that?

"Good morning, Beautiful!" Pratt greeted my daughter as he held her up in the air with his arms outstretched, her forehead above his, and her feet dangling toward the ground.

Zoe stuck her fingers in her mouth, smiled back at Pratt, and giggled. Pratt lowered her onto his hip and finally acknowledged me, as I would later tease.

"I see you survived the night, Ms. McCabe."

"Yes, thank you. I had a wonderful time," I blushed. "And you?"

"Yes. The evening's company was superb! So, what's on everyone's agenda today?" Pratt asked as he popped a slice of bacon into his delicious mouth, the same mouth I had surrendered to the night before.

"Sadly, I think Zoe and I should pack up and head for home. After breakfast, I'll see if Dex or Ginny can swing by with the Explorer to pick us up."

"Already taken care of. Kirk is out picking up a car seat for the Rubicon, and then I'll take you back to the beach house. It's my way of insuring you two get home safely."

"Safely?"

"Yes. First, we'll call Dex and Ginny to make sure everything has cleared out over there. Then, I'll call Lori in Dispatch to confirm that everything has quieted down around town."

I thought Pratt was being a little overprotective, but if it would put his mind at ease, I was OK with it. I wanted him to care that much.

We had a wonderful breakfast. Mr. and Mrs. Pratt were able to join us. Kirk had returned in time with the car seat; so he and Janice sat down to eat with us, too. Zoe LOVED Janice's Mickey Mouse pancakes. By the time breakfast was over, she had become quite the sticky mess. Janice could not have been happier. Mrs. Pratt, who seated herself on the other side of Zoe, seemed to enjoy Zoe's little antics and did not mind her syrupy fingers. Indeed, Janice and Mrs. Pratt were going to miss having Zoe around.

I looked at Pratt and silently wondered how any of this was going to remain simple? Pratt put a forkful of pancakes in his mouth and smiled back at me. He seemed to be so happy and content.

PRATT

Regrettably, it was time to take Susan and Zoe back to the Carter beach house. It was a short, quiet ride over the canal drawbridge and down to the Bay. In the warm Jeep, Zoe instantly fell into a deep sleep like a little person with narcolepsy. Susan commented that Zoe must have been tuckered out from all of the excitement. She also said that it would take weeks of retraining to correct all of the damage done by the over indulgence of my mother and Janice, and for that reason, she was never bringing Zoe back to the Pratt Canal House, again. It was an empty sarcastic threat full of complimentary wit and gratitude.

The landscape of the area was turning back to normal. Instead of oversized vans that were top heavy with their weighty towers and wrapped with network news identification call letters, the roads were once more filled with vans full of children, SUVs with beach tags, and trucks pulling boats on trailers. Things had calmed down considerably. The only thing the circus had left behind were the ruts alongside the roadways where the frenzied news hounds had parked their heavy vehicles. The few remaining ruts would serve to remind me of the dangerous rut I had been in for nearly a decade. Looking back, I could now see how clearly blinded I had been.

I looked over at Susan. She had her elbow propped up on the armrest and her chin rested in her hand. She was gazing out the window as the scenery floated by, the same scenery she had seen a million times before. I wondered if, like me, she was seeing it again for the first time. Perhaps she and I had more in common than I had calculated. I wanted our adventure not only to continue, but also to last. However, even though Gwen was behind bars and on her way to a federal prison, I feared that I had not seen or heard the last of her. I had never been that fortunate.

When we pulled up to 408 Bay Avenue, we could hear Gilda barking inside, announcing the strange vehicle that had parked on their lot. Ginny and Dex came downstairs to greet us, and Gilda bolted out the door as soon as they had opened it. When I hopped out and hit the ground on both feet, Gilda stopped, cocked her head, and looked quizzically at the Rubicon and then me. Susan was a little slower getting out, but as soon as her door opened, Gilda bounded over to her and started whining and dancing on all fours with her tail wagging like it was going to take off, or fall off. She knew Zoe was in the back seat. Zoe, sound asleep, missed all of the excited adoration of her best buddy. Susan unbuckled Zoe and hoisted her onto her shoulder and carried her into the house. Ginny and Dex invited me to stay for coffee. I was happy to accept their invitation. It always felt like home to be in their company. I hoped to be spending more time with Susan's "family."

"How are you doing? How are your parents?" Ginny asked as she poured coffee into four large mugs. I answered her as she reached into the fridge for milk and then refilled the sugar bowl.

"They are very relieved to say the very least. How are you guys holding up?"

"We survived. They weren't here as long as they were at your parents' place, but my God, they pushed the envelope! I started getting worried when they tried to set up on the beach. Please thank your co-workers for keeping them back."

"I'll do that. I'm sure life was very different for them, too!"

Ginny paused before handing me a mug of coffee.

"I'm really sorry about Gwen," Ginny politely apologized.

She sounded sincere.

"It's all right." I fiddled with the handle of the coffee mug as I pondered the correct way to express how I felt.

"It's very strange and downright debilitating when you think you really know someone, and then you find out they are not at all who you thought they were," I pondered out loud.

Susan emerged from the second floor and overheard my brief sentiments.

"I know exactly how you feel," she empathized, placing her hand on my shoulder as she passed by.

We do have a lot in common.

My cell phone rang as Susan reached across me to get to her coffee, and I placed a quick kiss on her cheek, all to Ginny and Dex's great surprise. I checked caller I.D. and knew that it was not good.

"I need to take this call. Will you excuse me?"

I kissed Susan one more time, this time on her soft lips, before I walked out onto the deck.

"We need you to come out here. Now. We believe she knows where we can find Koppelman and the child, but she says she'll only talk to you."

It was Wilson.

"Then put her on the phone," I responded, stating the obvious.

"In person. She says she'll talk if she sees you in person."

"You do realize that I'm at least four hours away?"

"We have a chopper on its way. They will pick you up at the Beebe Hospital Heliport. Be there in ten minutes."

I resented the way they thought they could dictate my schedule, my life, which I had hoped I could finally restart.

"And what if I don't want to see her?"

"We know you do because you want the child found and Koppelman locked up as much as we do," Wilson retorted, also stating the obvious.

He was right. Wilson knew I would go through fire to rescue the child, and I would be the first to strangle Koppelman, if given the opportunity.

"Alright. I'll meet the chopper. Can I assume you'll fly me back to Lewes when the meeting is over?"

"Yes, we'll get you back in time for dinner," Wilson joked.

"I'm really beginning to dislike you guys."

SUSAN

I was stunned. Just when I thought Gwen could never interfere again, Pratt had to leave to go visit with her.

Will I ever get a break from that woman? Or will she always be a part of Pratt's life? There is no way I want to spend the rest of my life with her dark shadow hanging over me.

"Who was that?" Ginny was first to ask.

"That was Agent Wilson with the FBI. They believe Gwen knows the whereabouts of Cal Koppelman, Corelli's fellow conspirator. They also have reason to believe that Koppelman has custody of the second child smuggled into the U.S. Apparently, Gwen's not cooperating. She says she'll only talk to me, so they want me to fly out to Cumberland, Maryland to meet with her."

I hated the thought of Pratt flying out there to spend even one more second of his time with her. It hurt to know that they would be in the same room together. I did not want him to look into her eyes, or care to ask how she was doing. I selfishly did not want them to have that "I wish things had turned out differently" conversation, the one I never had with Derek. I did not want her to try to walk him down the "Memory Lane of Happier Times."

However, none of it was about me. If Pratt was the key to finding the missing child, then he had no choice, no matter the cost. I just did not know if I could take much more of the roller coaster I was doomed to ride if I stayed with him.

As he sat his half-emptied mug in the sink, Pratt asked me to walk him out to his Jeep. I followed him down the stairs and out the door. Standing beside his vehicle, he took my hand in his.

"Susan, I'll be back in a couple of hours. I'll stop by here as soon as I get back. Are you OK with that?"

"Oh, Pratt," I sighed, "I don't want to sound like a big baby, but this whole Gwen thing is a real struggle for me. I feel like I am willingly allowing her to control me. It brings out the worst in me."

Leaning his back against his Jeep, Pratt dropped his head. He shifted his weight as he gave his response careful thought. He slowly raised his troubled face and looked into my eyes. His were dark, and deep regret peered out from within.

"I can't change the past, Susan, and neither can you. Either we learn to live with the choices we've made and the hands we've been dealt, or we quit, live a life of repressed frustration, and fight a battle we can't possibly win. I can't run from my past, and I certainly cannot run from a little girl who needs to be rescued. Neither of us could do that.

But, I also know I can't walk away from you. I will chase after you until you tell me I have to stop."

I brushed my hand across his late morning stubble. He intercepted my gesture and kissed my open palm.

"Susan, I can't make promises about how things are going to be. But I can tell you that my hope is that as soon as the child is recovered and Koppelman is taken into custody, we'll never have to spend another moment of time discussing or dwelling on what has been."

"When you run for office, Pratt, and live in the public eye, this will all be dredged up, over and over again. It won't ever stop, will it?"

"I don't have that answer," Pratt responded honestly. "For now, will you be here when I get back?"

"Well, I kind of live here!" I snickered.

"Oh, how I need to hear your laugh, and how I have waited all day to kiss your beautiful smile."

Pratt took both of my hands and wrapped them around his waist. He then drew me in, lifted my chin, and softly placed his warm, pleading lips on mine. As I responded, his low moan let me know that he would rather stay with me than be anywhere else.

"I have to go."

Pratt lightly touched my lips, again. "I'll be back for more of this!"

I watched as his Jeep pulled away.

The roller coaster left the station, and I was helpless to stop the ride and get off.

CHAPTER SIXTEEN

GINNY

The only time I had ever heard a siren on Bay Avenue was the night the old Carter beach house burnt to the ground. Usually, if a siren came across the drawbridge, it was to arrest a speeder or make a rescue at the public beach. However, not only did the siren come up Bay Avenue, it went past our house and stopped shortly thereafter.

Susan was running up the stairs as Dex and I were racing down.

"Ginny, Dex, the ambulance, it stopped at Mrs. Pollock's!"

Susan stayed in the house with sleeping Zoe while Dex and I ran up Bay Avenue. When we entered Mrs. Pollock's house, the customary aroma of fresh baked cookies was first to invade our senses. The result was an immediate calming effect. For a split second, I even thought I saw her standing at the counter, wearing her apron and donning a soft matronly smile. I was rattled back to conscious reality by the sound of unfamiliar voices coming from somewhere inside her house. Sadly, it occurred to me that before that day, I had never heard other voices, other than our own, in her house. Walking through the kitchen and past the dining room, we found the EMTs in the parlor. One was kneeling over her lifeless body performing CPR while the another was on a cell phone talking to someone I assumed was back at the hospital.

"Oh, dear God, with all of the commotion, we did not get out to visit with her today," I cried into Dex's broad shoulder.

Dex kept his arms wrapped around me and rubbed my back nervously as we watched and waited.

"It's OK, Ginny. She's going to be OK," he said, trying to convince the both of us.

"You don't know that! We should have been here."

Dex didn't know anything. He was wrong. She was not OK. Mrs. Pollock had suffered a massive stroke. We never had the chance to say goodbye. She was gone.

GWEN

Tom was escorted into the room. I was warned that a guard would be positioned outside. I knew there had to be hidden surveillance cameras, taping and recording everything I said and did. As soon as the door closed, I wanted to rush Tom and die a thousand deaths in his strong arms. But then again, *he* was the one that had set me up. I was arrested in *his* house. *He* had left me there, screaming.

We sat at opposite sides of the table, exactly where the chairs had been placed. Tom, always the gentleman whether I was dressed up in an evening gown or down in a prison jumpsuit, pulled out a chair for me and seated me before he circled the table and sat himself down.

"Gwen, where's Koppelman and the child?"

He was so cold. Distant. So matter of fact.

"Tom, I never meant for this to happen."

"Of course, you didn't. No one plans on getting caught."

"I didn't know that what we were doing was so wrong. At least, not at first."

"Come on, Gwen. How could you not know that kidnapping and selling children is a serious offense? Who do you think you're talking to? You brought me all this way to what, to try to justify some lame excuse with an insult of an explanation?"

Tom was angry. I knew he was hurt, too. I had hurt him.

"I thought that what we were doing was right. I thought we were bringing children to the States for medical treatment. I really thought we were working on behalf of Healing Wings."

"At some point you must have recognized that those children were not accompanied by parents or family members. You must have realized that they never returned home."

"Yes, I eventually learned that they were being given away for adoption, but they were being given a second chance, a better life here in the U.S."

"Given away? They were sold for profit! This is bullshit, Gwen!"

Tom nearly jumped across the table as he slammed his hands down and rose up out of his chair. For the first time, I thought he might actually strike me out of anger, but he didn't. He regained control of himself, and calmly sat back down before continuing.

"You believed what you wanted to believe. Koppelman was feeding you lies, bold-faced lies, and you should have been smart enough to see through them. But, you chose to stay with it. And do you know what the best part is? I no longer care. So, you decide, Gwen. If you want some leniency, then tell me where to find Koppelman and the child. Otherwise, I don't plan on wasting another moment of my time in the same room with you."

"She was for us," I whispered. I started crying. It was all too much. "She was brought here for us."

That time, Tom did reach across the table, and he grabbed my arm.

"Don't ever say that again. Do you understand? I never had anything to do with this. You did this."

He released my arm the way one throws away a bad card.

"I did it for us. It was my last arranged flight. This one was for me, for us."

"Shut up, Gwen. Do not pull me into your mess. Now, where's Koppelman and the child?"

In all our days, Tom had never once said "shut up" to me. We were in new territory, and I did not recognize the man across the table from me. I no longer held any sway over him. I wanted to howl. I wanted to wail as if I had just experienced the greatest loss of my life. Indeed, I had. In fact, I had gambled away life itself.

"It's Susan, isn't it?"

"For once, Gwen, accept responsibility for your own actions and realize that you checked out of what we had a long time ago."

"I made a few mistakes, Tom."

"A few mistakes? I will grant that you made plenty of mistakes concerning us, but when you take innocent children from their families, it's no longer a mistake. It's intentional, and it's evil. I cannot think of a worse crime. If you want any help whatsoever, then give up Koppelman's whereabouts, right now.

Tom was void of any sympathy for me. The soft spot in his heart that only I possessed had finally frozen over and had grown inflexible, like a deep scar. He was so strong in his own right that he no longer needed armor or any defense against me. Tom was on the offensive, and I would only find mercy in the truth.

I told Tom about a private island off the coast of Maine that Cal and I used as a "remote office." Cal was willing to pay the price for our seclusion and privacy. I allowed Tom's imagination to run with the suggestion of what had actually taken place on my many business trips with Cal. There was no need for me to go into any further detail. I waited for the excruciating pain of trying to manage inner rage to appear on Tom's face, or show in the clenching of his fists, but his countenance and body language never wavered. His jealousy for me had expired. He had conquered me. His battle won; the war was over.

"I believe he is holding the baby girl there until he finds a new placement and assurance that he can make the transfer without being discovered. If her delivery has already taken place, you can believe that he is long gone."

After Tom left, I cried uncontrollably. That little girl was supposed to be mine. She was going to be *ours*. Never had I wanted anything so badly.

DEX

Ginny and I followed the ambulance to the hospital. In the car, she questioned every visit we had made in the past several weeks. Was there anything we had missed? Were there any warning signs that we should have detected? Was she having symptoms that she deliberately kept hidden from us?

Mrs. Pollock was like that. She rarely, as in never, complained. She was always more concerned about others, especially our little household.

When the doctors confirmed what we already knew, Ginny broke down. She was inconsolable as I gathered her into my arms and held her head against my chest. She was distraught that Mrs. Pollock had died alone. The EMTs surmised that Mrs. Pollock had miraculously called 911 and then sat down in her chair. It appeared that she had not suffered long. Mercifully, it had to have been very quick. Mrs. Pollock was gone before the EMTs had arrived.

Back at the beach house, we found Susan in the den on the second floor, and in solemn, sacred whispers, we gave her the news. Susan was not surprised. She said she had had a bad feeling when the ambulance went by.

Susan and Ginny stayed in the den. I returned to Mrs. Pollock's house to clean up.

Mrs. Pollock always looked forward to my visits. She would bake my favorite cookies or pies, and if one of the girls came instead of me, she would box up her decadent desserts and send them down to me. Gilda loved visiting, too, because Mrs. Pollock always had a dog treat in the pocket of her apron for her. The night of the Carter beach house fire, Mrs. Pollock had miraculously made her way out to the beach to help Ginny, Gilda, and me. She provided warm, dry blankets and the use of her car in order to get Gilda to the Savannah Animal Hospital. She even made the call to make sure a doctor would be waiting for us when we arrived. She had given her husband's tools to me and allowed me to use his workspace. Sometimes she would watch from her kitchen window with a reminiscent grin on her face as I tinkered in the garage. In the week before her death, Mrs. Pollock had allowed us to use her car to get around unnoticed by the news media, and I got to chauffeur her around town for two days. What a treat that was! She always did her grocery shopping at Lloyds, an independent grocer who had been in town for decades. She was on a first name basis with every employee and vendor in the store.

We were going to miss her sage advice, welcoming smile, and warm treats. We were better people for having known her.

When I had finished removing her chair and cleaning the carpet, I came across several dirty dishes in the sink. I rinsed them off and threw them into the dishwasher. Though it was practically empty, it occurred to me that she was not returning to run it. So I added the liquid that she used and turned it on. I went upstairs to see if there were any unfinished chores that needed to be done. I threw her laundry into the washing machine and decided that I would stop back that night to switch everything over to the dryer.

I am doing laundry for someone who will never wear these clothes again. Ironically, it feels like the honorable thing to do. I don't think Mrs. Pollock would want a stranger to handle her dirty laundry.

I emptied all the trash, locked the doors, and walked home. I was not empty-handed, though. Her last batch of chocolate chip Toll House cookies were boxed up and left on the counter as if she had known. With tears in my eyes, I carried them home.

I never ate the cookies. I could not bring myself to "destroy" one of my favorite memories of her. In fact, to this day, I don't know what happened to them. I never asked, because I don't want to know.

Later that evening, I returned to put her laundry in the dryer and empty her dishwasher. When those chores were done, I was not ready to leave. I wanted to "stay with her" a while longer. I went into her parlor and poured a small amount of brandy into a snifter that Mrs. Pollock kept hidden in a sideboard. I made my way out to her deck, sat in a chair beneath the stars, and pondered her journey. Mrs. Pollock was finally reunited with her husband, a man I wished I had met. She had said many times that I reminded her of the young Mr. Pollock. Every once in a while, she would drift off to a different place and remark how excited she would be the day of their reunion, so I knew she was happy, I could feel it in the night air. I knew in my heart of hearts that she was dancing somewhere across the stars and planets. I knew she was OK and that she would want those of us left behind to carry on and to be happy for her. Her waiting was over. I grinned as I recalled the vision of her kind, angelic smile.

I stayed and thought about some of our more memorable conversations: the numerous times she shook a finger at me like I was an errant child, or the times she encouraged me to follow my heart and to do what was right. I knew I would reflect back on her words in times of trouble.

My brandy snifter emptied, I slapped my knees, stood up, looked heavenward, and said one last goodbye. I rolled back the awning on her deck. No longer would we sit in the shade with her and discuss the things that really mattered.

Good night, Mrs. Pollock. I love you.

SUSAN

Ginny and I were working on dinner when the intercom buzzed.

"It's got to be Pratt," I said under my breath.

"I'm surprised Dex locked the door on his way out. How funny is that?" Ginny laughed.

I was glad to see her sadness dissipating.

I grabbed Gilda's collar and spoke into the intercom.

"Say 'Hi' to Gilda so she doesn't bark when you open the door.

"Really?" Pratt laughed.

"Yes. It's something we've been working on so she doesn't wake Zoe. We have a lot of strange visitors here, you know."

I was being sarcastic. Other than the mailman, the UPS man, and Ginny's students, rarely did anyone come just to visit.

"OK. Hi, Gilda!"

Gilda sat and I buzzed Pratt in.

It was good to hear his footsteps coming up the stairs. I was beginning to recognize the rhythm of his gait.

"Hey! It worked! I'm so glad to see you!" Pratt grinned.

Gilda's tail was wagging wildly as she waited for Pratt to pat her head. I proudly rewarded her with a dog treat. I recalled Mrs. Pollock's apron pockets and sighed heavily.

"Oh, Pratt, I am so glad you're here!"

"Why wouldn't I be here? I said I would stop in as soon as I got back."

He was rightfully confused.

As Pratt held me, everything I had been holding in, from his visiting Gwen to Mrs. Pollock's sudden death, came pouring out as I tried desperately to restrain my tears and runny nose. I was part overjoyed to see him return and part sad at the loss of a great woman.

"Mrs. Pollock died of a massive stroke, today," Ginny explained.

"Oh, I'm so sorry. On my way out, I saw the ambulance cross the drawbridge and continue down Savannah. I had no idea."

I felt his arms tighten around me as he kissed the top of my head.

"What can I do to help?" Pratt offered.

Even though he had been going nonstop all day, Pratt sincerely wanted to do something.

"Dex is up there now, cleaning and closing up the house. He should be back soon. I'm not sure there is much more we can do today," Ginny answered.

Pratt's cell rang. He held me with one arm and took his cell phone from his pocket with his other hand.

"I am so sorry, but I need to take this call."

He held on to me as he spoke. Still leaning against his chest, I could hear both parties.

"Wilson?"

"It's over Pratt. They've got Koppelman and the child."

Pratt took a deep breath and exhaled.

"Thank God. How is the girl?

"I've been told that she's going to be OK."

"Will you be able to locate the family?"

"Now that we have her, we'll be able to work with the Bolivian authorities to have her returned home. Good work, Pratt. We could use more guys like you on our team.

It's been a pleasure working with you. Take care of yourself and that new girlfriend of yours."

"What?"

"We don't miss much, Pratt. We had to watch you, too. Personally, I had no doubts, but it's what we have to do. By the way, the pictures are safe. As soon as the trial is over, we'll destroy the hard drive."

I gasped.

CHAPTER SEVENTEEN

GINNY

Mrs. Pollock's attorney called a meeting for all those mentioned in her Last Will and Testament. We met at Courtney and Dylan's and then caravanned over to Georgetown.

Mrs. Pollock's attorney was a kindly older gentleman whom Courtney knew well. They shared a few professional pleasantries before we were seated in the conference room to get down to business.

The first item: Mrs. Pollock named Poindexter Thurman Lassiter as the Executor of her Will.

"I assume that's you, Dex?"

"Yes, sir."

Dex sat up straight as he answered.

Mrs. Pollock knew Dex's real name?

Fortunately, Mrs. Pollock wrote down exactly how she wanted everything to be handled. It was Dex's job to carry it through to completion. Mrs. Pollock requested that she be cremated and her ashes were to be spread in the Bay as she had done with her husband's.

"You all know that her request is illegal, right?" her attorney winked.

"Yes, we understand."

"Mrs. Pollock had a life insurance policy that named Poindexter Thurman Lassiter as the beneficiary. More recently, she set up a trust for Zoe Virginia McCabe. Susan, I understand that Zoe is your daughter?"

"Yes."

"Very good. You are the trustee of the fund until Zoe reaches twenty-five years of age, and then it will be turned over to her."

Boy, that sounds familiar . . .

"Thank you," Susan whispered.

"Mrs. Pollock has asked that Dex take inventory of her belongings and distribute them to whomever he would like, as he sees fit. Once that task is completed, he may auction or donate whatever is remaining. All proceeds of the sale are to go to the Sable-Carter Women's Shelter."

"That is so generous of her," Courtney commented.

"Oh, just you wait," the attorney paused. "There's more. Mrs. Pollock owned her home free and clear of any liens, and upon her death, she has stipulated that it is to be sold and all proceeds of the sale are to go to into an endowment for the Sable-Carter Women's Shelter."

Courtney's mouth fell open. She had no idea. Tears of great gratitude formed in her eyes. She understood the value of the Pollock property, and Mrs. Pollock understood the value of Courtney's cause. Unbeknownst to us, Mrs. Pollock had been married once before and was beaten senseless several times by her first husband. Mr. Pollock was her rescuer. The room fell silent upon hearing the revelation in a letter she had left for us and read aloud by her attorney.

"I would have killed the bastard," Dex whispered enraged by the thought.

DEX

Ginny and I had spent the prior day scrubbing down and polishing up the Right Tackle. We wanted everything to be perfect for the event. The weather did its part, too.

The morning of Mrs. Pollock's burial at sea, Ginny had dressed in a whimsical dress, sandals, and wore a sun hat with flowers. Susan wore a long sundress. Like Ginny, she also brought a floppy sun hat. Zoe wore a little dress with a big sunflower on the front of its bib and matching sandals. It was a gift from Mrs. Pollock.

Pratt met us at the beach house and drove Susan and Zoe over to the boat. Susan mentioned that she believed a car seat had taken up permanent residence in his Rubicon.

Courtney and Dylan met us at the dock. Courtney brought bouquets for all the ladies, including a small one for Zoe, and boutonnieres for the gentlemen. Courtney wore a short sundress and a floppy sunhat. It was obvious that the girls had had the "what to wear" conversation. Dylan, Pratt, and I were wearing tropical shirts and shorts as dictated by the women in our lives. It was sadly obvious that they felt they had to tell us how to dress, as well.

Gilda was also onboard for the trip with us. Ginny had purchased a new pink collar for Gilda with tiny green palm trees embroidered into it.

Charles was onboard the "Morning Starr" as we all gathered on the decks of the Right Tackle. When he saw us, he started laughing.

"You all look like you're off to a Jimmy Buffett concert!" he joked, or not. "Do you want me to take your picture?"

To this day, that photo is one of my favorites.

As we slowly cruised past the outside deck of Irish Eyes, diners and patrons at the bar clapped and cheered for us, raising their drinks high in the air as if they were saluting Mrs. Pollock. As we made our way out Roosevelt Inlet, those fishing from the rocky bulkhead waved and whistled. Mrs. Pollock would have been thrilled.

Rather than ride on the fly bridge with me, as she normally would have, Ginny sat in the cockpit, tightly clutching the oak box that contained Mrs. Pollock's ashes. Mrs. Pollock specified that she did not want an urn and nothing ornamental, just a plain box. It was beautifully her.

The Bay was relatively calm. Once we crossed the breakwater, I opened up the Right Tackle and let her fly out to the shipping lanes half way between Lewes and Cape May. I wanted to give Mrs. Pollock one last ride. When we reached our destination, I cut the engines, threw out a sea anchor, and let the Right Tackle drift. We made sure there were no other witnesses before we started the ceremony.

Standing in the cockpit, we each shared our favorite Mrs. Pollock memory and said our farewells. Dylan offered a beautiful prayer. Pratt led us in singing several verses of "Amazing Grace." Then, Ginny carefully opened the wooden box and broke the seal on the plastic that contained her ashes. She handed me the box.

Standing at the stern I held the box over the water.

"According to the wishes of a great lady, I now commit her ashes to the Bay that she loved. May she find peace at sea and joy in her reunion with her loving husband. Until we meet again . . . "

Making sure the light breeze was blowing off the stern, I carefully turned the box over. We watched as her ashes floated down to the water's surface and slowly vanish from sight. Susan, Courtney, and Ginny threw their bouquets into the water. Gilda barked because we would not allow her to retrieve them! Zoe wanted to hold on to her flowers, which we allowed, knowing that Mrs. Pollock would have wanted it that way.

We sat adrift for another half hour, realizing that once we went ashore, we were landing in a world without her.

I never had to list Mrs. Pollock's house. It sold within days to an anonymous buyer who accepted it in "as is" condition. The home inspection was waived. The proceeds of $2.6 million went into an endowment as stipulated by Mrs. Pollock's Last Will and Testament. Courtney immediately named another wing for the Pollocks. I had made quick work of distributing several items from her home. An auction house removed all of her other belongings and furnishings. I intended to hire a cleaning company; however, the new owner said that it was not a necessary expense.

GINNY

Of all the things that Mrs. Pollock had left in her Will, perhaps the most treasured was a personal letter she wrote to Dex, a letter that he has cherished more than anything ever put to pen and paper.

Dear Dex,

I hope you do not mind that I have often thought of you as my own son. While Mr. Pollock and I never had children of our own, you have been kinder and more caring than most natural-born children could have ever been. Because of you, I never felt alone, forgotten, or afraid. For this, I am most grateful. Because of you, I was able to live out my days in my home. I can never explain to you how much that has meant to me. One day, you will understand.

There is a very special place in Heaven for men such as you. I know that when you arrive, Mr. Pollock will thank you for looking after his bride. It was as if God, Himself, sent you to me.

For now, I pray that you will live your life to the fullest! Enjoy all the rich treasures in store for you. Allow troubled times to make you stronger, and don't forget to celebrate the love that surrounds you every day.

I love you, my dearest son,
Mrs. Marjory Pollock

CHAPTER EIGHTEEN

DYLAN

Things had finally settled down in Slower Lower Delaware, and with the weather cooperating through the winter months, we were able to focus on the construction of the Sable-Carter Women's Shelter. Once the foundation was poured and the walls went up, Courtney went to work on recruiting administrators and staff. With Dex managing the construction, the shelter was completed and the Certificate of Occupancy was in hand two weeks ahead of schedule.

The fifty-three acre site allowed for a large footprint, and Courtney decided to exploit it and build something spectacular for its future occupants. It was set back from the road for privacy. The main entrance and common areas were under the roof of what looked like a large plantation house with a wrap around porch on all three floors, the bottom floor being screened in. The third floor housed four administrative apartments. The second floor housed the offices and several conference rooms that could be opened up for multi-purpose use. Downstairs was the entrance, grand hall, kitchen, and dining facilities. Connected to the main building were four wings of private units. Each family would have its own private quarters: living room, two to three bedrooms, and a bath. All meals were to be taken in the main dining area, including snacks, which were provided 24/7. Courtney wanted to ensure a sense of community among the residents and believed nothing would accomplish that more than communal dining and chores. She even said it was biblical. Go figure. She never ceased to surprise me.

Behind the main building was a large gymnasium, the size of two basketball courts. Connected to the gymnasium were a low-impact workout room and a daycare facility for infants through pre-school ages. Before- and after-school care was also provided for kindergarten through the twelfth grade.

To be a resident at the facility, one had to volunteer their time for the good of the facility and other members of the community. They would be added to a schedule of chores, including kitchen and cleaning duties. Daycare was provided on site 24/7 so the women had no excuse for not actively pursuing a job and/or further education. It goes without saying that drugs and alcohol were strictly forbidden.

Once the main building and offices were completed, Courtney worked like a crazy person to fully staff the facility. She eventually had to hire a recruiting service. Susan and Ginny donated their time to shop and haggle, acquiring the best furnishings at the best prices for the shelter's offices and future residences. Many local retailers worked with their corporate headquarters to provide deep discounts and donations. For Ginny and Susan, it was a labor of love. The end result was a beautiful décor inside the facility and a network of new friends on the outside.

"Big sacrifice you two are making," I would often tease them. "And I should turn you in for corrupting the morals of a minor," I would add, because Zoe always happily tagged along during their shopping excursions.

The girls also tapped the talents of local artists, of which there were many, for the wall hangings and other items needed to fill empty spaces. They put out the word that they were looking for pieces that would provide inspiration and hope. All different kinds of medium were donated, including several large pieces of pottery, sculptures, and quilts.

Though it was very old, we saved the Kranich & Bach upright piano from Mrs. Pollock's house and moved it into one of the community rooms. A piano store out on Route 1 also donated a reconditioned Yamaha grand piano, which went into the main hall.

With the help of a group of volunteer students from the Delaware Technical Community College, who graciously dedicated their weekends, we designed and built a playground area comprised of elaborate tunnels and bridges leading to swings, climbing nets, and monkey bars.

Courtney was overwhelmed by the generosity of people and businesses from all over the Delmarva Peninsula. She wanted to show her gratitude and decided to do so in the best way a Sable knows how. Once the Certificate of Occupancy was in hand, the law firm of Sable & Sable threw another smashing big party: The Grand Opening of the Sable-Carter Women's Shelter. Held on site, the event began at 10:00 AM with a carnival and ended that evening with a formal dinner dance.

The carnival included several child appropriate rides and games, but the main attraction was the playground. The DTCC students realized their ideas and dreams were a hit when the guests flocked to their creation and the area became filled with young energy and laughter.

The caterers arrived at 3:00 PM, commandeered the kitchen, and began setting up inside. Courtney and I retreated to one of the residences to shower and change. We decided to make one of the residences our base camp for the day for several reasons: it would allow us to stay on campus all day, saving us travel time, and it would give us a sense of how it would feel to live there.

Finally in our own space and out of view of the public eye, Courtney relaxed her face.

"My facial muscles hurt from smiling all day," she whined.

"Here, let me help."

I placed my hands on either side of her face and gently massaged her cheeks, kissing her lightly after several passes.

"How are you holding up?" I asked with sincere concern. "Is everything as you had hoped it would be?"

"Everything is more than I ever expected. In fact, it is so grand that it has added its own level of pressure. I want to make sure the shelter matches or exceeds everyone's expectations because they have put so much heart and soul into it."

"That's why you have paid administrators. You make sure they know what is expected. Have a follow-up plan and assess if they are doing their jobs. Reward them generously. Let them know how much they are appreciated. Treat them as they are to treat the residents, and they will take care of the rest."

"You make it sound so simple," Courtney remarked.

"You're right. It's easier said than done, and I have very little experience with management."

"Oh, Dylan, don't sell yourself short. You did an amazing job working with those students. You encouraged their creativity and challenged their design specs. The end product was the highlight of the day. Did you watch the children playing? They had a great time! You are a fabulous teacher and supervisor. Someday, you'll have your own little crew to raise up. You're an amazing man, Dylan Carter, and one day, you are going to be an awesome father."

"I hope so, Court."

Behind closed doors, in the privacy of the newly painted room, on clean linens with curtains drawn, I made love to my extraordinary wife on a single bed as the sounds of innocent giggles and laughter could be heard outside. I was sure we broke a rule, but I was sure that being with an executive had its privileges.

"This can never happen here again," Court whispered at the height of it all.

"Never . . ." I groaned.

God, how I loved her.

PRATT

As soon as my shift was over, I ran home and jumped into the shower. I told Susan that I would pick up the babysitter at 5:00 and bring her to the Carter beach house when I came by to pick up Susan and take her back to the Carter-Sable celebration. Susan and Zoe had already spent much of the day there, but Susan needed to bring Zoe back to the beach house, and then Susan and I would return for the dinner-dance.

Family logistics . . . Phew!

The babysitter, Bethany Sickler, was fifteen and had a sterling reputation. She was also one of Ginny's piano students, one that actually practiced!

"Hi, Officer Pratt!" Bethany chirped as she greeted me at her parents' front door. "What car are we riding in tonight?"

"I thought we'd take the Lotus. Will that work for you?"

"You betcha!"

The Sicklers lived within a mile of my parents who probably lived less than two miles from the Carter beach house. So Bethany's exciting ride in the Lotus lasted all of five minutes. But she was more than satisfied.

I announced our arrival on the intercom and Dex buzzed us up.

"Glad to see you're locking up these days!" I complimented the newly developed habit at the Carter beach house.

"Only because you were becoming such a pain in the ass. So, shut up about it and come on up!"

"You have to forgive him," I said to Bethany. "He's just a cranky old man."

Bethany appropriately giggled at our jests.

All was quiet on the second floor. I could hear the shower running and Zoe must have been asleep. I escorted Bethany upstairs, and she immediately went to the piano.

I met Dex in the kitchen. He was dressed in a suit with a beer in hand and ready to go."

"You clean up nice, Dex!"

"Thanks, you didn't do so bad yourself. Beer?"

"That would be great."

"Mr. Pratt, do you want to hear what I'm learning to play?" Bethany asked from the piano bench with total confidence in her voice.

"Well, sure."

Bethany sat down, adjusted the piano bench, placed her fingers in position on the keys, and began playing Beethoven's "Pathetique." It was actually quite lovely, yet something was missing.

"You know, Bethany, that was really quite good. In fact, Beethoven would have been very proud. However, it was missing something."

"It was? What?"

"You. You played it exactly as it was written, but I didn't hear anything that told me how it made you feel."

"Me?"

"Yes, you. You are the most important part of the piece. What I heard was the accuracy of your technique, but I did not hear how it made you feel. May I?"

"You play the piano?" Bethany asked in shock.

"A little," I responded humbly.

Bethany shot off the piano bench. I took my seat behind probably one of the most incredible instruments ever built. To mentally prepare to play the "Pathetique" as I had described, I thought about Mrs. Pollock and how much she loved this family of friends, and then began playing: softly—slowly—leaning on the notes as the melodic line rose. When the phrase repeated, I made the dynamic even more dramatic with just the slightest acceleration. I lifted my hands and looked at Bethany.

"What did you hear?"

"I heard the 'Pathetique,' " she answered, somewhat puzzled.

"What was I feeling when I played it?"

"Sad. Like you were missing someone. Someone who was far away."

"Very good! So you could hear and feel the difference?"

"Yes! Yes! Let me try again."

I traded places with the accomplished Bethany. She sat still in meditation before replacing her fingers on the keys. She closed her eyes and played the same phrase twice, as I had done. Only this time was different. She had succeeded in making the magnificent instrument sing.

How is it that a fifteen-year-old child can express that much emotion?

"How was that, Mr. Pratt?"

"Simply beautiful!" Susan complimented as she reached the third floor. "That was absolutely beautiful!"

"Officer Pratt would make a very good teacher. Not as good as Miss Ginny, but pretty close!" Bethany crowed!

Ginny stepped out quietly from the master suite.

"My God, that was beautiful, Bethany!" Ginny exclaimed!

"Thank you, Miss Ginny! Officer Pratt told me to play it the way it made me feel."

"Well, he told you right. That was simply beautiful!"

Susan gave Bethany a schedule for Zoe and all the contact information she would need. Ginny mentioned that there was a lasagna and salad in the fridge and plenty of snacks in the cupboards.

As the music trailed behind us, I escorted Susan down the stairs and out to the Lotus.

"So, to which hobby are we appealing to most tonight, Mr. Pratt?"

"Both. A man can dream, can't he?"

GINNY

By the time we had showered, dressed, and returned to the Sable-Carter Women's Shelter, the place had gone through a total transformation. Gone were the carnival rides and games. Tiny white lights were strung in all of the small trees lining the walk to the main entrance. Inside the entrance hall, the ceiling was accented with large sweeping swags of very sheer silk and lace, alternating in colors of white and lilac. I do not know how it was accomplished, but above the silk and laced sheers of varying depths were stars that seemed to twinkle.

"Fiber optics? Lasers?" I asked Dex.

"I have no clue. That's incredible!"

The entrance was filled with all of the donors. Whether they contributed their time and /or their money, everyone was invited, and all seemed to be stunned by the décor.

Courtney spotted us first and came dancing up to us. She was on cloud nine and probably running on fumes after the busy day she had had thus far.

"Courtney, this is amazing!" I could not conceal my stunned awe.

"Thanks! And thanks again for everything you guys have done to make this all possible. Dylan and I are the luckiest when it comes to family. You guys are the absolute best!" she gushed and we all fell into a big group hug.

"Where's Dylan?" I asked, noting his absence from our overt display of affection.

"He's over by the desk. He's supervising the student volunteers who are giving the tours."

"What a great idea!" Dex affirmed. "Are you ready to open on Monday?"

"As ready as we're going to be!" Courtney boasted, when she suddenly caught herself and grabbed Pratt's shoulder.

"Are you alright?" Pratt asked as he sensed her imbalance and caught her.

"Yes, I'm just a little lightheaded. Probably from being out in the sun all day," Courtney rationalized.

"I'll get some water," Dex volunteered and then left the group.

"Do you want to sit down?" Pratt suggested.

"No, I'll be all right. I just need a second."

A half hour later, we were seated for dinner, catered by one of our favorite restaurants: "Fish On!" Located at Five Points, it has a fabulous menu and because it's located outside of town and features a large dining area, there's never a long wait. Most of all, the food never disappoints and that night was no different.

During coffee and dessert, Dylan took to the podium. He graciously thanked everyone for being there, and more importantly, for making "all of this" possible. He introduced his lovely wife, who received an immediate standing ovation.

"Since when did he become such a dashing statesman?" I leaned over and asked Dex just loudly enough to be heard over the applause.

"I think we just witnessed it!" he chuckled in agreement. "Who knew?"

After everyone took their seats and the applause faded, Courtney personally thanked everyone, again. She then introduced a video that showed the progression of the project, starting with photos taken at the fundraiser held in Dover. She and Dylan made sure that Gwen and Marco were not in any of the photos. Several shots included meetings held at Delmarva Architects where Dan had worked before his untimely death. The main feature of the video was a time-lapse production of the building from foundation up, ending with a shot from the day's carnival and ribbon cutting. It was amazing.

Dylan rejoined his wife at the podium.

"As many of you have seen by now, we have four wings of residential units," Dylan began. "Two have been named for donors: " 'The Thomas and Anna Pratt Wing' and 'The Raymond and Marjory Pollock Wing.' "

Everyone applauded the announcement, and Dylan happily waited until the show of appreciation quieted down.

"We have two more wings to be dedicated tonight. It is my great pleasure to announce that the third wing will be named 'The Dean and Elizabeth Sable Wing.' "

As the audience applauded again, Dylan invited Mr. Sable to the stage to receive the plaque that would later be placed in the wing.

I was not prepared for what happened next. Courtney took the microphone.

"I want to thank my best friend and husband for helping me through my own personal tragedy. Without his support, I would never have been able to stand here in front of all of you with any sense of self-worth.

"My husband comes from an incredible family and group of friends. I have learned so much from them in just the short period of time that I have known them. I may have learned the most from a family member who has left us, yet still remains our family's glue. Dylan and I would like to name the fourth wing the 'The Daniel S. Carter Wing.' "

A great lump formed in my throat. I couldn't breathe. I felt Dex's gentle kiss on my cheek. Somewhere in the background was a muffled thundering applause and the room rose up. Dex helped me to my feet and escorted me to the podium where I fell into Dylan's arms and we both cried on each other's shoulders. In front of hundreds of people, we openly cried tears that had been concealed for more than three years. Courtney stood aside with the plaque in her hand, applauding with the audience, and gave us time to have our moment.

"I miss him so much," I whispered in Dylan's ear.

"I know, Ginny. But he never really left us, did he?" Dylan asked.

"No, I guess not."

"He will always be a part of us. All of us," Dylan assured me.

I knew in my heart that Dylan was right.

I gathered myself together and thanked Courtney as she handed me the plaque. I kissed her cheek and I kissed Dan's name beautifully etched into the brass plate. Dex reappeared and escorted me back to my seat.

Very slowly, I returned from the dimension I had entered at the mere recognition of Dan's name. Dex, bless his loving heart, somehow understood.

Just when I thought the night had reached a climax, there was still more to come.

Dylan took the microphone, again.

"Now, before we close the evening presentations and open the dance floor, we have one more important announcement to make."

Dylan handed the mic back to Courtney. She intentionally addressed her father.

"Dad, you're going to be a grandfather!"

There is no way I can put into words the excitement of the room, and especially at our table as I screamed with delight and Mr. Sable nearly knocked the table over as he jumped from his seat and ran to the stage to embrace his daughter and son-in-law.

"I am the happiest man on earth!" the mic picked up as he hugged them both.

SUSAN

"Wow, that was some night!" I commented as Pratt and I walked out to the car.

"That's putting it mildly!" Pratt chuckled.

When we reached his car, he did not open my door for me as he had always done in the past. Instead, he stood and waited for my eyes to meet his.

"I love you, Susan McCabe. I love everything about you."

I reached up and put my hands on either side of his face.

"I love you, too, Thomas Pratt. I think I always have."

"And I think I will *always* love you, Susan. In fact, I am sure of it," Pratt added.

Standing beside the red hot Lotus Elise, Pratt's lips burned into mine. We melted together as his tongue swirled around mine and his breathing intensified.

"Hmmm . . ." he moaned into the side of my neck, trailing kisses down to my shoulder.

"Let's see if I can get you home before you run away this time!" he laughed as he reached around and opened my door.

CHAPTER NINETEEN

SUSAN

In May of the following year, Marien Merck was appointed the Mayor of "The First Town in the First State," Lewes, Delaware. There was no need for her to run a lengthy or dirty campaign. No one opposed her. It was a virtual appointment.

Pratt did resign his job as a Lewes Police Officer, just as he said he would. He felt challenged by the illegal adoption case and decided to join the FBI. He had hoped to become a special agent while still young enough to do so. Then, he would see where the future would lead him within the bureau. He asked my blessing. I think he already knew my answer.

Pratt later joked that he wanted to join the FBI so he could personally insure that my photos never surfaced again! He could be so overprotective at times that I almost believed his rationale.

In solidarity for the cause, Ginny and I held a ceremonial photo burning in the fire pit Dex had constructed between their house and the dune. Fortunately, only Ginny and I were present, because as the envelope burned away, some of the photos were exposed, exposing parts of my body before bursting into flames. Ginny and I were howling. It seemed like it would never end as one by one the glossy photos caught fire.

"You are one hot momma!" Ginny yelled.

We were laughing so hard; tears were flowing from our eyes. Dex came out to make sure we were OK and not setting the beach on fire.

"Get out of here!" I screamed. "Don't you dare come out here!"

It was a moment to remember. I will never look at that fire pit the same way again.

Pratt had another surprise up his sleeve. He was the anonymous entity who had purchased the Pollock beach house. He had to confess it when he decided that he might want to raze it and rebuild. Bless his heart; he felt he needed Dex's and Ginny's permission to do so. He knew how Mrs. Pollock was like family to them, and he wanted to make sure that razing the Pollock house would not upset either one.

Ginny said that had it not been for the fire at the old Carter beach house, she would have never been able to tear it down. There were too many emotions attached to the old structure. She acknowledged that there were several blessings in the tragedy. One: no one was hurt; even Gilda was able to escape the flames. Two: it forced her to rebuild. She said that trying to maintain what was there would have been throwing good money after bad. Instead, she made a good investment by rebuilding, providing a nice place for everyone to live, and in the end, it greatly improved the value of the property. Ginny strongly advised Pratt to raze the Pollock house.

"What about Zoe?" he asked me. "Zoe adored Mrs. Pollock. Will it upset her?"

"You're right about that, Pratt," I validated his assumption. "Zoe did adore Mrs. Pollock. All of us will miss her. But Zoe won't remember the house. She's too young; she may not even remember Mrs. Pollock when she's older. We just won't take her up there during the demolition. We have plenty of time. We'll know when to take her back. Let's not over complicate it. Are you looking for complicated, Agent Pratt?" I winked.

Pratt looked at me and laughed quietly.

"You are a treasure. I have another question. Will you help me design the new house? I'm going to hire Delmarva Architects, but I need you . . ." he stopped. "I need you, Susan. It's as simple as that."

"Did you say 'Yes'? Did you? What did you say?" Ginny demanded to know when I gave her the news later that day.

"Whoa, slow down, girl. He's not proposing," I cautioned sternly.

"I know that!" Ginny defended her exuberant prompting. "But if *you* help, then that means that *I* get to help, too!" she said, stating the obvious.

Zoe had entered the Terrible Twos and began to display a real stubborn streak. One evening, she threw one of her worse temper tantrums during a family dinner at the beach house. In my frustration, I slipped.

"Sometimes, she is just like her father!" I stormed as I picked up my screaming and kicking daughter.

Once I realized what I had just done, Pratt and Ginny chuckled while Dex, Dylan, and Courtney looked a little stunned.

Dex gave Pratt the "all-knowing" glare.

"It's not what you think!" Pratt laughed defensively.

Ginny shook her head and snickered.

"Zoe is Derek's," I quietly confessed.

Zoe immediately stopped her little fit, as if she understood, which she did not. She was probably aware that the air around her had changed. No longer were her actions the center of attention.

"Well, now. There's a surprise. Not," Dylan responded with a welcomed defense of my character.

Zoe was beginning to resemble Derek in so many ways. Only someone who didn't know Derek and our history would question Zoe's paternal roots.

I thank God everyday for bringing Tom Pratt into my life. He convinced Derek to allow me one visit.

To say that I underestimated my reaction is an understatement. However, I think Pratt knew what to expect, so he drove me there and waited. He refused to come in with me, stating that I needed to do it on my own and that the time belonged to Derek and me.

"Keep in mind, Susan, when you leave, you go to a place you call home where a beautiful little girl, his daughter, waits for you. Derek returns to a cell, his personal hell. Your visit can either bring him some sense of peace, or fan the flames of condemnation."

"Thank you, Pratt. But how can I bring him anything less than pain and resentment?"

"Be honest. Answer him directly."

"I know, keep it simple."

"Right. Don't try to overcomplicate matters by analyzing, questioning, and commenting on what you see or hear him say. Take everything at face value and nothing more."

I tried to prepare myself as best I could, but it had been three years, almost to the day.

I sat down in the chair and waited for a guard to escort Derek to his seat on the other side of the glass wall. With my head down, I saw the shadow of a man take his place opposite me. I looked up and gazed into the eyes that I never got to say goodbye to a million lifetimes ago. They were tired. They had seen too much. They no longer knew me, and I no longer knew them.

Derek picked up the phone and placed it to his ear. I did the same.

"Susan, I am so sorry. Can you forgive me?"

They were the words that I needed to hear. As always, he gave me what I desired.

"Yes. I forgave you a long time ago."

CHAPTER TWENTY

GINNY

The Sable-Carter Women's Shelter opened and rapidly reached sixty percent occupancy. Courtney had no doubt about its need; however, we were all surprised at how quickly the need was realized. I'll leave it at that. Within six months, Courtney reported that the center had reached eighty percent occupancy. She and Dylan started making plans for another fund raising campaign to support an addition to the facility. It already had several success stories under its belt. Not only was it meeting the needs of families in distress, only two of the original families remained on campus. Because of its strength in counseling, education, and training services, the facility was exceeding its expected turnover rate.

Speaking of new additions, Courtney was due any day. They were going to have a boy. I found myself praying every night for his safe delivery and could not wait to meet him. Dylan was going to be an amazing father, and Dex was looking forward to becoming an uncle, once again.

Dex and I decided to squeeze in one last overnight on the Right Tackle before the weather turned too cold and all of the excitement of a new family member hit. We packed up and left Gilda with Susan and Zoe. We speculated as to whether or not Pratt would spend the night there. He was so overprotective of "his girls."

Pratt was an extraordinary man and loved Zoe as his own. Susan shared with me that even Derek said that if she had to be with someone else, he took comfort in knowing that it was Pratt. It meant the world to Susan.

It took Susan a full week to recover from her visit with Derek, and as a testament to Pratt's patient understanding, he gave Susan space as she recovered from the shock of visiting "the man she thought she no longer knew." Susan shared with me that when she received Derek's heartfelt apology, she was finally able to recall the man she had married years ago and realized that she had indeed forgiven him.

When Susan was back on her feet, Pratt became her constant companion whenever he was in town. Pratt had been accepted into the FBI and was training to become a special agent. He had basically turned over the design of the new house to Susan ... and me! *(Ha ha!)* Dex and I also suspected that it would only be a matter of time before Pratt married Susan and brought her and Zoe under his roof.

Dex anchored the Right Tackle in the Bay, about a hundred yards off the beach. The Carter beach house had become our home, and from the water it looked warm and cozy inside. Once again, with autumn on the horizon, the Carter beach house was becoming one of the few remaining signs of life on the beach.

Dex and I sat in the cockpit of the Right Tackle and huddled under a familiar blanket. I was sitting on his lap as he kept the blanket wrapped tightly around us.

"It's been quite the summer," he remarked reflectively.

"That it has," I agreed as we both gazed upon the house behind the dune.

Dex pulled me in a little closer.

"I have no idea where I would be right now had I never met you," he said, lightly kissing the side of my face.

"Me, too. I can't imagine a single day without you."

Dex said nothing. He remained silent as he buried his face in my shoulder momentarily.

I parted his arms and turned around so I could straddle him and look into his eyes.

"What?" he asked innocently.

"Well, I have this crazy idea."

"Oh, no. Your plans lead to nothing but trouble."

"Rest assured. This means trouble of the most serious kind."

"All right. Give me a moment to prepare."

Dex teasingly squinted his eyes, then opened them and smiled back at me."

"OK. I'm ready. What's this great plan of yours?"

DEX

Ginny has always been full of surprises. Sometimes I think she lives to shock me. At anchor, she gave me the surprise of my life.

"Marry me, Dex."

"What? Really?"

"Yes. Marry me tomorrow. Marry me the day after. Marry me. Let's not wait another day. In fact, I'm not going home until you say you will."

"Whoa, baby. Why would you want to become a Lassiter?"

"I don't. I want *you* to become a Carter. Take *my* name. Dan would give us his blessing, I'm sure of it. Please, Dex, say you'll marry me."

"Yes."

If you have enjoyed the **"BAY AVENUE"** series, consider reading another novel written by Jill Hicks.

"The Long Climb Back"

The Long Climb Back is a story about an adventurous young woman who strikes out on her own after an over-the-top marriage proposal from a winery heir. Her travels introduce her to two engaging brothers. Will she be able to return to her fiancé with her mind, body, and soul intact?

"Adrift"

Adrift follows the journey of Carly Young Mariner, a devoted wife, mother, and second grade teacher, who walks in on an encounter that upends her ordinary life. Over time—but not out of time—she distances herself from her family and everything that has given her a sense of purpose. With the hope of finding contentment and a place to contemplate her options, Carly escapes to the Outer Banks of North Carolina. Shortly after her arrival, a minor accident transforms her and those around her.

ACKNOWLEDGEMENTS

First, I would like to thank my husband, Bill Hicks, for encouraging me to pursue this project that began with a simple conversation as we rode bikes on the Breakwater Trail between Lewes and Rehoboth, Delaware. Three years in the making, he has patiently encouraged me and listened intently as I tried to sort out how each character would act and react. While the "BAY AVENUE" series is a work of fiction, I wanted the characters to hobnob with reality. Bill often helped me discern when a character could, and should, take license, and when they were overstepping reasonable boundaries. Bill pressed me to push through the limitations of my own experiences and to try walking, in detail, in someone else's footwear. Without Bill's support, I never would have attempted this venture.

Second, I want to thank my sister, Jane, and her husband, Mike, a.k.a. "Monkey Mike" to his nieces and nephews. Jane and Mike are two of the kindest and most generous people God has put on this earth. Over the years, Bill and I have had the pleasure of taking several extended vacation adventures with them. Because of their sense of humor, can-do spirit, and great curiosity with the world around them, they are the best travel companions, ever. "The Long Climb Back" and another book, currently in the works, were inspired by our travels together. Jane and Mike have also been instrumental in encouraging me to pursue the dream. They have helped me edit each book. You guys are the best! Where are we going next?

Third, I would like to thank my sister, Dr. Joan Yarnall, DVM. Joan helped with the editing and proofing of BAY AVENUE II and III. In life—and she arrived on this earth before I did!—she has always been the one to push me beyond what I would have thought possible. She continually raises the bar and expects one to at least strive for it. She accepts no less than the best from herself and those around her. Knowing that she would also demand excellence on this project, I asked her to give me her best shot. Thanks, Joan, for the enormous amounts of care you put into all that you do! I should also note that Joan is an exceptional veterinarian. She and her staff at the Animal Clinic at Thorndale, in Pennsylvania, have been guardian angels to all of our family pets.

Fourth, I need to thank a man who has coached and inspired me to be a better writer. Ralph Painter, a long time friend of the Hicks family, worked as a typesetter through high school and college. He is an avid reader and a wealth of knowledge. I could spend hours listening to Ralph explain uses of grammar and best practices in writing. I appreciate how he sends me notes when he comes across new literary ideas and expressive techniques. Never in a million years would I ever believe that writing could be so fascinating, until I met Ralph and he began sharing his wisdom and experience with me. Ralph, you have given me the confidence to continue in my pursuit of literary expression.

Most of all, I want to thank all of the "BAY AVENUE" readers, especially those who have written reviews, forwarded their comments, have generously invited me into their homes to attend their book clubs, and have attended my book signing events. What a great experience for me to hear first hand from my readers what they thought and felt as they journeyed through the series. Thank you so much for your continual support and encouragement. You have inspired me along the way.

And now, it is time to say farewell to the Carter "family." Thank you letting us into your lives and sharing it with others.

Blessings!
Jill Hicks

ABOUT THE AUTHOR

Jill L Hicks was born and raised in West Chester, Pennsylvania, and currently resides in Lewes, Delaware, with her husband, Bill. Together, they have two daughters. Tragically, they lost their eldest, Jamie, in an auto accident when she was just twenty. Jamie is survived by her younger sister, Jessie, and her half-sister, Jenn.

Jill is very close to her extended family. She draws on her personal experiences and the stories of others to express the joys and sorrows of life and love.

Jill is a graduate of Penn State University with a degree in Music Education. In her spare time she loves to read, play piano, ride her bike, sail, and spend quality beach time with her husband, family, and friends.

Ironically, Jill loathed reading until just several years ago. Suddenly, poring through twenty to thirty books a summer, she ran out of beach books to read and decided to write her own, ergo her first novel, "BAY AVENUE: The Inheritance."

Made in the USA
Charleston, SC
01 March 2017